int... ...
and froze.

Silhouetted against the thin gray light coming through the back window was the dark form of a man.

Her heart rushed to her throat. When she flipped the light switch, the sight that met her gaze did nothing to dispel her terror.

He was huge, well over six feet tall, with broad shoulders and thick, bulging biceps. Tawny hair hung in waves to his shoulders, framing a hard face and amber-colored eyes.

"What do you want?" Her words came out breathy.

Her mind screamed, *Run!* But she couldn't. Heart thundering, she gathered every last scrap of courage, rose to her full five foot five, and lifted her chin.

"Get out of my house."

A single, tawny eyebrow rose. "Bare your right breast."

By Pamela Palmer

HUNGER UNTAMED
RAPTURE UNTAMED
PASSION UNTAMED
OBSESSION UNTAMED
DESIRE UNTAMED

PAMELA PALMER

DESIRE UNTAMED

A FERAL WARRIORS NOVEL

AVON

An Imprint of HarperCollinsPublishers

This is a work of fiction. Names, characters, places, and incidents are products of the author's imagination or are used fictitiously and are not to be construed as real. Any resemblance to actual events, locales, organizations, or persons, living or dead, is entirely coincidental.

AVON BOOKS
An Imprint of HarperCollins*Publishers*
10 East 53rd Street
New York, New York 10022-5299

First Avon Books paperback printing: July 2009
First Avon Books special printing: February 2009

Avon Trademark Reg. U.S. Pat. Off. and in Other Countries, Marca Registrada, Hecho en U.S.A.
HarperCollins® is a registered trademark of HarperCollins Publishers.

Printed in the U.S.A.

10 9 8 7 6 5 4

To Keith, Kelly, and Kyle.
My family, my support, and my heart.

Acknowledgments

I'd like to thank the following people:

Laurin Wittig and Anne Shaw Moran, extraordinary writers and dear friends. You're always there for me and, though I hate it sometimes, you're always right. I'd be lost without you two.

My agent, Helen Breitwieser, for your wise counsel and willingness to follow me to the dark side in your reading. Your enjoyment of this story moved me more than you know.

My editor, May Chen, whose enthusiasm and support for this project changed my life. Your wisdom and vision are my guiding lights.

My dad, for borrowing Mom's romances when you found out I was writing one, so you'd understand the genre I loved. My mom, for sharing your love of reading with me and for being the perfect role model, always. And my brother, Bud Palmer. You're all the good and honorable things I aspire to make my heroes, even if you can't quite bring yourself to read my books.

Fellow writers Denise McInerney, Kathryn Caskie, Sophia Nash, and Elizabeth Holcombe for your sage advice and friendship. And the incomparable Anna Campbell for friendship, chocolate, and laughter. Wish you lived closer!

And, finally, thanks to my web designers, Emily Cotler and Misono Yokoyama at WaxCreative Designs, and my right hand, Kim Castillo, for your tireless efforts on my behalf.

Chapter One

One woman, in all the world, held the key to the survival of life on Earth.

And they'd lost her.

The Therian race called her the *Radiant,* for it was through her that nature channeled the energy to their guardians, the Feral Warriors, enabling them to track and destroy the Daemon remnants, the *draden,* before they snuffed the life from Therians and humans alike. In return, the Feral Warriors protected the Radiant with their lives.

Which was damn hard to do when they didn't know where . . . or who . . . she was.

Lyon grimaced as he led his eight warriors along the dark, rocky trail high above the falls of the rugged and deadly Potomac River. Hell, they'd lost *two* Radiants. The old one to death. The new one, the one marked by the goddess to take her place, had never come forward. And the situation was growing dire.

The rocks felt cold beneath Lyon's bare feet as he left the trail and climbed down toward the goddess stone wearing nothing but a silk shirt and a pair of jeans. In his hands he carried two deadly switchblades in case of a draden attack. Below, the glow from the full moon tripped over the bounding water, shooting brilliant shards of light into the night air.

"What in the hell are we doing out here at 3:00 A.M.?" Jag's tone, as always, challenged.

Anger rumbled deep in Lyon's throat, the sound of an irritated lion. Which he was, down deep.

Jag had no use for any of them, and the feeling was more than mutual. Lyon cut his gaze toward the warrior, taking in the oh-so-familiar belligerence in Jag's eyes and the sneer forming on his cynical mouth. In his camouflage pants and army green tee, Jag took his role of warrior a bit too literally. None of the Ferals had ever served a day in the United States military. As a rule, they stayed out of all things human.

"Cat got your tongue?" Jag prodded.

"What do you *think* we're doing out here at this hour? We're raising the power of the beasts." He leaped down to the path he sought, Jag close behind him.

"So you haul us out here in the middle of the

night because *you*, mighty chief, couldn't do your job?"

Raw violence clawed at Lyon's self-control, his beast's instincts begging to rip the asshole's throat out. His control, battered by their increasingly critical situation, snapped. The tip of his fingers burned a moment before his claws sprang out. With a growl, he shifted both his blades to one hand while he whirled and sank the claws of his other in the man's neck as he slammed him against the rock.

Blood trickled down Jag's throat, but no fear flickered in his eyes, only a spark of malicious amusement that he'd pushed Lyon too far. Even if Lyon completely lost it, he'd be hard-pressed to do Jag any real damage. Physically, they were a match. Shape-shifters simply didn't break that easily.

What he longed for was a comeback to Jag's snide remarks, something to put the surly warrior in his place. The bitch of it was, he didn't have one. Jag was right. Lyon had failed to find their new Radiant. With a jerk and a snarl, he released the man and shoved himself away, sheathing his claws. Every muscle in his body vibrated with frustration as he climbed down to the goddess stone.

Within a couple of months of their old Radiant's death a Therian woman should have woken to find a mark upon her breast like a long-healed scar. Four-inch-long claw marks.

The mark of the chosen one.

It was Lyon's job to find her and get her ascended to her power, renewing and empowering all the Feral Warriors. As the *finder,* Lyon was the only one who possessed the ability—the senses—to seek her out. He'd waited, knowing the marking wouldn't happen immediately. But now too much time had passed. The only thing he could figure was that she was out of range of his human senses. Worse, his Feral strength had drained to the point he could no longer access his deeper, more primal power—the power of the beast that lived inside him.

Without an ascended Radiant to renew them, the Feral Warriors—the guardians of the Therian race and last of the true shape-shifters—grew weaker by the day. Except for the occasional show of claws, fangs, and animal eyes, they'd all lost the ability to shift. With each passing sunrise, Lyon's ability to find the woman diminished.

He had one chance left. Tonight.

Vhyper joined him, his bald head glistening pale in the moonlight, a silver earring hanging from his right lobe. "So, what do you say we build a campfire and make s'mores while we're out here? We could send the cub back to the house for marshmallows and grahams and those little chocolate squares."

Lyon threw the man a rueful glare.

"You're a moron, Vhype." Tighe's short pale hair gleamed in the moonlight as he threw his arm around Vhyper's shoulders, buddy style, in the easy manner of most shape-shifters.

An ease Lyon had never understood. "Let's get this over with."

"Are we really going to bleed ourselves?" Foxx had a shaggy fall of orange hair and the pale complexion and freckles to go with it. The youngest of the Ferals, he showed surprising power and great promise, if he ever matured.

Lyon glanced at him. "Didn't you bring the ceremonial blade like I told you?"

"Yes. But I thought . . ."

"We're going to invoke the Feral Circle, pooling all our energy into a single force. The ritual requires blood."

"Well, shit," Vhyper drawled, tugging on his earring as Tighe released him. "I'd rather sing a few campfire songs."

"Shut up, Vhyper," Jag snarled.

Lyon clapped his hands. "Let's do it." His palms were damp, the muscles in his neck tense with worry as he prayed they still had enough power among them to make the ritual work. Raising the power of the beasts would steal what little mystic energy they had left. They wouldn't get a second chance.

Lyon shoved his knives into his pockets since the draden couldn't reach them within the mystic circle, then pulled his shirt off over his head and tossed it onto the rock. The chilly, early-spring air felt good against his heated flesh. While the others stripped to the waist, Lyon continued, pulling off his jeans. If this worked, he was shifting. And unlike a couple of his comrades, he possessed no odd strains of Mage blood that would allow him to keep his clothes intact. Only the thick gold armband that snaked around his biceps and channeled the Earth's energies stayed with him through a shift.

The nine formed a circle on the flat, wide goddess stone, golden armbands gleaming as the men stood bare-chested against the clear night sky.

Lyon held his hand out to Foxx. "The knife."

Foxx slapped the hilt onto his palm. Lyon turned the blade on himself and made a shallow, searing cut across his chest. An odd surge of energy twined with the pain, sending a jolt through the blade and into his flesh. He handed the knife to Tighe, glad the mystic powers were with them this night. He slapped his right hand to the burning wound, then fisted his hand around the blood and thrust his arm into the air in front of him. Tighe followed, slicing his chest and slapping his bloodied hand around Lyon's fist, then handed the knife to Jag. One by one, they added their slick hands to the knot of flesh until only one remained.

Vhyper carved his chest with the knife as the others had, then jerked, the knife clattering to the rock. "*Damn* this is a bitch. We need some new rituals."

But as Vhyper squatted to reach for the blade, his hand stilled, his body going rigid. "*What the hell?*" He grabbed the knife's handle and surged to his feet, whirling to face Lyon. "*It's the Daemon blade!*"

The words sliced through Lyon's mind, icing his skin. He thrust out his hand. "Give it to me."

As Vhyper laid the blade on Lyon's palm, faint etchings snaked over the flashing steel in the moonlight. Lyon's eyes widened, shock washing through him as his hand closed around the blade's handle.

With a snarl, Lyon sprang across the circle, grabbed Foxx around his thick neck and jerked him off his feet. *"What have you done?"*

The kid looked as shocked as Lyon felt. "Nothing. I mean . . . I didn't know. You said get the ceremonial blade, and I did. I swear, I didn't go near the vault. *Why would I get the Daemon blade?"*

Lyon felt his eyes turn feral as fury had his claws unsheathing. Blood began to run freely down Foxx's neck. *"You. Tell. Me."*

Foxx's face began to turn red. "Can't . . . talk."

With a growl, Lyon retracted his claws and dropped him to his feet. *"Tell me."*

Foxx coughed and backed up a step, his hand against his throat, his eyes wide and confused. "I wouldn't. I didn't. I swear."

Vhyper grabbed the kid's arm and jerked him back from Lyon's reach. Tighe stepped in front of Lyon, his mouth grim. "We're blooded. Let's finish the ritual before we mete out punishment. We can't accidentally free the Daemons."

But Lyon wasn't so sure. "Hawke?" If anyone knew, it would be the whipcord-lean warrior with more college degrees than most of his men had weapons.

Hawke shook his head. "The first step in freeing Satanan and his horde is the same as raising the power of the beasts—the blooding of the nine. But there's far more involved. A complex ritual requiring the free will of all the Ferals and the blood of their Radiant. The ancients made certain the Daemons would never rise again."

"Then there's no problem," Vhyper said, shielding the kid from Lyon's fury.

Hawke frowned ruefully. "Every time that blade comes out of the vault, there's trouble."

Lyon gave Foxx a look that promised deep and painful retribution, then turned back to the others. "Tighe's right. Let's finish this before the blood dries and we have to start over." Lyon shoved his fist into the air. The warriors resumed their positions, covering his fist, one by one.

Lyon began to chant. "Spirits rise and join. Empower the beast beneath this moon." The others joined in, the murmured words flowing around him, over him, sliding across his flesh. Thunder rumbled in the clear sky. The ground beneath his feet trembled as the great force of Mother Nature herself rose from the depths of the Earth, through the vessels of bone and skin and up through their arms to the blood raised to the heavens.

"Empower the beast of the lion!"

A flash of lightning lit the sky, burning through the flesh of Lyon's palm, sending energy and power flooding his body like a wash of hot oil. Power. Strength. He thought of his other half and shifted into his animal form at last. Fierce joy surged through him at the change. The others moved back, circling around him as he raised his thickly maned lion's head to the starred canvas above and let out a deep, rumbling roar. It was a damned good thing the mystic circle enclosed all sight and sound or they'd have Fairfax County Animal Control on them within minutes.

Lyon paced in the tight circle, reveling in the rush of power flowing through him as he used his beast's senses to search slowly in every direction. Tens, dozens, hundreds of miles.

A spark lit his mind, a connection formed that could not be severed. Relief surged through his brain.

He'd found her.

His nose high in the air, he let out another fierce roar and shifted back into his human form. Around him, his fellow warriors watched, their eyes glowing with the feral light of the animals they'd shift into once they got their Radiant ascended.

"Did you find her?" Vhyper asked.

Lyon grabbed his jeans and pulled them on while the knowledge from his beast's senses flowed into his brain. "West. Beyond the Blue Ridge. Beyond the Mississippi."

Vhyper grunted. "How did she get all the way out there?"

"Beats the hell out of me."

"You'll take someone with you?" Tighe asked.

"No." Lyon shook his head once. "I go alone."

Vhyper frowned. "I wonder if she even knows what the mark means."

Jag laughed, an ugly sound. "If she doesn't, our little Radiant is in for one hell of a surprise."

For once, Lyon had to agree.

Kara MacAllister paced the floor of her mother's blue-sprigged bedroom, frustration and grief shredding her insides as rain slashed at the windows.

"Kara, honey." Her mom's words sounded pained and slurred as she eased out of another drug-induced nap. "Why don't you hire a nurse?" The same question every day.

"No nurse, Mom." Kara's heart shriveled as she met her mother's pain-filled gaze. Propped up on thick pillows stuffed into white, lace-trimmed pillowcases, her mother looked twenty years older than she had just a few months ago. Her once-full cheeks lay sunken in pools of skin, the pasty gray of the terminally ill. The doctors had opened her up to remove a tumor on her left lung only to close her back up and send her home to die. A few weeks, they'd said. Maybe a month. That was two weeks ago.

It felt like two lifetimes.

"But your job, honey. You'll lose your job."

Kara squeezed her mother's thin hand. "It's okay, Mom. I found someone to cover my class until I get back." If she *went* back. For nine years, ever since high school, she'd been content to stay in tiny Spearsville, Missouri, to share the old farmhouse with her mom and teach preschool in the basement of the local church. Maybe it wasn't the most exciting life, but her mom had begged her to stay, and she'd been okay with it. Even happy.

Until three months ago. Two days after Christmas, she'd woken up a frustrated bundle of restlessness as if overnight she'd developed a chronic, severe case of PMS. Everything annoyed her all of a sudden. Her boyfriend, her friends, her life, even the preschoolers she adored. She'd felt as if she needed something, but didn't have a clue what.

The only thing she knew for certain was that her mother's dying wasn't it.

Her mom squeezed her hand, her grip weaker even than yesterday. "I want you to . . . have fun, honey. Not watch me die."

Fun. As if she could possibly enjoy herself doing *anything* under these circumstances. Kara leaned down and kissed a fragile cheek. "I love you, Mom. I'm right where I want to be." For now.

Her mother was all the family she had, all the family she'd ever had, and her cancer was killing them both. If only Kara could share with her a bit of her own remarkable health. It was so unfair. Kara was never sick. And her mom lay dying.

She rose, unable to remain still a moment longer. "I'm going to heat some soup and make a batch of blueberry muffins. After dinner we can watch a movie. How's that?"

"Lovely."

On her way out of the room, Kara reached for the television on the dresser and flipped on the local news. Glancing back, she caught her mother's sad smile twisting in pain.

It wasn't fair. She slammed the heel of her fist against the blue-painted wall as she started down the stairs. Her mom didn't deserve this. *She* didn't deserve this.

Kara blinked back the film of moisture that suddenly clouded her eyes. In a few weeks' time, she'd be all alone. Orphaned.

Could you call it orphaned at twenty-seven?

The sun had set while Kara was upstairs, and the main level of the old farmhouse was shadowed with dusk. But she'd grown up in this house, lived here all her life, and could find her way blindfolded.

She slipped into the dark kitchen . . . and froze.

Silhouetted against the thin gray light coming through the back window was the dark form of a man *inside the house.*

Her heart rushed to her throat. Her stomach buckled beneath the slam of fear even as her logical mind screeched, *It's just a neighbor.* But when she flipped the light switch, the sight that met her gaze beneath the fluorescent strips did nothing to dispel her terror.

He was huge, well over six feet tall, with broad shoulders and thick, bulging biceps. Tawny hair hung in waves to his shoulders, framing a hard face and cold amber-colored eyes. With his dress pants and expensive-looking shirt, he could never pass as one of the local farmers even if she hadn't known everyone within a ten-mile radius of town. This man was a total, and frightening, stranger.

"What do you want?" Her words came out breathy, forced around the constriction in her throat.

Her mind screamed, *Run!* But she couldn't. Not with her mother upstairs and helpless. Heart thundering, she gathered every last scrap of her courage, rose to her full five-foot-five, and lifted her chin.

"Get out of my house."

A single, tawny eyebrow rose. "Bare your right breast."

Kara gaped at him as the full realization of his intent sent her pulse into a grinding thud in her ears.

As if reading her mind, the man rolled his eyes with an exasperated grunt. "I'm not going to hurt you."

Kara choked out a laugh. "Right. You just want to see my breast, then you'll go."

"Something like that."

She stared at him, her terrified mind grasping for a plan. Any plan.

He started toward her. Kara lunged for the knife rack, but as her fingers curled around the handle of a small paring knife, the stranger closed the distance between them. He hauled her against his chest, face to pecs, his large hand clamping around her wrist, immobilizing her.

Swallowing a scream, she struggled against his ironlike hold, but she might as well have been a fly in a spiderweb for all the good it did her. *He was too strong.* Kara tried to kick him, to knee him, but he only pressed her against the counter, his hips tight against hers as he towered over her.

Terror flashed in her mind like an explosion of light. He was going to rape her. Murder her.

Her pulse began to slow, the terror slipping away as if someone had opened a drain in her head. Even her shallow, desperate breathing evened out as if she'd suddenly, inexplicably, lost her fear of the huge man.

He eased the knife from her hand and returned it to the knife block. "I'm calming you."

And that's exactly what it felt like, she realized. A strange, unnatural calm settling over her as if an invisible hand were squashing her fear.

"How?" Though the word rang incredulous in her head, her tone, as it left her lips, was one of simple curiosity.

This wasn't right. He shouldn't have this kind of control over her. Her pulse tried to leap fearfully but was instantly stroked into complaisance.

"Stop it." She *needed* to be afraid of him. He overpowered her. Overwhelmed her. Her senses swam in his nearness, in the elemental scent of wind and earth and pure, raw male. The intoxicating blend teased and tantalized, sending the blood rushing to the surface of her skin in a hot flush of awareness. An awareness that horrified her.

"Let me go."

"I'm not going to harm you. I need to know that you're the one I'm looking for."

"I'm not."

He stepped back, putting a slight distance between them even as he kept tight hold of her wrist. Feeling utterly detached, she watched him reach for her with his free hand, felt the pad of his finger slide down her upper chest to hook into the top of her scoop-neck tee and tug downward.

His eyes flared, those well-sculpted lips compressing as his thumb brushed over the flesh rising above the lace of her bra, tracing the odd stretch marks she'd noticed for the first time around Christmas.

Her gaze caught on his lips, mesmerized by their perfect fullness as a single, disturbing emotion finally broke free of his unnatural control to sweep her imprisoned body. Lust. Delicious fire skimmed over her skin, burrowing deep into her bones and blood, rushing straight down to her core.

He released her shirt as if he'd been burned and met her gaze, his own cool and shuttered. "You are the Radiant."

"I'm the what?" She stared at him, trying to make sense of his words. Of any of this. "What do you want?"

Those amber eyes glowed with a dark determination that would have made her heart pound if he hadn't been tamping her emotions. He slid his free hand over her jaw, his palm rough and callused, his touch not ungentle as his forefinger hooked around the back of her jaw, coming to rest beneath her ear.

"*What do you want?*"

"You."

The sudden, sharp pressure at the base of her ear stole her thoughts and vision, sending Kara tumbling into a dark, unconscious abyss.

Rain fell heavily on Lyon's head and shoulders as he carried the unconscious Radiant out to his BMW, keeping her tucked tight against his body. A surge of protectiveness tightened his arms.

Damn his finder's senses and the connection that linked him to the chosen ones. That connection had to be at the root of the sudden, sharp attraction he'd felt the moment he saw her, though he was certain he'd never been attracted to a Radiant before. Not like this. He tried to focus, tried to escape the awareness, but even through the rain the scent of her, a sweet smell, almost of peaches, pumped the blood straight to his groin.

As he laid her across the backseat, the raindrops on her cheeks glistened in the overhead light, drawing his gaze to her flawless skin and the sweet curve of her mouth. Her features possessed a simplicity, a girl-next-door freshness, that pleased him. She wasn't beautiful so much as cute, with her blond ponytail and that one crooked eyetooth. Perhaps not beautiful, but decidedly appealing.

As he released her, the fall of her damp hair brushed his hand like a silken caress, a touch that sent heat spiraling through his veins. He gave a rueful snort. He had a miserable couple of days ahead of him if he didn't find a way to curb the unfortunate rush of need he felt every time he touched her. Slamming the door closed, he slid into the driver's seat and started the car.

The windshield wipers kept a steady rhythm as the road cut through the center of the small Missouri town, past a strip of nightclubs and burger joints. Cars lined the street on both sides as he headed east on the two-lane toward the highway that would take them back to Great Falls, Virginia, and home.

The sound of a feminine groan behind him had his neck muscles spasming. She shouldn't be waking. The pressure he'd exerted should have been enough to knock her out for hours. Barely ten minutes had passed.

The woman was stronger than he'd thought.

Lyon glanced in the rearview mirror as she pushed herself upright, brushing a loose strand of hair out of her face with groggy awkwardness.

"Where am I?" He knew the moment she remembered. A thick wave of tension rolled off her, her eyes widening in alarm. "Take me back!"

"Easy, Radiant. I'm taking you home. I don't know how you got all the way out here, but you've been marked by the goddess."

Pitching forward, she leaned between the front bucket seats. "*You're going the wrong way*. Take me back!"

"Your life here is over."

"You idiot. She's dying!"

She sat back . . . or he thought she had until her hand shot past his face and grabbed the steering wheel, jerking it hard to the right as they passed close to a row of parked cars.

Lyon wrenched the wheel, but it was too late. The car slammed into the back of a Toyota, inflating the air bag in his face, knocking him back, stunned. When his head cleared, he whirled to find himself staring at the empty backseat, a gust of damp, chilly air blowing in from the open door.

"Mick, I need to borrow your keys!"

At the sound of the woman's voice, Lyon twisted toward his own door and caught sight of the Radiant hopping into an old blue pickup truck across the street. Before he could disentangle himself from the deflated air bag, the truck squealed away from the curb and took off, leaving two young men watching, bemused.

Dammit to hell.

Lyon tried to back up, but the bumper of his

BMW was caught on the Toyota. Swearing, he threw open the car door and leaped out in a frustrated fury as the two men sauntered across the street to inspect the damage.

"Jerry's going to be pissed when he sees what you done to his car, man."

"Jerry will get over it," Lyon snapped, and lifted the front of the BMW until the bumpers unhooked.

"Dude!" One of the men laughed. "Fucking Superman."

"Yeah." Lyon climbed back into the car, pushed the air bag out of his way, then spun the vehicle in a tight circle and headed once more to the farmhouse. Anger slicked his palms as he gripped the wheel. What was the matter with her? Every Therian female dreamed of waking with the mark of the chosen one on her breast and finding her true mate among the Feral Warriors. Yet this one had run halfway across the continent and was still running.

Vhyper's words replayed in his head. *I wonder if she even knows what the mark means*. Was it possible she didn't even know she was Therian?

Sweet goddess. That would explain much—why her fear had leaped at the sight of him, why she'd fought to escape.

Lyon pushed the air from his lungs in a harsh burst. He'd thought he was dealing with a reluctant Radiant, or at the very least, a Therian who'd intentionally turned her back on her people. Now he had to consider the possibility she thought herself human.

Pulling into the driveway of the yellow clapboard house, he parked behind the old truck and debated the best way to extricate the woman from her human world. There was no time left to ease her out.

As he opened the car door and stepped into the rain, he heard a shout behind the house.

"Mom?" The alarm in the Radiant's voice twisted something deep inside him. "Momma!"

Lyon took off at a run, the rain stinging his face with small, cool pellets, soaking his hair and clothes. When he reached the corner of the house, he found her kneeling in the wet grass beside the slight, prone form of a woman. In the swath of light from the open back door, the downed woman's soaked white gown clung to her emaciated frame like a second skin.

Crying and frantic, the chosen one tried to lift the woman without success. Even an unascended Radiant should have double the strength of a human, simply from absorbing the energy of other Therians over the years. But this one had none, a sure sign she'd been cut off from her own kind for most, if not all, of her life. The new Radiant of the Ferals had most certainly been raised human.

Hell.

As he neared her, a twig snapped beneath his boot, drawing her wild, hate-filled gaze.

"My mother must have heard us in the kitchen. She tried to come after me. You killed her!" Emotion swirled around her like harsh fire in the cold rain.

"She's not dead." His boots slurped in the muddy grass as he reached her side. "I can feel her life force." Barely. The woman's hold on life was as thin as the finest thread. "She's human. She's not your mother."

A sound of disbelief escaped the Radiant's throat on a burst of humorless laughter. "You're insane, you know that? Just leave us alone."

"Radiant . . ."

"Don't call me that!"

"I don't have another name to call you." Pushing his dripping hair back from his face, Lyon knew he was handling this badly. He was the wrong warrior to woo her back into the fold. Tighe would turn on the charm. Vhyper the humor.

Lyon had no softness in him to give this woman. To give any woman. He was the chief. The leader. And she would simply have to do as she was told.

"I'm Kara. Just . . ." The anger on her face crumbled, tears welling in her eyes until her face was a solid sheet of moisture. "Help me. *Please*. She's going to die right here if I don't get her inside. I'll give you whatever you want. Just help me save her."

Her plea, trembling with desperation, tore through his determination, slamming him with guilt and the harsh understanding of the damage he would do . . . had already done . . . by trying to extract her from her human world with as much finesse as a berserker on a rampage.

Kara stumbled up the rain-slicked steps to the back door, a desperate pounding in her ears as she glanced over her shoulder at the stranger following with her mother. There was a terrible irony in the fact that her kidnapper was the only one who could keep her mother from dying in the rain.

She held the door for him, then ran for the phone. "I need to call an ambulance."

"Kara . . ." Her mom's voice carried to her, thin as worn cotton. "Don't. The doctors . . . can't do anything."

A sudden crack of thunder rattled the windows and doused the lights, blanketing them in utter darkness. The portable phone in her hand went dead. Kara slammed the phone on the counter in a burst of helpless fury. With the electricity out, she was trapped. Cell phones had never worked out here, and her closest neighbor was almost a quarter mile away.

"Carry her to the car. I'll drive her to the hospital myself."

"No . . . Kara." As weak as her mother's voice was, the determination rang clearly. "Stay here."

Kara wanted to scream her frustration. Instead, she rummaged through the drawers until she found a couple of flashlights. If they were staying here, her mom needed blankets and towels, dry clothes and maybe some hot tea to warm her insides. Kara refused to let her die from this. Not from this.

Flicking on the flashlights, she stabbed the darkness with two steady beams of light, illuminating the big man, wet and dripping, holding her mother with surprising care. His expression remained closed, but no longer quite as cold or forbidding as before. The tiny bit of softening did nothing to ease her wariness of him. Her fear, however, was all for her mom.

Kara turned toward the living room and motioned the stranger to follow with a sweep of one flashlight. "Put her on the sofa." She set one light on the coffee table and took the other with her as she ran to the downstairs linen closet and grabbed a couple of blankets.

Hurrying back, she covered her soaked and shivering parent from shoulder to feet, then grabbed a towel and sank to her knees beside the sofa, dabbing her mom's trembling face as she tried to ignore the stranger looming behind her like the grim reaper.

"You're not human, Kara," he said. "You're Therian. And you've been marked as our chosen one."

His words vibrated through her like the discordant notes of a song. The man was certifiably crazy, but he could sing the alien national anthem for all she cared as long as he left her alone to tend her mom.

"You think you belong here," the man continued, his voice a deep, pleasant rumble so at odds with the absurdity of his words. "But you don't."

Her mom's lashes fluttered, her pain-ridden eyes filling with distress as she looked toward the stranger.

"Stop it," Kara hissed, turning halfway around. "What is *wrong* with you?"

"You need to understand the truth."

Kara turned her back on him, but he moved beside her, standing over her. "Tell her."

"Tell her what?" But when Kara glared up at him, she found his gaze not on her but her mother.

"She deserves the truth," he said.

Kara lurched to her feet and faced him, anger snapping her patience. "Leave her alone. She's been through enough tonight, thanks to you."

A hint of regret warmed his amber gaze. "For that I'm sorry, but her time in this world is almost over. Yours has just begun. And you need to know the truth."

"What *truth*?"

"That you're not her daughter."

"Of course I'm her daughter." But she found herself turning to her mother, seeking confirmation . . . and found tears and denial swimming in the woman's eyes.

Kara sank to her knees beside the sofa and took her mom's icy hand in hers. "I'm yours. Of course I'm yours."

Tears pooled on her mother's ashen cheeks, her body no longer shivering. Her head moved from side to side in tiny, damning movements, a single word escaping her lips.

"No."

"Mom? What are you saying?" A chill that had nothing to do with the rain lifted goose bumps on her arms. It wasn't true. It couldn't be true.

And suddenly she understood. Kara swung her furious gaze on the stranger. "This is your doing. You're manipulating her just as you manipulated me."

He shook his head, his wet locks brushing his shoulders. "You're mistaken. The only wrong I've done is take you away when she needed you."

"I don't believe you."

His gaze fell to the sofa behind her, and his eyes flinched. "Radiant. *Kara*. Her spirit has fled. I'm sorry."

Kara jerked at his words and whirled back to where her mom lay still as . . .

"Mom?"

She grabbed her mother's thin wrist with frantic gentleness, searching for a pulse, but there was none. "Momma?"

It was over. Just like that, she was gone.

"No, Mom, no." Tears clogged her throat, choking her, as she sank to her knees beside the sofa and touched the cool skin of a papery cheek. "Please don't go. Don't leave me." Sobs broke over her in a torrent of grief as her head sank to the once-strong chest upon which she'd cried countless tears over the years. "I need you."

Misery swallowed her in a loss so deep she was

afraid she'd never escape. She didn't even notice the hand on her shoulder until the weight that crushed her heart started to lift enough that she could breathe again.

He was trying to steal her grief as he'd stolen her fear.

Kara surged to her feet in a sudden, blinding fury. "Get away from me! She's dead, you monster, and it's *your fault*."

She launched herself at the man, slamming her fists against his massive chest, unthinking, uncaring that he was twice her size and could snap her in half with his pinkies. But he didn't move. He took her blows without trying to defend himself, without touching her at all.

The maelstrom finally ran its course, leaving her exhausted and aching as if she'd been the one beaten instead of the one administering the blows. But before she could move away, he grabbed her and shoved her behind him.

"*Shit*." The word exploded under his breath even as he yanked two knives from his boots and held them aloft.

The man was certifiably . . .

The thought fled as she eased around his broad back and saw what was coming through the windows . . . the closed windows.

A scream lodged in her throat.

Draden.

Lyon shifted his weight to the balls of his feet, twin knives at the ready as half a dozen of the semicorporeal fiends flew straight for him, each of their bodies little more than floating gas beneath a head shaped like a hideously melted human face. His only thought was to protect the Radiant from the monsters that would drain the life force from her just as surely as the disease had stolen the spirit from the woman who'd raised her.

"What *are* they?" Behind him, Kara's fear washed over him like an icy stream.

"Stay behind me." He had no more time to talk as the enemy closed in. Lyon dodged fanged mouths, stabbing cleanly through the bodies and popping out the hearts of one, two, three . . .

The fourth latched onto his scalp from behind as the fifth went for his throat.

The sixth . . .

He heard a shriek and whirled, two draden still attached to him. The sixth swooped in on the Radiant only to collide with her upraised fist. Kara screamed with pain as her hand disappeared inside that razor-sharp mouth. Her gaze slammed into his, her eyes twin pools of blue terror.

"Grab the heart!" Lyon fought the creatures locked on to his neck and head, desperate to help her. Six months it had taken him to find her. He'd be damned if he'd lose her now.

*Chapter
Three*

Panic engulfed her, pain ripped through her hand and body as Kara struggled against the monster, hitting its gelatinous head with her free hand, trying to pull her captured hand loose of its fiery mouth.

Pain shot up her arm as if she'd stuck her hand into raw flame. The thing was trying to suck her in. She could feel it pulling at her as if it meant to swallow her whole. Terror threatened to cut off her air.

"Pull out its heart!" The man's words barely penetrated the fog that encased her brain.

Its heart. Its *heart*? How could a body with no form have a heart? But her free hand reached inside the ghostlike body as if she'd been doing this all her life, and closed around a beating, pulsing glob. *Holy cow*. With a hard yank, the creature disappeared in a puff of smokelike energy, freeing her ripped and shredded hand. Bone showed through ribbons of bloody flesh.

Her head spun with dizzying lightness. Her legs refused to hold her, and she slid to the ground, curving around her injured hand. Beyond screaming, beyond crying, all she could do was shake, her body quaking with pain. Disbelief. Shock.

She couldn't think. *Refused* to think about what she'd just seen. About all that had just happened. Her world had gone insane.

Cold. So cold.

Her mom was dead.

"Radiant." Out of the corner of her eye, she saw the stranger lower his big body to the floor beside her until he was sitting, his back against the love seat, his long legs stretched out in front of him. "Let me see your hand."

"No. I'm fine." Words were coming from her mouth, but she wasn't sure what she was saying. She barely recognized her own voice. So cold.

She felt a warm, callused hand slide across her jaw and cheek, one long finger curling behind her ear as it had earlier just before she'd lost consciousness.

"Do it," she whispered. "Knock me out."

"You want to escape."

"I can't . . . do this." Tears burned and slid down her cheeks as the pain in her hand nearly rivaled that in her chest, but the grief was worse, tearing so much deeper. "It hurts too much."

The man released a heavy breath. "Making you sleep won't get rid of the pain." Slowly, he removed his hand. "I can't take it all, but I can help. I owe you that much."

His hand slid beneath her hair to curl around her neck, but instead of easing her pain, misery swamped her, a hundred times worse than before.

"Oh, God. Oh, God."

"Easy, little Radiant. I had to strip away your defenses to get to the real emotions. Give me a minute."

Grief tore through her body like a muscle-wrenching poison, doubling her in half. "I can't do this. I can't . . ."

All at once, the pain eased, and she began to breathe again. In the space of half a dozen heartbeats, her grief lessened, aging, as if she'd been living with it for weeks or months, instead of minutes, dulling around the edges and slowly losing the ability to cut. The fear and confusion quieted in her head. Only her hand still swam with pain.

Kara lifted her gaze to his, meeting enigmatic amber eyes. "How do you do that? Are you some kind of healer?"

"It's just a skill."

She stared at him, really looked at him, her gaze skimming over the hard bones of an undeniably arresting face. His expression remained cool, perhaps guarded, but his eyes had warmed considerably.

"What's your name?"

"Lyon."

"Is that your first name or your last?"

"My driver's license would say my last. But only humans use the first."

She looked away, a succession of chills snaking through her body before being snatched away, one after another, through the man's touch. *Only humans.* As if he wasn't one himself.

With a breath-stealing slam of understanding, she knew he wasn't. The things he could do . . .

She dipped her forehead to rest on her updrawn knees. "I can't deal with this."

His thumb slid down her neck and back up again in a gentle and oddly sensual caress. "You can. Any woman with the courage and presence of mind to kill a draden the first time she sees one can handle a bit of truth."

Kara laughed, the sound more hysterical than humorous. "A *bit* of truth?" She raised her head to meet his gaze. "You're not crazy, are you? All that talk earlier of a different race . . . it's real."

"Yes."

"You're not human."

"No. Neither are you."

And somehow she knew that. She'd always known in some dark corner of her mind that she wasn't normal. Her cuts healed much too fast, and she never got sick. Had never, in twenty-seven years, even run a fever. Was that why her mother never let the doctors near her?

Had she known?

"What are we? Aliens?"

The man's smile, wide, crooked, and utterly charming, was so fleeting she almost missed it, but for an instant it transformed his face.

"We're Therians. A race similar to humans, but far less fragile. We don't age, and we heal most wounds quickly."

"So we're immortal?"

"To the humans, yes. Or virtually so. But we can die like any creatures. We just do it far less easily."

Questions crowded her mind as fear tried to clutch at her heart, but he held the emotion at bay with his touch.

"There's no need to be alarmed, little Radiant."

"Why do you call me Radiant?"

"You are the caller of the energies of the Earth. It's through you that your race renews its strength."

"I don't understand." She squeezed her eyes shut and shook her head. "I don't care. I don't want to be your Radiant."

The very thought that she was some kind of immortal chosen one was absurd. She was just Kara MacAllister, preschool teacher. A woman of average looks, average intelligence, average athletic ability. She was average in so many ways her picture ought to be inserted beside the word in the dictionary.

"I can't possibly be the one you're looking for. There's got to be a mistake."

She curled in on herself even tighter, inadvertently

squeezing her injured hand. The wave of fresh pain brought tears to her eyes.

"I've got to heal that injury, Kara."

"It'll heal on its own."

"No. It won't. A wound from a draden is different. Let me see your hand." His thumb slid under her chin, and he tilted her face up to his. "I won't hurt you."

She believed him, though she figured he was probably forcing trust into her while he was taking the other emotions out. As she eased her hand away from her body, the pain exploded. Breath hissed into her mouth between clenched teeth.

Lyon took hold of her wrist and lifted her mangled hand to his mouth.

She looked at him in disbelief. "Kissing it is not going to make it feel better." No matter how much her preschoolers believed otherwise.

Her words seemed to amuse him. "I heal through my tongue."

"Your . . . ?" She gasped as her aching thumb slid into a cocoon of warm silk. His velvet tongue stroked her skin, stealing the pain, sending shivers of heat flowing into her blood.

Her eyes widened as she felt her body begin to melt. Her breath quickened with a desire that shouldn't be there. A desire she didn't want.

He watched her with sharp eyes as he released her thumb and took each finger into his mouth, one by one, healing the flesh, easing the hurt, ensnaring her in a web of restless need. Her fingers healed, he pulled the back of her hand to his mouth and stroked his warm tongue over the cuts until the only pain remaining was from the raw tears on her palm.

When he turned her hand and pressed her palm to his mouth, fire leaped deep inside her, a living ache centered low in her body, at her very core. An ache that built and grew with every stroke of his tongue.

"Lyon . . ."

Her breaths came in small gasps as the pressure between her legs built. She was racing toward . . .

No. This wasn't right. Her mother lay dead only a few feet away. She clamped her knees together, fighting the rising tide, and lost. The orgasm broke over her in a sudden rush, tightening her womb in spasms of hot joy. Wave after wave of glorious sensation ripped through her, release singing through her veins. The best . . . the absolute best . . .

With a shudder of pure perfection, she collapsed against the coffee table and met Lyon's shocked gaze.

"Oh, God." She buried her face in her free hand in a useless attempt to hide from the utter mortification. How had she gotten so excited from such a simple touch?

She hadn't. Not by herself. She peeked between her fingers, then lowered her hand and glared at him.

"*You* did that to me. You're a master of manipulation, aren't you?"

He opened his mouth, then closed it with a snap. "We need to get going." His voice was gruff, almost strained, as he released her hand and rose to his feet. "The draden found us once. They'll find us again."

Kara shuddered and stood, happy to drop the subject of her small sexual overreaction, even as aftershocks tightened her womb, refusing to let her forget.

"What about my mom?"

"She's dead, Kara. We can leave her for others to dispose of in a more traditional manner, or we can bury her now. Your choice. But we can't stay. The longer you're here, the more likely other draden will find you. And there's no protection."

Kara opened her mouth to argue, then sighed, feeling her control over her life slipping from her hands. She was going with him. Tonight. Not only was it no longer safe for her here, but she had to know who she was. *What* she was. And there was only one way to get the answers.

Lyon.

"You found her," Tighe called, hopping down from the cockpit of the small Cessna several hours later.

Lyon nodded as he ushered Kara across the dark tarmac. The rain had finally stopped while they'd dug the grave for Kara's adoptive mother. He'd called Tighe to come get them, deciding to leave his BMW behind. After the evening's events, he'd given up any thoughts of driving cross-country with the woman. They faced the danger of another draden attack, of course. But the bigger danger, he'd realized, was to himself.

He'd always been somewhat sensitive to others' emotions, but he seemed to read Kara's extraordinarily clearly.

Sweet goddess, all he'd done was heal her injured hand, yet with every stroke of his tongue, her excitement had risen, driving his own right along with it until he'd been on fire for her. When her passion broke, he'd nearly lost it in his pants. Since he hadn't . . . quite . . . he was still hard as a rock and painfully aware of her. Her sweet scent, the curve of her jaw, the fine silk of her skin.

Goddess help me. The last thing he wanted was an obsession for any woman, let alone the chosen one. Yet every time he touched her, he felt need power through him like a charge of pure lightning.

When they reached the plane, Tighe greeted him in the usual fashion, extending his hand as they clasped one another just below the elbow in a slam of hard flesh.

Tighe looked at Kara curiously as he bowed his head. "Radiant."

"I'm . . . Kara." Wariness and exhaustion laced her voice. "Kara MacAllister."

Tighe threw Lyon a questioning look over Kara's head.

"She's the one," Lyon confirmed. "She was raised human, with no knowledge of the Therian race."

Tighe whistled low. "That's awkward." He took Kara's suitcase from Lyon, then turned to Kara, flashing a pair of dimples that had slain too many feminine hearts to count. "So, it was a bit of a surprise to you, huh? Being chosen to live with a bunch of sh—"

"Tighe . . ." Lyon warned, silencing the man with a look. She wasn't ready for any more surprises. "Kara's had a tough night."

Tighe nodded. "Understood." He slipped on his dark shades, then slung his arm across Kara's stiff shoulders, ushering her to the plane.

Something dark and jealous deep inside Lyon sprouted claws. There was only one reason Tighe put on sunglasses in the middle of the night. He was becoming aroused. When this particular warrior's interest was piqued by a female, his eyes turned from green man's eyes to golden cat's eyes. A change that would send a human woman screaming into the night. Or a woman who had been raised human.

A growl rumbled low in Lyon's throat.

Tighe glanced back with a questioning look, then dropped his arm with a smile that conceded nothing. He followed Kara up the steps, leaving Lyon to follow.

"Would you like to ride up front with me, Kara?" Tighe asked, closing the hatch. When he took Kara's hand, Lyon sprang, pulling her down beside him.

"*Leave her alone.*"

Tighe stared at him for one startled moment before his face broke into a grin. "Looks like the Pairing Ceremony may not be necessary after all, eh?"

"Like hell." What was the matter with him? He was acting like his beast had already claimed her. But she wasn't his and probably never would be. Hell, he didn't want her to be.

But the thought of anyone so much as touching her burned a hole in his gut the size of his fist.

Lyon dug his hand in his hair, raking it off his face.

He was so screwed.

Kara stared out the window of the Land Rover as Tighe pulled off the narrow, thickly treed road onto a long drive. Though dawn was breaking to the east, the heavy blanket of trees held the morning at bay like a shield against the encroaching light. And made the approach to her destination, possibly her new home, dark and unsettling.

In the front seat, Lyon and Tighe discussed their ongoing war against the terrifying draden. Tighe turned toward Lyon, his strong face animated. With his fashionably short, sun-bleached hair and wicked smile, he was every bit as good-looking as Lyon, though in an entirely different way. Though both men were far larger than most, Lyon had the broad shoulders and chest of a linebacker. Tighe had the sleek, muscular build of a quarterback and an overabundance of sexy charm.

But it was Lyon, with his intense amber eyes and air of command that pulled at her. And when he glanced back, meeting her gaze, made her breath quicken and her pulse kick up. Was this attraction real, or yet another thing he was forcing on her?

Kara clenched the fingers of her entwined hands, pressing them against the tense knot of her stomach. *What am I doing, coming with him?* The refrain had echoed like a litany in her head since the plane took off from the small airfield hours ago. Her first plane trip had whisked her away from everyone and everything she'd ever known. Everything.

Kara pulled her jacket tighter around her. With each passing minute, the events of the night seemed more and more unreal. Talking with immortals, or almost-immortals. Fighting a creature who could fly through a pane of glass without harming it yet tear her flesh to shreds. Burying her mom . . . who was not really her mom.

The ache of grief had settled in her chest, aged and mellow as if she'd been living with it for months, if not years.

How could any of this nightmare be real?

Yet it was. Even as she questioned the insanity that made her agree to this trip, part of her shook with the nervous excitement of discovering who and what she really was.

Ahead, scattered lights peeked through the trees until the car drew close enough to illuminate the whole of the house. Feral House, they called it. The home of the Feral Warriors. And their Radiant.

The house was nothing short of a small mansion—three visible dark brick stories with dormers on the top floors and black shutters at each of the windows. In the dark, the house appeared cold and forbidding like something out of a gothic novel. All it needed was a rollicking thunderstorm and a few crows to make it a perfect setting for a horror movie.

The thought did nothing to ease the apprehension twisting her insides into knots.

The drive widened and curved in front of the house and was lined with expensive-looking cars. A couple of low-slung sports cars, a Hummer, and a yellow Porsche among them.

Tighe parked the Land Rover behind a red convertible and glanced at her in the rearview mirror. "Welcome home, Kara. We're a lot to take in all at once." He grinned, the smile carving deep dimples into his cheeks. "But you'll grow to love us."

"I'm sure," Kara murmured, but the thought of living with *nine* men like these two was enough to take her breath away.

Lyon held the car door for her and ushered her out into the damp morning chill. She glanced at his profile as they started up the short brick walk to the house. "Are there draden here, too?"

"They're everywhere we are. But the house is protected. You're safe."

"Why haven't I ever heard of them before?"

"Humans can't see them and generally don't attract them. The draden feed off Therian energy. Lost among the humans, with your energy untapped, you were safe enough. Until I showed up. You'll be safe here as long as you stay inside at night."

"They're nocturnal?" Kara followed him up the wide brick steps to the front door.

"Yes." Lyon ushered her into a circular, high-ceilinged foyer dimly lit by a pair of electric sconces. Twin stairs curved to the second floor, framed by ornately carved wood railings, then traveled up to a third. Her wide-eyed gaze traveled down, following the line of chain from which hung the biggest chandelier she'd ever seen, teeming with hundreds of crystals. Her gaze slowly descended farther, taking in ornately papered walls covered with paintings of gardens and flowers, coming to rest on the magnificent scene painted on the wood floor beneath her feet. Like something out of an ancient temple, naked men and women played hide-and-seek in a woods teeming with unicorns and centaurs and all manner of mythical creatures.

Feeling as if she'd stepped through the doors of a small palace, she met Lyon's gaze. "How many women live here?"

"Pink is the only female, besides the Radiant, who resides here on a permanent basis. Some of the men bring in girlfriends to stay for a time, but none of the men are currently mated. Pink does the cooking and keeps the house." He led her across the painted floor to the right-hand stair. "Why? Looking for allies?"

"No, though a friend would be nice. I'm trying to reconcile the fancy decor with a house full of males. I expected wood paneling, maybe some stags' heads on the walls."

Tighe made a half-choked sound behind her. "We're not much on mounting animal heads." He started up the stairs. "I'm going to catch a few more hours of sleep."

Lyon nodded and turned back to Kara. "Believe me, the decorating was Beatrice's doing, not ours. Beatrice was your predecessor. The previous Radiant."

"What happened to her?"

"She died six months ago."

"How?" Kara frowned. "I thought you said we were all but immortal."

"We're not indestructible. We can, and do, die. Beatrice fell asleep with her window open. The draden got to her before we knew what happened."

"I'm sorry."

Lyon nodded. "No one lives forever. Not even Therians."

Kara shivered at the thought of being overpowered by those horrible little fiends, their teeth ripping her to shreds as they sucked the life out of her. Definitely not the way she wanted to go.

Lyon swept his hand outward, encompassing the foyer. "You're free to redecorate any way you like."

Redecorate. The thought was so absurdly mundane she almost laughed out loud. She was in a strange, unsettling house full of powerful males who claimed she was their chosen one. She didn't know who they were, who she was, or what they really wanted from her.

The wallpaper could wait.

She followed Lyon up the stairs and down a long, dark hallway lit only by the faint glow of dawn. Lyon seemed to have no trouble finding his way in the near dark as he led her to the end of the hall and into one of the rooms. He flipped on a bedside lamp, illuminating the biggest bedroom Kara had ever seen. The decorating was so overwrought, it made the foyer seem plain by comparison. A mammoth tester bed draped in burgundy velvet and gold silk sat in the middle of a room papered in a busy pattern of lush foliage and birds. Even the ceiling was plastered with heavy gilt scrollwork and painted with fat, playful cherubs.

"This was . . . Beatrice's room?" Kara asked.

"Yes. She was a great collector of art." He motioned to the many oil paintings hanging on the walls. "They're all originals."

Lyon set her single suitcase on a carved chest at the foot of the bed, then closed the red velvet drapes and retreated to the door.

"Sleep, little Radiant." His expression was closed, yet not unkind. "You can unpack when you're rested. If you need me, you have only to call my name, and I'll hear you. My room is directly above yours."

Lyon strode to the door, and Kara started to follow, her pulse rocketing at the thought of being alone. She forced herself to stop. As badly as she wanted to beg him to stay, there was only one way he could possibly construe such a request, and she wasn't that kind of girl. Kara MacAllister didn't have sex with strangers, not even ones who sent her hormones into such paroxysms of excitement that she orgasmed from the simple stroke of their tongues on her hand.

As Lyon closed the door behind him, Kara groaned, mortified all over again. What must he think of her? She pressed the heels of her hands against her closed eyes, easing the tired ache. Lyon was right. She needed sleep.

Pulling her nightgown out of her suitcase, her gaze was pulled to one of the paintings on the wall. An African lion with his head thrown back in full roar, stood with one massive paw pinning a disembodied human head to the ground. Painted on the cheek of the male head was a shiny copper circle. And in his eyes, the brightness of life and disdain.

With a small shiver, Kara stripped out of her clothes and pulled on her nightgown, then walked to the window and peered between the heavy drapes, looking out over the woods that pressed in from all sides. The sky was beginning to lighten now. The sun would be up soon. A new day.

Her first without her mom.

Sadness rolled over her, triggering the burn of tears. Kara swiped away a lone drop that slid down her cheek and pressed her palm to the cool glass.

Why had she come? She should have refused. But with a despondent sigh, she knew it wouldn't have mattered. Lyon would have knocked her out and brought her anyway. He'd come for her for a reason. And until he was through with her, she knew with total conviction, he wouldn't let her go.

Chapter Four

"Did you find her?" Paenther asked, stepping back for Lyon to enter even as he extended his hand in greeting. As their forearms met, the black-eyed warrior flicked the wall switch to his bedroom, squinting against the sudden light, telling Lyon in no uncertain terms he'd woken the man from a sound sleep. If the blinking eyes hadn't told him that, the barely controlled rage permeating the room would have. The sharp edges of a rage that had been burned into the shifter's soul centuries ago and which he kept under control only by dint of his granite will.

"She's here."

"Thank the goddess." Paenther released him to rake a hand through his straight black hair, sending it swinging down to brush his shoulders. One lock fell forward, tangling with the harsh feral marks that cut across his left eye. "How soon can we get her ascended?"

Lyon shook his head. "She was raised by humans."

"She's had *no* preparation?"

"None. It's going to take time."

"Shit. We're going to play hell getting the draden swarms back under control if this goes on much longer. We need to be able to shift, Roar."

"What about Foxx and the Daemon blade?" The moment Lyon had sensed Kara's whereabouts, he'd left to track her down, leaving Paenther, his second-in-command, to deal with Foxx. "Did you get to the bottom of it?"

Paenther shook his head. "One minute he swears he didn't go into the vault, and the next he says he only wanted to look at the Daemon blade and accidentally got it mixed up with the ceremonial blade. Then he's back to swearing he didn't take it out of the vault at all. I don't think he did it intentionally. I think the problem is the lack of radiance. He's young, Roar. Those first couple of years after you're marked are a bitch as it is. He's going to be the first to suffer."

"Keep an eye on him. On all of them. We can't afford any more mistakes like that one."

"Agreed."

Lyon left to find some sleep, but as he started down the long second-floor hall toward the stairs that would lead to the third floor and his room, a trill of feminine laughter drifted to him from the far end. Zaphene's laughter. Foxx's girlfriend of . . . what was it now? Five months? Six? Zaphene seemed to be spending more nights in Feral House than whichever Therian enclave she now called home. Though he was beginning to think that arrangement might turn permanent. The young Foxx had been exhibiting all the signs of a man foolish with love.

But as the pair walked into the light of an electric sconce, Lyon saw the sultry redhead was not with Foxx, but Vhyper. Though they weren't touching one another, there was something about the look of them together that made him wonder if Foxx's dreams were about to come to a crashing end.

"Did you find our Radiant?" Vhyper asked, as they met at the stairs.

Lyon nodded. "I did."

A grin split Vhyper's face. "Good. That's good."

Lyon's gaze flicked between the couple. "You're up early. What are you two up to?"

"Coffee. I couldn't sleep."

"Where's Foxx?"

Vhyper shrugged. "Still licking his wounds from the thrashing Paenther gave him last night." He grabbed Zaphene and pulled her tight against him as she gave a sultry laugh. "I'm keeping his woman entertained until he snaps out of it." Vhyper waggled his brows. "The cub better get out of his sulk soon, or he may need to find himself a new woman."

Lyon assumed Vhyper was pulling a major flirt, but there was something in his eyes that set off Lyon's instinct for trouble. He gave a silent groan. The last thing he needed right now was to have to play referee in a battle over a woman.

Zaphene's cool laughter grated on Lyon's ears as she slipped out of Vhyper's hold and stepped up to him. Her warm fingers trailed down his forearm until she gripped his hand. "If I'm back to shopping for a man, maybe I'll have to start at the top this time."

Lyon pulled his hand from her grasp. "I'm not for sale." He tossed Vhyper a hard look. "Do me a favor and keep your hands to yourself until things get back to normal around here. Foxx doesn't need this right now. None of us does . . ." The walls and floor started spinning.

"Easy, Roar."

Lyon felt himself being eased down until he was sitting on the top step of the stairs.

Zaphene laughed. "I didn't mean to fluster you, Warrior."

"You didn't . . ." Goddess, but he was dizzy.

"It's the lack of radiance." Vhyper squeezed his shoulder. "Get some sleep, Chief. You'll feel better in the morning."

As Lyon watched Vhyper and Zaphene descend the stairs, his head slowly cleared. Apparently Foxx wasn't the only one suffering from the lack of radiance. Dammit to hell. They had to get Kara ascended, and fast.

He pushed himself to his feet and walked the

few steps to the upper stair. As he reached for the rail, his gaze caught on Kara's door. He imagined her sprawled in sensuous abandon across the gold satin sheets of that big bed, her unbound hair splayed like fingers of silk, her creamy skin beckoning.

Clenching his jaw, he forced his feet onto the steps, climbing with slow deliberation. He returned to his room, stripped, and fell back onto his bed, flinging his forearm over his eyes as if he could erase the image of Kara from his mind. His senses, opened to her in order to find her, had become drugged by her quiet beauty and aching vulnerability. But it was over. She was home. It should be a simple matter to turn off his interest in a woman he'd known fewer than a dozen hours.

A simple matter.

Just as soon as he figured out how to get her out of his blood.

Kara woke to find gray daylight seeping into the room, framing the dark drapes in a colorless glow as rain pattered on the windows. She levered herself up from the rumpled sheets and sat up, pushing her hair out of her face as she looked at the cavernous room.

It was real. The whole accompanying-an-immortal-to-his-castle thing really should have been a dream.

And her mom . . . Kara closed her eyes, bracing for the grief to steamroll her. But the pain didn't come. Only a dull ache, a heavy sadness. Blinking, she opened her eyes again, suddenly glad for Lyon's intervention. This she could handle.

Her thoughts clung to her mother, to the woman she'd grown up with, strong and healthy, and full of love.

Had she known Kara wasn't human? Kara's brows lowered as thoughts cascaded through her mind, one after another, bringing a near certainty that she had. Her mom's insistence that she never go near a doctor, nor ever play sports, had probably been intended to keep anyone from learning how quickly she healed. And the reason she'd begged Kara to stay in Spearsville when she finished high school? She'd always believed her mom was afraid she'd miss her too much. Now she wondered if her mother hadn't known there were dangers waiting for her if she wandered too far.

All these years, it seemed, she'd protected Kara's secret. Even from Kara herself. For twenty-seven years, she'd thought she'd known who she was. For twenty-six and a half of those years, she'd been perfectly happy. Until three months ago when she'd suddenly become restless and dissatisfied with her life. Until the mark appeared on her breast, she realized. Her restlessness had almost certainly begun when she'd become the Radiant.

Tossing back the sheet, Kara climbed out of bed. As her bare feet hit the plush rug, she stopped, a sudden, inexplicable feeling of dread welling up to tighten her throat. Why? Her gaze darted around the room. With a shiver of fear, she dropped to her knees and looked under the bed, but there was no one there. By the time she stood again, the sharp dread had dulled to little more than a faint disquiet.

Weird. Was there more to this house than she could see? Was there a ghost or some other invisible creature they'd yet to tell her about lurking in the shadows? The thought sent goose bumps skating over her skin and had her starting for the door.

Lyon would know. He could tell her if there was anything to be afraid of. He'd keep her safe.

The thought had her pulling up. Whoa. How had this happened? How, in a matter of hours, had Lyon gone from being a frightening stranger to her security blanket?

Was he really? Or was he merely playing with her emotions again, this time from a distance?

She refused to race out of the room like a scared little girl letting her imagination run away with her. Not that her current situation didn't warrant some trepidation, but feeling ill at ease about the unknown didn't mean there was some evil presence breathing down her neck.

For heaven's sake, she was still in her nightie. And it had to be late. She looked around for a clock. Almost five o'clock. In the evening, she supposed. She'd slept all day.

Kara grabbed the toiletries from her suitcase and headed for the private bathroom. But despite telling herself there was nothing to be afraid of, the feeling of disquiet wouldn't go away. She raced through her shower in record time chanting one word over and over and over.

Lyon.

Fifteen minutes later, Kara started down the stairs, her eyes darting and watchful as she followed the sound of male voices somewhere in the house. All through her shower, and since, the unnatural dread had ebbed and flowed, rising to chill her skin and make her pulse race, then falling again. She hoped she was just being paranoid, prayed that when she found Lyon and asked if there was any reason she should feel spooked, he'd tell her no, of course not. Then he'd introduce her to the rest of the Feral Warriors, men as nice and charming as Tighe, and give her the full tour of the house, which would include a swimming pool or gazebo, or something equally luxury-mansion-ish, and she'd laugh at her completely unfounded misgivings.

She really hoped that was what happened, because right this moment she wanted to bolt from the house and not stop running until she crossed the Mississippi.

Her nose caught a whiff of roast pork as she stepped onto the painted floor of the foyer, making her empty stomach growl in complaint. She'd never had a chance to eat that soup last night . . . or anything since. Her trepidation took a sudden backseat to hunger. Maybe Lyon was in the kitchen. And if not? She'd grab something to eat before she continued her search.

The mouthwatering aroma seemed to be coming from the same direction as the voices, down a long, wide hall lined with more paintings. The voices became clearer as she walked.

"I can beat you, dog."

"Don't call me *dog*."

"Tonight at midnight. Outside the wards. No knives."

The second man grunted. "Deal."

"Morons," said a third voice Kara thought she recognized as Tighe's. "If they swarm, you're both dead."

Kara eased into the doorway of a spacious, window-lined room. Outside, the budding trees dripped with rain against a gray sky, darkening with dusk. Inside, large blue-and-gold birds covered the wallpaper in a dizzying explosion of color lit by a pair of chandeliers half the size of the one in the foyer, yet no less grand. At a table that looked like it might have been stolen from the court of one of the old French kings, sat four huge men. They ate and talked with one another as naturally and casually as if they sat in a rustic kitchen instead of a painfully formal dining room.

"Let 'em swarm," the first man said. She could see him, now, sitting facing the doorway, a shaggy thatch of red hair framing a youthful, freckled face. "Wulfe and I are going hunting, aren't we, my man?"

"I'm not your man."

The red-haired one looked up and saw her, then

rose to his feet, prompting the others to do the same. Kara felt her cheeks grow warm. The only one she recognized was Tighe, who was even now slipping on a pair of sunglasses.

He motioned to her with a friendly grin. "Come join us, Kara."

Four pairs of eyes pinned her, watching her with varying degrees of interest and curiosity, making her feel ill at ease in a way that was utterly foreign to her. At home, she was never self-conscious, but there had never been a reason to be. Everyone knew her and had since she was a baby. She was just Kara. Miss MacAllister to her preschoolers.

But she wasn't Miss MacAllister anymore. She was the chosen one. And what exactly did *that* mean? How did they expect her to act? Immortal VIP wasn't a role she'd ever imagined for herself. But she did know how to be Kara MacAllister, and she supposed that would have to be enough for now.

Kara took a deep breath and forced her feet to cross to the table where the men stood waiting for her. Watching her. Four of the most physically imposing men she'd ever seen other than Lyon.

Reaching them, she thrust out her hand to the nearest man, the biggest of the bunch. As she looked up into his face, she caught her breath in a small, startled gasp. She had to force herself not to jerk back at the scars that crisscrossed his hard, rugged face. Had he been in an accident? A bad one, by the looks of his nose, which had to have been broken at least half a dozen times.

The scowl on his mouth was only partly due to the scar tugging his lip downward, and she realized she was staring. And still standing with her empty hand outstretched.

"I . . . I'm sorry." Her hand dropped self-consciously as her gaze rose to his. In his eyes she saw not so much anger as a hardness. And maybe a hint of resignation. "I'm Kara. Kara MacAllister."

Something flickered in his gaze, softening the harsh lines of that badly scarred face. Easing, if only slightly, that scowl. He lifted a hand the size of a dinner plate to the spot hers had been moments before.

"I'm Wulfe."

Kara took the proffered olive branch without hesitation and managed to smile at him. "Hi, Wulfe."

His huge palm closed around hers. "At your service, Radiant." To her surprise, his other hand landed softly on her shoulder, and he started to close the distance between them as if he meant to hug her.

Kara stiffened involuntarily. Wulfe's scowl returned full force as he jerked back and turned away. She opened her mouth, uncertain what to say to apologize, but an arm around her shoulders startled her into silence.

"Welcome, Radiant." She looked up into the face of the redhead. He was definitely younger than the others, his eyes friendly. "I'm Foxx." He pulled her against his side and slid his hand down her arm.

Were they all coming on to her? Or were they just way too touchy-feely?

She didn't move, couldn't move without risking offending him, too. Finally, he released her and stepped away. All she wanted to do was step back and establish a little personal space, but there were still two men crowding around her.

Tighe stroked her hair gently, then stepped back, as if sensing her keen discomfort. His dimpled smile helped to calm her. "How'd you sleep?"

"Hi, Tighe. I . . . slept fine."

"I'm glad. You hungry?"

She felt a true smile lift her lips and make it all the way to her eyes.

"Starved." She'd almost forgotten the fourth man until he moved beside Tighe. He was as tall as the others, but without the heavy musculature.

He kept his hands clasped behind his back as he smiled at her. His face was long and strong-boned, his brown eyes alight with curiosity beneath a pair of dark, sharply winged brows. Unlike the others, he made no move to touch her, and she relaxed further.

"I'm Hawke, Radiant."

Hawke was a cool name. So was . . . Kara blinked. Wulfe. And Foxx. *And Lyon*. Her gaze flew from one man to the next. "You're all named after animals."

Hawke started to say something, but Tighe coughed, and the man went quiet. "Nicknames, Kara. Someone once said we had the manners of a bunch of wild animals, so we decided to call ourselves by their names."

Kara cocked her head. "Then why are you just Tighe?"

He grinned. "Tiger."

Kara smiled, but the fear that had ridden her since she woke tightened her throat. She sensed nothing amiss. The men were all friendly enough, in their way, yet the feeling she was in danger persisted, as did the certainty that only one man could keep her safe.

"Where's Lyon?"

"You won't find him here." Foxx started back around to the seat she'd seen him in when she entered. "Our chief never eats with his foot soldiers."

"Lyon keeps to himself." Tighe pulled out the chair he'd been sitting in for her, moving his plate down a space to seat her between Foxx and himself. He smiled at her with those incongruous sunglasses, a flirtatious smile that should have had her pulse racing. "Have a seat, pretty girl. When you're through eating, I'll take you to him. Unless I can convince you to stay with me." His grin turned boyish, carving dimples into his cheeks.

Kara found herself smiling back. She hesitated only a moment before she nodded and sat. Tighe grabbed a clean plate from a stack in the middle of the table and handed it to her.

"We have pork medallions, ham steaks, and roast beef. What are you in the mood for?"

Kara looked at the three platters. The only food on the table. "It's all meat."

The men stilled, an odd tension rippling through the air of the room.

Kara wished she could crawl under the table. "It looks wonderful." She felt like she'd made a terrible gaffe. They'd offered her a king's feast, and she'd had to comment.

"I can have Pink make you something else," Tighe said.

"No, this is fine. I didn't mean to imply . . . I wasn't complaining. I like meat."

As she reached for the serving fork on the nearest platter, Foxx leaned toward her, dipping his head until his face was only inches from her own.

"So, where have you been all my life?"

Kara bit her tongue to keep from laughing. All his life? He couldn't be more than twenty. But at the same time, she felt her cheeks heat from the obvious come-on.

"Have some mercy on her, Foxx." Hawke shook his head, his expression sympathetic. "Why don't you tell us something about yourself, Kara?"

But Foxx wasn't through toying with her. He looped his arm around her shoulders and tilted his head toward her, conspiratorially. "Be careful of Hawke, Radiant. Once he starts asking questions, he never stops. You'll be crying for mercy within the hour."

Hawke's smile was bland. "Better that than having her crying from boredom, kit."

Foxx's smile turned wicked. "Give me an hour

with any woman, and she'll be crying, all right. Crying for more."

Kara's cheeks went from warm to hot, her body stiffening. She needed space. She wanted Lyon.

"Cool it, Foxx," Tighe said sharply. "Show a little respect. She's not used to us, yet."

Foxx made a sound deep in his throat that almost sounded like an animal's growl, but his arm slipped from around her shoulders.

Tighe gave her shoulder a quick, gentle nudge with his. "Eat, Kara. You've got to be hungry."

"I . . . yes. I am. Thanks."

"She can answer your questions later, Hawke."

Finally, they began to talk around her, the discussion turning to knives and how far they could throw different kinds of blades. At the rabid one-upmanship, so typical of any Friday night bar party in Spearsville, Kara began to relax enough to be able to eat, and even taste the food, which was truly delicious.

Beside her, both Tighe's and Foxx's heads rose in unison. When she lifted her own, she saw three people walking in the door, two more of the large men and an auburn-haired woman who looked like she'd stepped out of the pages of a fashion magazine, her slinky, emerald green dress slit nearly to the top of her thigh. In her black stilettos, she carried herself with a seductive grace that left Kara feeling like the country bumpkin she probably was. She wished she'd dressed in something nicer than her khakis and cotton sweater. She wished she *had* something nicer.

"Any food left?" one of the men said. "Or did you animals wolf it all down?" The man was bald in a sexy-pirate kind of way, though he was dressed more like a lean, muscular biker. A belt hung low on his waist, carrying an impressive, if somewhat disturbing, collection of knives. His black leather vest hung open, revealing a chest as devoid of hair as his head and a short row of scars on his neck that looked oddly familiar. Like the mark on her breast, she realized. Did they all have them?

The man on the other side of the woman had a seriously sinister look to him with his mustache, goatee, and pale, pale eyes. Eyes as cold as they were curious. She realized the newcomers were eyeing her with as much curiosity as she was them. As they approached the table, the men around her rose.

Kara was suddenly uncertain what to do. What was the proper protocol? Should she stand, too? Or was that something only the men did? Her mother had taught her basic table manners, but considering the fanciest restaurant she'd ever eaten at was Bill Barton's Steakhouse, this was way out of her realm of experience.

Tighe exchanged greetings with the bald man in the same way she'd seen him do with Lyon. Almost a handshake, but more, while their free hands clasped the other's shoulder. When they separated, Tighe took the woman in his arms and kissed her full on the mouth. But all he exchanged was a glance and a brief nod of the head with the scary-looking man.

To Kara's bemusement, every one of the men went through the same ritual, greeting each in exactly the same way Tighe had. Except for Foxx, who took the woman aside and gave her a kiss befitting long-lost lovers.

Were these three visitors, or just the stragglers coming in to dinner late?

Did they really do this all the time?

Foxx released the woman, and Kara felt the woman's cool, assessing gaze turn to her. Kara rose, disliking the feeling of everyone towering over her.

"Could this be our new Radiant?" the bald man asked, releasing Wulfe to turn to her. His gaze was sharp and assessing.

"Kara, Vhyper. Vhyper, Kara," Tighe said with a wave of his hand. "Sit, Kara. Don't make her quit eating, Vhype. The poor woman's starving."

But Kara stayed where she was. She'd sit when the rest of them sat.

Vhyper started around the table, but Tighe called him off.

"You can all greet her properly later. She wasn't raised Therian and isn't used to our physicality." Tighe touched her shoulder briefly, drawing her attention to the other man. "This is Kougar and Zaphene, who is soon to be Foxx's mate. His wife."

Kara swallowed, then nodded and smiled, encompassing the newcomers in a single, quick gaze. "It's nice to meet you."

"Charmed," Zaphene murmured, but something in her tone made Kara feel like the woman was laughing at her.

If Kara could have slunk away without being noticed, she would have.

Tighe urged Kara back in her chair. As soon as she sat, the others took their seats. Foxx grabbed his plate from across the table and placed it beside Zaphene as the three newcomers took seats at the far end of the table.

Kara took a bite, then felt Zaphene's gaze on her and began to grow even more uncomfortable than before. The woman's eyes, filled with an amused pity, stripped her of her quickly waning supply of confidence. She didn't know the first thing about this culture or this world. With growing mortification, she wondered how many mistakes she'd already made without knowing it.

Her discomfort grew until her fork slipped from her fingers with a clatter, jerking all gazes her way. Her cheeks flooded with heat as unwanted tears pricked the backs of her eyes. She just wanted to go home.

"Oops," she murmured, and picked up her glass of water as casually as she could manage, desperately trying to ignore the woman at the other end of the table with her too-sharp eyes.

"Can I get you anything else?" a pleasant, though oddly pitched feminine voice said behind her.

Beside her, Tighe groaned. "Pink . . ."

Kara glanced over her shoulder and froze, her heart shooting into her throat. The woman was . . . the *creature* was . . . a bird! She was the size of a person, but her legs . . . were those of a flamingo, and her human-looking hands and face were covered in pink feathers. *Feathers instead of skin.*

Her glass slipped from her numb fingers and shattered on the plate in a spray of water that soaked her shirt.

Kara jumped up and backed away from the mess . . . and the bird . . . her entire body shaking, her scalp tingling as if the hair on her head were trying to stand on end.

"Kara," Tighe said.

"I'm sorry," she murmured at the stricken look on the creature's face.

The sound of Zaphene's low laughter only sealed her humiliation.

"Kara, I'm sorry. I should have . . ."

As Tighe started to stand, she shoved her palms toward him. "Don't." To her mortification, she felt tears starting to leak from her eyes. "I'm fine. Excuse me."

She half walked, half ran from the room. Immortals. She'd assumed that meant humans or humanlike. The woman was a *bird*.

And the others . . .

Her hand clutched at the wall as she doubled over for one long, horrified moment. Lyon, Kougar, Foxx. *Nicknames?*

She pushed away and stumbled down the hall, fearing she was going to be sick.

Lyon. Where was Lyon?

The pounding of her pulse in her ears drove her forward. She had to find him. The sound of some kind of sports game on television caught her ear, and she ran toward it. She rounded the corner to find a large, dark-paneled rec room filled with leather furniture and the biggest television she'd ever seen.

Another of the huge warriors sat on the sofa, one arm across his knees, the other casually curling a metal dumbbell with weights the size of bowling balls.

The man saw her, set down the weight, and rose.

"I'm . . . looking for Lyon."

"Are you, now?" The man was dressed in army fatigues, his hair an unstyled shaggy brown, his lower face covered in a two-day growth of beard stubble. His eyes were hard as he came too close, crowding her.

Kara stepped back, knocking against the wall behind her.

"Are you our new Radiant, then?" he growled.

A desperate lump formed in her throat as she nodded jerkily. "I need to find Lyon."

The hint of curiosity in the man's eyes transformed to something unpleasant, and he pressed his fists against the wall on either side of her, towering over her.

"What do you want with Lyon?" He leaned forward, nearly touching her cheek with his nose, then made a low, animal sound in his throat. "I can smell him on you."

She couldn't move, caught between the wall at her back, the table at her side, and the man himself. "He's not on me. I haven't even seen him since I got up."

"He's marked you. Which was foolish of him since there's been no Pairing. But if he wants to play that game, so can I." He pushed his pelvis against her hip, pinning her to the wall as he rubbed himself hard.

Kara choked, slamming her hands against his chest. "Stop it! Get away from me!"

And suddenly he was gone, jerked backward by yet another stranger, a furious black-haired man with skin the color of a Native American and a scar across one eye that looked exactly like the marks on her breast. Cold fury filled his black eyes.

Her heart froze. The dread she'd been fighting since she woke leaped, sending her into a spiraling panic.

But the black-haired warrior turned that heated gaze on her attacker. "Jag, *you go too far.*"

With a snarl, Jag swung at the other man, raking his fingernails across the man's face. No, not fingernails. *Claws.* Huge, razor-sharp cat's claws.

Kara shrieked, then clapped her hand against her mouth as ribbons of blood bloomed on her rescuer's face. A face that, even as she watched, transformed into something out of a horror flick. Black eyes shifting, the irises expanding until no white showed, changing to the green eyes of a jungle cat. His teeth grew, both canines and incisors elongating, sharpening to daggers.

With a roar of fury, the two men attacked one another, tumbling onto the floor in a slash of claws and fangs, barely missing her feet. She stood frozen, staring at them, her mouth wide, chills racing down her spine in a continuous, icy flow. Tremors coursed through her limbs until her entire body was shaking.

They weren't human. She'd known they weren't human, but . . . but . . .

Panic raked at her mind as one word, a single desperate cry, screamed through her head and finally found its way out of her mouth.

"Ly-on!"

Chapter
Five

At the sound of Kara's scream, Lyon leaped from his desk chair and started running. As he turned the corner to the media room, he saw Jag and Paenther in a full-out feral battle. They were tearing one another to shreds at the very feet of their brand-new, very human-minded Radiant. A Radiant who he'd intentionally *not* told they were shape-shifters.

Dammit to hell.

Well, she had a pretty good clue now and appeared none too happy about it if the look of raw terror on her face was anything to go by.

"Cease!" At his roar, the combatants tore apart and sprang to their feet, their gazes locked on one another for a long, heated moment, before slowly turning his way.

Blood striped the carpet and drenched what was left of their shredded clothes.

Lyon's gaze swung to Kara, taking in the unnatural paleness of her skin. Her wild-eyed gaze locked on his, and she flew at him. He barely had time to open his arms before she pressed herself against him.

"Everything okay?" Tighe asked, rushing into the room, Hawke close behind.

"Yeah." Lyon closed his arms around the quaking woman slowly, awkwardly, feeling both stunned and awed by her sudden lack of fear of him. By her trust. He was a man used to wariness in others, and he'd certainly instilled that in her well enough last night. Yet now she clung to him as if he were all that stood between her and certain death.

Thanks to his two warriors, who only now were beginning to sheathe their beasts.

He slid his hand beneath Kara's soft hair, pressing his palm to her bare neck to ease some of the panic pouring out of her.

Tighe met his gaze with a grimace. "I guess she got an eyeful." He shook his head with regret. "She saw Pink. I should have warned the bird . . ."

"It's my fault. I put off an explanation that shouldn't have been delayed." He looked to Paenther. "The Pairing takes place in an hour."

Paenther nodded.

As Lyon peeled Kara away from him, she looked at him with eyes that, while no longer petrified, were still more wild than he would have liked.

"Come." He held out his hand, and she took it without hesitation and followed him from the room. His palm pressed against hers, calming her as he led her up the stairs. But while her fear ebbed away, he sensed rage rushing in to fill the void.

The moment they reached her room, she jerked away from him and grabbed her suitcase. "I hate this place! I'm going home."

No. She wasn't. But he was wise enough not to voice that thought out loud. Not yet. Not until he'd had a chance to ease her anger. He crossed the floor and slid his hands on her tight shoulders, but she whirled out of his reach and faced him, her color high, blue eyes flashing.

"Stop it! Stop manipulating my emotions. I *like* feeling angry." But with each word, he felt her anger draining away. "I hate feeling afraid." Her hands rose and splayed over her skull, her gaze scattering like shot over the floor. "This place is driving me crazy."

Finally, her hands fell, and her gaze rose to spear him. "You neglected to tell me a few things."

"Yes." *Avoided,* was more like it. "I'm sorry. I didn't think you were ready for the whole story, but you shouldn't have had to find out that way."

"I think you'd better tell me everything now." Her voice was brittle, but no longer jagged with emotion.

Lyon nodded. He'd known he'd have to tell her sooner or later, though he'd been opting for later.

"Why don't we sit down?" He needed to be able to reach her, touch her, if she became agitated. *Yeah, right.* He just wanted to be close enough to smell the sweet scent rising from her skin.

But Kara refused. "I don't want to sit."

Lyon settled himself on the upholstered chair by the window where he could watch her.

She met his gaze. "What are you? Werewolves or something?"

"Shape-shifters." He could almost see the wheels turning in her head.

"Just eyes and fangs? And claws?"

"No. The partial shift comes about when emotions run high. Usually negative emotions. We call the partial shift *going feral*. When we're in full power, we can also shift completely into our animals when we want to. That takes control, and is usually not done in the heat of anger."

She looked away, as if processing that. "Am I one? An animal?"

"No."

Her focus returned to him, her sweet mouth moving, her teeth playing with her lip. On a burst of air, she sank onto the chest at the foot of the bed. "You'd better tell me the rest, Lyon. I need to know."

She wanted the truth. Deserved the truth. And yet there were things—things about the rituals—she was not ready to hear. He'd tell her what he could.

"All right." He settled himself more comfortably

and recited the brief version of their history he'd learned as a youth. "Eons ago, before the rise of human civilization, two immortal races battled the Daemons for control of the Earth. The Mage, or magic ones, and the Therians, the mighty shape-shifters. Though traditional enemies, the Mage and Therians banded together to overcome the High Daemon, Satanan, ending his reign of terror and destroying his armies."

Kara watched him, her blue eyes deep as the sea, her expression, for once, giving nothing away.

"The cost of victory was high," he continued, still reciting. "To win that ultimate battle, both races were forced to mortgage nearly all their power. Only one Therian among each of the ancient lines of shape-shifters was left with the power of his animal. They became known as the Feral Warriors. Today there are only nine of us left. Our job is to hunt the remnants of the Daemon empire, the draden, and to guard the blade that imprisons the High Daemon and his horde."

"So you don't . . . attack people?"

Lyon felt his lips twitch. "No. We're not monsters."

"What about the draden? Do they attack people? Humans?"

"Rarely. They're mindless beings, pure predators who feed off Therian energy. They can feed off us just by being near us, though they'll attack if they get the chance. As long as we keep their numbers low, there's enough energy to go around.

If their numbers grow too large, though, as they're in danger of doing now, they'll turn on humans. Humans give off such low levels of energy, a draden can only feed by stealing it all. Killing the person."

She stood and began pacing, her stride sure and graceful. "Where does the Radiant . . . where do I come into all this?"

"It's through you that we access the Earth's energy that gives us the power to shape-shift and thrive."

Her gaze snapped to his. "How?"

"Initially, through the ritual that ascends you. After that, just by living." And making love with her mate.

An unwanted image blasted through his head, sending the blood rushing to his groin. Kara lying sprawled across the sheets, thighs wide and welcoming.

He didn't want to be her mate. Being chief already took up all his time. A woman would demand attention he didn't have time to give. He didn't *want* a mate. But damned if she didn't keep making him forget that.

Shifting uncomfortably, he leaned forward. "We need to be able to reach our animals, Kara. And we can only do that through your Ascension."

She stopped pacing and faced him. "I don't want to be your Radiant. Find another one, Lyon. Please. I'm not right for this job. I don't belong here."

Her unhappiness wove a tight web of misery

around them both. "You'll belong here soon enough. You just have to get used to us."

"It's not going to work."

"Kara . . . you've been here less than a day."

"I know. It's just . . ."

He rose and went to her, cupping his hands over her shoulders without trying to quell her emotions. Her scent rose to engulf him, filling him with a heady rush of pure lust. His hands tightened, and he had to struggle to keep from pulling her against him, to keep from covering her mouth in a kiss that would shatter them both.

She looked up at him, her blue eyes pools of confusion. "You don't understand, Lyon. I'm a preschool teacher. I'm not cut out for this job."

"You're wrong, Kara. You're strong. As strong as any woman I've ever met."

She snorted in disbelief. "I'm not."

Lyon released her. "It doesn't matter, Kara. There's only one Radiant at a time. Only when one dies will the next be marked."

Understanding dawned slowly over her features, and her jaw dropped, her eyes going wide. "So I'm stuck here until I die? That isn't fair! Someone should have asked me if I wanted this job."

"Kara . . ."

She waved her hand as if flicking away his words . . . or her own. "Don't. Don't say it. I know it was a silly comment. It's just . . . I don't like it here. I don't like this house. I don't feel safe here."

"There's nowhere safer for you. You just have to get used to what we are."

"What if I never do?" Fire leaped into her eyes. "I won't be a prisoner here for the rest of my life, Lyon. I won't."

Lyon cursed whatever fates had sent her mother west. Kara should have been raised Therian. How much easier this would have been on all of them.

"I'll make you a promise," he said, as she stood before him, hugging herself, watching him. "After your Ascension, if you want to leave, you can live among the humans as long as you stay in this area."

She wouldn't. He was sure of it. The Radiant was the one among them whose true mate, body, heart, and soul, was preordained. Chosen by the Earth. Once she found her mate, she'd never choose to go. But she didn't need to know that. Not now. The woman needed to think she had choices.

"How long until the Ascension?"

"As long as it takes to get you ready. Hopefully, no more than five or six days, though your lack of preparation may cause it to take longer. The first of the rituals will take place within the hour. We need to get started. You must be prepared."

He'd intended to have Pink do the preparation. No male should be expected to perform such a task, especially with a woman who stirred his senses like a spring thunderstorm. But after the debacle in the media room, and the earlier encounter with Pink, he knew she wasn't ready for close contact with the flamingo servant.

"Five days. Six, max," he said. Maybe longer. "Can you stick with us that long?"

Her breath left her on a snort. "Who are we kidding? We both know you're not going to let me leave."

Lyon felt one corner of his mouth lift as his admiration for her grew. Though her emotions at times got the better of her, she had a strong, clear mind.

"Let me ask it another way, then. Will you cooperate until we get you ascended?"

She lifted a single, dark gold brow. "That's the real question, isn't it?" The challenge in her gaze made him smile.

"That *is* the question."

As she watched him, the challenge slid from her features. "I'll cooperate if you promise to keep Jag as far from me as you can."

"Agreed. He'll be part of the rituals because he has to be. But if he comes near you again, I'll lock him in the prisons."

A flash of humor softened her features for only a moment before she dropped her hands at her sides and shook them as if preparing for a road race. "What do I need to do to get ready for this?"

He had to struggle not to laugh because he knew she was dead serious. She amused him and pleased him on new levels every time he was with her. Unfortunately, that did nothing to diminish the raging attraction he'd felt for her from the moment he saw her. An attraction that was going to test him to his limits in a few minutes.

The thought of what he had to do made him long for an ice-water bath.

"Kara . . . usually a woman is prepared for this first ritual, the Pairing, by another woman from her line . . . her family. But we don't know who your line is, and the only women in the house are Zaphene and Pink."

Kara's gaze snapped up, her eyes wide. "Pink? The bird?"

"Yes. The only ones who can prepare you for the ritual are one of them . . . or me."

"You." The word came out of her mouth like a shot. "Please."

"You don't know what you're asking. The preparation requires you to be fully undressed."

Her jaw dropped, then closed with a snap as her eyes narrowed. "Just what kind of ritual is this?"

"It's not a mating, if that's what you're thinking. The purpose is to determine the one . . . the only one . . . who can safely see you through your Ascension. Your biological match. There's magic in our world that humans can't reach and don't understand. Our rituals call forth that magic. You have to trust me. And we don't have much time."

"You want me to just . . . get naked?"

Yes. No. He wouldn't survive such an assault on his senses. "Put a towel around you."

"Lyon . . ."

He could see her uncertainty even as he could smell her blossoming arousal. The purpose of the preparation was to ready her body, cleansing and opening, so that when she entered the Feral Circle, her passion would rise to the surface of her skin. But the mere suggestion of baring her flesh to him had done the trick. What would happen when he touched her, as he must? *Where* he must?

Goddess give me the strength to carry this through.

"I have to rub drops of ritual oil into your body in seven key places."

"*Where?*"

"Get ready first. And put your hair up. I'll explain as we go."

When Kara retreated to the bathroom, Lyon pulled the ritual oil from the drawer where he knew Beatrice had stored it and removed the stopper. He took a whiff of the erotic substance and immediately wished he hadn't. There would be no slaking his own desire. No slaking hers. She must come to the ceremony with her passion ready to rise from her skin. Unfortunately, she was going to enter with her body more than ready. As would he. His body was already as hard as the hilt of a sword.

Moments later, Kara emerged, clinging to the thick royal blue towel wrapped around her with a charming self-consciousness. His gaze rose from her perfectly shaped legs over the slender curves hidden by the towel to the gentle swell of breasts and the sweep of her silken shoulders.

The breath caught in his throat as heat spiraled

low inside him in a raw, pulsing ache. And he hadn't even touched her.

I can't do this. But when his gaze rose to her eyes he saw an odd combination of uncertainty and trust. It was the latter that did him in. She trusted him to do what must be done. The least he could do was trust himself.

He motioned her to stand by the bed. "We'll make this as quick as possible." Which wouldn't be nearly quick enough. He lifted the oil jar into his hand and poured a drop onto his palm. Rubbing it between his thumbs, he closed the distance between them.

Her sweet scent rose up through the floral scent of shampoo, wrapping itself around him, swamping his senses.

"The first is your temples. The opening of the mind." He slid his fingers into her hair, gripping her small head as his thumbs slid over her temples in a circular motion, rubbing the oil into her beautiful skin. She was so near, the warmth of her flesh ignited his own as she watched him with luminous eyes framed in gold lashes. His gaze slid lower to the light dusting of freckles on her pert nose and the lush curve of her lips parting with her quickening breath.

Her sighs slid over his skin, the need to taste her becoming almost a physical pain. He began to chant softly in the language of the ancients, a chant designed to call her passion. But her need rolled over him in a wave of heat that almost buckled his knees.

"*Sweet goddess.* No more chanting. Talk. Questions. Ask me questions." The oil was a must, but the passion was going to drown them both if he didn't change the direction of their thoughts.

How in the hell was he going to survive what was left to come?

Chapter Six

Questions?

How did he expect her to think of questions when she was standing in nothing but a towel, so close she could feel his breath in her hair? Kara's gaze caught on the small triangle of hair in the open vee of Lyon's shirt as his masculine scent sent a river of heat flowing between her legs.

He stepped back and poured a dab of oil into his palm, then dipped his fingers into the oil and traced the scar on her right breast.

"The opening of the heart," he murmured, pressing his fingers into the sensitive flesh and rubbing.

Her chest rose and fell against his fingers in a quickening movement as she pressed into his touch, wanting more. So much more. She looked up into his face and saw her thoughts mirrored perfectly in the passion-filled amber of his eyes.

"Ask me a question, little Radiant," Lyon begged, his voice pained.

Kara struggled for a thought besides the heat swirling through her veins. "I thought . . ." she breathed, triumphant over the lust that held her in thrall. "I thought you said there were only nine shape-shifters. Pink makes . . . ten, right?"

"Pink's not actually a shape-shifter so much as a half-animal. When a Feral dies, his animal flees to another within his line. The strongest. Usually it's an adult male. Occasionally a woman or a child, though children are rare in our society. Pink was an identical twin. In Pink's case, we believe the animal flew to her shortly after conception, just before the egg split. The animal became trapped between the two girls. They were both born half-human, half-flamingo. Pink's sister was killed in the belief doing so would free her half of the animal spirit, allowing the entire spirit to go to Pink. But it didn't work. Pink has been trapped within that half-animal body for nearly six hundred years."

"*Six hundred?*" The true realization of what it meant to be immortal nearly lifted her out of the sensuous haze. "I saw Pink in the dining room. I'm afraid I reacted badly to the sight of her. I need to apologize."

Lyon lifted his hand from her breast and stepped back as if he needed to regroup, giving her air to breathe even as the oil's scent slid through her in a wash of erotic warmth.

"Pink understands," Lyon assured her. "She's used to reactions such as yours." He made a circular movement with his finger. "Turn around."

"Where now?"

"Your spine. The source of your strength."

Kara caught her breath. "My spine is covered."

"Leave it that way for the moment."

She turned, and he settled his thumb gently against the base of her skull and started a slow, downward motion between her shoulder blades as far as the top of the towel, then back up again. Twice. Three times.

"Drop the towel, Kara." His voice sounded strangled. "Hold perfectly still. And *ask questions.*"

She heard him kneel behind her. The thought of baring her naked rear to him turned her breathing shallow and erratic, and sent a rush of liquid heat to moisten her thighs. Mortifying her.

"Lyon . . ."

"Quickly, Kara. I don't know how much more of this I can take."

With a scrunch of her face, she pulled the towel away and held it in front of her, clutching it tight to her breasts.

She felt his thumb between her shoulder blades as it began a slow decent down the curve of her back. An involuntary shiver had her arching her back, sending her bare rear brushing against his arm. With a jerk, she straightened, even as she felt that thumb slide lower. And lower, to the very base of her spine where it nestled between her nether cheeks.

The groan that escaped her throat was half embarrassment that she was letting this virtual stranger touch her like this, and half pure erotic feeling.

"*Questions, Kara.*" Lyon's voice was husky with raw desire. At least she wasn't the only one affected.

"*You're kidding.*" All she could do was feel his thumb rubbing, dipping into that crevice, wishing it would go lower. Down, around. Inside.

"*Kara.*"

"Right. What were we talking about?"

"Pink. Shape-shifters."

Her breath came in fast, shallow pulls as if she'd been running up the stairs. Her thoughts whirled with carnal images of where she longed to feel his fingers next. But he wanted questions. About shape-shifters.

She struggled to reconnect her brain. "How . . . you said . . . you hunt Daemons in your animal form. Don't people notice lions and cougars and tigers roaming the D.C. suburbs at night?"

With a mixture of relief and hot regret, she felt his thumb lift from her spine. She tensed, waiting for the next place, hoping . . .

She felt his thumb at the back of one knee and let out a sigh of disappointment.

"We have . . . talents." His warm breath wafted over her lower back. "What you would call magic. When I hunt in my animal, I can alter my size and shape to fit the landscape."

"What do you mean?"

He gave a snort that was half amusement. "I prowl D.C. as a tomcat."

"You're kidding."

His hand shifted to the back of her other knee. "It took me years to perfect the ability, but it works. Some of the others do the same. Wulfe can't change his form, so he stays out of the city to hunt."

He released her knees and rose. "Put the towel around you again." His words were sharp, almost harsh, but she knew he was struggling as much as she was. She had no illusions that she was pretty enough to drive a man mad with lust when she was clothed. But a man with his hands on any naked woman was going to want her. That was just the way men were. And this one, shape-shifter or not, was all male.

Lyon strode to the window and stood there staring out, every line of his gorgeous body as taut as a cat ready to spring.

Kara wrapped the towel tight around her as she had before. "What's next?"

Lyon didn't turn around. "The palms of your hands. The soles of your feet. And . . . are you covered?"

"Yes."

He turned and met her gaze. Even across the room she could see the need in the harsh lines of his face. She wanted him. Never had she felt such desire for a man. His touch aroused her more than she'd ever thought possible and his tongue . . .

Just the thought of his tongue sent a flurry of small spasms rippling through her womb.

Lyon started toward her, moving with a sleek grace that almost made it seem possible he could become the great cat in truth. The raw desire that filled his amber eyes made her breath catch and sent heat flushing her body.

She was trembling, she realized, as he closed the distance between them. *She wanted him.* How could she take any more of this? How could *he*?

To her surprise, he didn't stop in front of her as she'd expected, but fully closed the distance between them. Her heart leaped, her senses spinning as he pulled her against him, dug his hands into her hair, and claimed her mouth.

The moment his lips touched hers, desire exploded, sending her world tilting on its axis. She grabbed him to steady herself, holding on to him as he held her, as his mouth claimed hers in a kiss that was as intense and barely controlled as the passion that flared between them. His mouth opened over hers, his tongue swept inside, strong and fierce, as if laying claim. She welcomed him, sliding her tongue against his, the gloriously masculine taste of him transporting her out of herself and into a lush, erotic jungle. Lyon groaned and pulled her tighter against him, tilting his head as if he sought to climb inside her, his desperation sending her into a tailspin of lust.

Slowly, his mouth gentled, coaxing instead of dominating, tasting instead of devouring. His tongue slid over hers in a sinuous dance, every stroke sending a lick of fire to her sensitive core until the throbbing between her legs became almost unbearable. Every stroke tightening, twisting, until she writhed against him, small whimpers escaping from her throat.

Dear heaven.

His tongue stroked hers once, twice more before the pressure deep inside her crested and broke, the orgasm ripping through her in furious, glorious spasms. He pushed the hand at her back lower, grabbing her rear and pressing her hips tight against the thick ridge in his pants. And still he kissed her. Still his tongue rode hers, sending her scattered passion into a whirlwind of a spiral, shattering her a second time.

Lyon pulled his mouth away with a last sensuous slide of his tongue against hers, then kissed the tip of her nose and held her tight against him as the spasms slowly subsided, and her legs finally remembered how to stand.

"I shouldn't have done that," he murmured against her hair.

"Oh, I think it was a grand idea."

Lyon chuckled, his chest rumbling beneath her cheek. "It was necessary."

"Yes." She blinked. "Why?"

He pulled back, releasing her to stand on her own as he picked up the oil jar and dribbled a few drops into his palm, then knelt before her.

"Because, to open you to life," he murmured, then slid his oiled finger beneath the towel and between her legs. "I must oil the gates of your womb. Spread your legs, Kara."

She took a ragged breath and widened her stance,

doing as he asked. Squeezing her eyes closed, she struggled to stand still as his fingers slid over that moist, sensitized flesh when all she wanted to do was buck and writhe until he buried himself deep inside her.

"Lyon . . ." she groaned.

"Stay in your skin, little Radiant."

"Stay where?"

"A shape-shifter saying. It means to calm down."

She groaned. "*How?*" She was out of control. She'd just come . . . twice . . . yet it hadn't been enough. Her body wanted him. Hips rocking, she pressed against his hand, unable to control the need raging through her. "I want you inside me, Lyon. All of you."

"I know. Sweet goddess, you're wet." His words were brittle with restraint. "But I can't take you. If I slake my desire on you now, the ritual won't work. I'll never know if I was the one."

"Lyon . . ." She was dying. *Dying.* "*Lyon.*"

He shoved a finger inside her, then a second, and she moaned with relief. In and out, harder and faster, feeding her frenzy as she rode the waves of sensation. Never had she felt like this, so out of her head with desire she barely even remembered the word *inhibitions,* let alone knew what she'd done with hers.

She gripped his shoulders, feeling the towel slide down and away and not caring. When his mouth closed over her breast, she felt a hot spurt of triumph. Her hands moved to his head, his

thick hair sliding between her fingers as she
held him against her. She arched into his touch,
rocking against his hand as his fingers dove into
her, over and over, in a hard, desperate rhythm.
Within moments, she was shattering yet again
and knew she'd never felt anything so wonderful
in her life.

Lyon pulled his fingers and mouth away and held
her from him with shaking hands. His white-hot
gaze scorched her naked body.

"Kara," he croaked. "Put the towel on. I'm hanging on to my control by a thread, and we're not
done." He released her and reached for the oil as
she struggled to wrap the towel around herself. In
record time, Lyon rubbed the oil into her hands
and feet, then strode to the closet with fast, urgent
steps.

He returned with a simple, if elegant gown. The
dress reminded Kara of a loose-fitting spaghetti-
strap sundress, but longer. And silkier. A cocktail
dress, she supposed, white with gold embroidery
at the neck, and a spray of gold flowers running,
diagonally from left breast to right hem.

"Drop your towel and lift your arms," he directed, keeping his gaze fixed on the far wall. She
did, and he slipped the gown over her head and
let it fall to a few inches below her knees in a soft
cloud, caressing her skin with a sensuous softness.

Lyon turned away and stalked to the window.
"Brush out your hair, and we'll go."

"What about shoes?"

"No shoes," he said, his voice hoarse, his hand gripping the window frame as if he meant to tear it off the wall.

She watched his rigid back a moment longer, then crossed to the bathroom where she'd left her hairbrush and pulled the rubber band out of her hair. As her hair tumbled around her shoulders, she caught her reflection and stared at herself in the mirror in bemused fascination. She barely recognized the woman she saw there. With her hair down, her cheeks and lips flushed, and the gown flowing over her slender curves, she almost looked like something out of a Greek play. As she moved toward the vanity for her brush, she caught the flash of light between her legs from the room behind her. Her gaze fell to her breasts, and her eyes widened. While one of her nipples was strategically hidden by a gold flower, the dusty bud of the other showed plainly against the sheer white of the gown.

The dress was indecently see-through!

Kara snatched up the brush and returned to the bedroom, where Lyon still gripped the window frame.

"I have to wear a bra with this. And I need a slip. And panties."

"No." The word was softly spoken, but laced with steel.

A dark suspicion had her catching her breath. "You told me there was no sex involved in this ritual."

"I told you the truth."

A harsh burst of strangled laughter escaped her throat. "Then why did you have to . . . turn me on? Why no underwear? Why the porn-queen dress?"

He turned slowly, his hot gaze skimming the dress and every one of her curves, setting her on fire all over again. But when his gaze finally met hers, his mouth twitched in what might have passed for a very strained smile.

"That *porn-queen dress* has been worn by our Radiants for nearly a thousand years."

A thousand . . . ? Kara's eyes widened.

"My intent wasn't to turn you on, as you put it, but merely to ready your body for the passion that will rise naturally during the ceremony. Passion opens the body and mind in ways nothing else can. It's the way nature finds . . . the one who will help you ascend."

"Passion." Why did she get the feeling he wasn't telling her everything. "But not sex?"

"No."

She met his amber gaze, searching for the truth. "You promise?"

He met her gaze, then crossed to her and took the hairbrush from her unsteady fingers. Turning her, he began to pull the brush gently through her hair.

"There is no sex involved in the ceremony, Kara. Nothing for you to fear. We would never hurt you." His deep voice soothed her senses, easing her disquiet with every word, with every stroke of the brush. "You're our Radiant. The conduit to our power. You hold our very lives in your hands."

Tossing the brush onto the bed, he turned her around to face him, then stepped back, as if afraid to touch her. His gaze slid over her slowly, his eyes hot, admiring, heating her all over again. He took a deep, unsteady breath and motioned toward the door. "Let's go."

They descended one flight of stairs and crossed through the empty and silent house. As they started down a second, much longer flight to what she assumed was the basement, the dread she'd felt earlier returned, tightening like a band around her chest until she could hardly breathe. And she began to wonder what her real role was destined to be in this strange world.

What exactly did it mean to be the Radiant and lifeblood of the Feral Warriors?

In this dress, with her hair down and her feet bare, she was beginning to feel more like a blood sacrifice.

Chapter Seven

Lyon lifted Kara onto the foot-high pedestal in the center of the sacred circle, his hands shaking with need for her as they splayed at her narrow waist. It was all he could do not to bury his face in her neck and drink in the sweet scent of her skin. It was all he could do not to lift the hem of her dress and sheathe himself deep in her heat.

He'd done too much as it was. Kissing her. Fondling her. Hell, he'd done everything *but* make love to her. Never had he struggled so hard for control and lost it so badly. The lack of radiance was definitely getting to him, too.

"What's going to happen?" Kara's voice quavered as her gaze slid around the smoky, dark-paneled room. The flames of the six sacred fires cast shadows over her face. "It's spooky down here." Her gaze caught his, whispers of fear in her eyes. "What's going to happen, Lyon?"

A fierce protectiveness rose inside him, a need to fight back her fears as he'd been doing since he found her. But her fate was in the hands of the goddess, now.

"It's just ritual, Kara. You have nothing to fear. All you have to do is stand here as we call on the Earth's wisdom to pair you with the one who will aid your Ascension to your power."

"All I do is stand here?"

Lyon hesitated, deciding he'd put off the explanation as long as he could. At least the part she needed for now.

"One by one the men will approach you . . . kiss you . . . until the one is found."

Her blue eyes widened, her mouth dropping open in disbelief. "You're making that up."

"No."

"I'm not kissing all of them," she hissed.

"It's the only way." Out of the corner of his eye, he saw the last two warriors, Vhyper and Paenther, enter the room. The slap of forearm to forearm echoed through the ritual room as his men greeted one another, along with a few low, ribald comments. One man would indeed be well bedded tonight.

"It's time," Kougar said. The fires that ringed the circle were lit and flaming. The men all there.

Lyon pulled his shirt off and tossed it to the ground outside the circle, as did the others, standing in nothing but his pants. The Pairing required flesh. Against flesh.

He took his place in the circle. Each man was bare to the waist except for the golden armband that curved around his right biceps, an armband with the head and jeweled eyes of his beast. Lyon gazed at Kara standing before them, proud and wary. More beautiful than any Radiant before her. The goddess personified. A rumble started deep in his chest, vibrating through him as his animal fought to stake his claim.

Mine.

He clamped down on the beast within. She wasn't his, and he didn't want her to be. The last thing he needed was the time-consuming responsibility of a mate. But, heaven help him, she filled his senses. Never could he remember feeling this insanely attracted to a woman. Attracted, jealous, possessive.

Damn, but this ceremony couldn't happen quickly enough. When she was paired, he'd be free of this obsession once and for all. He had to believe that.

But the wildness inside him tossed its head in denial. He wanted Kara. Not just in his bed, but by his side. Sharing her thoughts and doubts, gifting him with a smile, and in time, maybe even laughter.

Mine. His beast's claim raged through him, demanding he attack every man in the room and protect what was his. But he was not a beast tonight. He was a man. And the ritual would reveal the truth he would live with.

Kara turned, the firelight catching in the hair that brushed her shoulders, turning it to spun gold. The diaphanous gown whispered over her skin, revealing hints of the woman beneath. Passion rode her skin, ripe and seductive, making Lyon sweat.

Goddess help him, he wanted her. As did every other man in the room. He could see the hunger in their eyes.

Kara's gaze found his, clung to him as if he were her lifeline. Even from where he stood, a good ten feet away, he could see the pulse pounding thickly in her throat. She was afraid. It was all he could do not to go to her.

Kougar, the oldest of the Ferals and the ceremonial head of the circle, pulled out his switchblade, flicked it open, and slit a vein in his wrist. Tighe, standing beside him, handed him the ceremonial bowl that had once been the top of the skull of an ancient and long-dead shape-shifter. Kougar let his blood seep into the bowl, then passed the bowl to Tighe, who did the same. One by one, the warriors added their blood to the bowl until it was Lyon's turn. As the chief, he was last. He slit his own wrist, ignoring the searing pain. Moments later, when blood no longer flowed from the quickly healing cut, he handed the bowl back to Kougar.

Intoning the ancient chant, Kougar moved into the circle. Kara watched the warrior with wide-eyed wariness as he dipped his fingers into the blood and dripped it onto the ground as he circled her slowly three times. Finally, he returned to the main fire, where he poured the remaining blood. The fire spit and rose, turning as blue as the fingertips of the man who would ultimately be chosen tonight.

Kara's gaze flew to Lyon. The gazes of every man in the room turned to him as well. He was Chief of the Feral Warriors and it was his place to go first . . . or turn the honor over to another.

Mine, his beast raged. Lyon clamped down hard on the wildness of his animal, but he was nearly out of control.

"Paenther," he called, his voice tight with the effort. He would not touch her until he was certain he could kiss her and back away.

"Roar?" Paenther questioned. "Are you sure?"

"It's my right to choose the order," Lyon snapped. "Go." He clenched his fists at his sides as the beast within him railed at the betrayal, and his body shook with the need to have her.

As Paenther strode forward, Kara's gaze locked on Lyon and he could see plainly that his beast wasn't the only one who felt betrayed.

Paenther stopped in front of her in his black leather pants, his black hair loose about his shoulders. Tentatively, Kara turned to face him, her shoulders tight, her arms trembling at her sides. The warrior reached for her and she reared back.

Only Paenther's quick hands on her forearms kept her from falling. "Easy, Radiant. I won't hurt you."

"I don't like this," she murmured, her pleading gaze flying back to Lyon.

His chest tightened, yet he steeled himself against her silent plea.

"This is the way it is done," Paenther said, his voice low and tight.

Jealousy curled deep in Lyon's gut as Paenther covered the soft flesh of Kara's shoulders with his hands and pulled her against his chest, skin to skin, slowly leaning forward to kiss her.

Rage tore through him, his beast ripping to get free. *Mine!*

Paenther pulled back and stepped away from her, holding up his hands. Hands that held no blue flame within their tips.

Lyon was shaking. He couldn't do this. He couldn't stand here, watching, as the others kissed her, wondering if she was somehow meant for him.

"Me next?" Tighe asked.

"No," Lyon growled. He wanted this over with. Either she was his, or she wasn't, and he wasn't waiting any longer to find out. If she wasn't, he'd at least get a last kiss. And if she was? No one was touching her ever again. *Ever. Again.*

The relief and welcome in her eyes as he approached nearly drove him to his knees. His hands shook with the need to pull her into his arms. For once he didn't have to fight the urge. He cupped her bare shoulders and pulled her against him, his passion igniting and flaring into a wildfire with the first brush of his heated flesh against her silken skin. Her breasts pebbled against his bare chest. Her scent rose up, clouding his mind, ensnaring him in a haze of lust that was almost too thick to breathe.

When he covered her mouth, reason fled. Her sweetness drugged him, stealing all thought but the certainty she was the only sustenance he would ever need. His hands pressed against her back, pulling her closer as her own hands swept up to catch in his hair, holding him tight.

His tongue swept inside the lush cavern of her mouth, seeking its mate, drawing small moans from her throat that grew in force until she was rocking against him. In a far, distant corner of his mind, he remembered where they were. Remembered they stood within the circle of his fellows. He should let her go and step back.

But his beast roared, *Mine!* and he increased the pressure of his tongue strokes instead, marking her, his beast daring the goddess to ignore his claim. In a trembling rush, Kara came apart in his arms, clinging to him as soft whimpers escaped her throat.

Lyon continued to kiss her, drinking in the heady taste of her release until the torrent passed, and she clung to him. Slowly, regretfully, he released her mouth and held her tight against him until she could stand on her own.

Sweet goddess, he wasn't letting her go. She had to be his. His logical mind took up the cry of his beast. *Mine.*

But she would only be his if his fingertips glowed in the mark of the true mate.

His scalp began to tingle with cold realization. Glowing fingers would have triggered a shout. A cheer. The only sounds that met his ears were the crackle of the fires and the stunned and utter silence of his brothers. He knew. Before he ever pulled away from her and looked at his hands, *he knew* there would be no glow.

Mine! his beast roared in anger and betrayal. But he lifted his hands and stared at the traitorous normalcy of his flesh.

Kara wasn't his.

He released her and stepped back, her gaze clinging to him even as he turned away. Pain lanced his aching body.

This was good, his logical mind cried. He didn't have time for a mate. But his beast growled at the treacherous fates, and he knew his beast was right.

All his life he'd been alone. And hadn't realized it. He'd thought it was just him, just the way he was. Until Kara. The first time he touched her, he'd felt an awakening deep inside, a stark and painful illumination of the lonely hollows within him that he'd never acknowledged, perhaps never even known existed. An ache that eased when he touched her.

But she wasn't his. The goddess, in her cruelty, had given her to another. And those hollow places inside him, raw and open, would bleed for the rest of his life.

He would never touch Kara again.

* * *

Kara covered her face with her hands, longing to sink into the ground and disappear. Never had she been so humiliated. Every time Lyon kissed her, she came. It was embarrassing enough to do in front of him, but she'd just done it in front of *eight men*. Men she was supposed to live with!

Oh, God.

She lowered her hands and saw the men exchanging glances, felt the unnatural silence blanketing the dungeonlike room. Had something gone wrong, or were they merely horrified at the sluttiness of their new Radiant?

The odd cherry-sweet smell of the fire smoke teased her nose as Tighe approached her, his muscular chest bare above his low-slung blue jeans, a golden armband with a tiger's head tight around his upper arm, glinting in the firelight. Above his right nipple he had the scar, the four claw marks just like her own.

Tighe stopped in front of her, demanding her attention. For once, he was without his sunglasses, and she gasped when she saw his eyes. No whites rimmed his irises. Instead, golden tiger eyes stared back at her with the same disconcerting hunger she saw in the others'. A chill slid down her spine.

Never had she been the object of such attention, and never from men such as these. While it was a heady experience to have so many men desire her, there was only one among them whose attention she wanted.

Lyon.

Tighe's gaze caressed her face. "Look at you," he breathed. "You're glowing. Absolutely glowing." He shook his head, looking mystified. "He should have been the one."

He slid his hands over her shoulders, his hands shaking ever so slightly, telegraphing the hunger she saw on his face. "I feel like I'm encroaching on something sacred." But he pulled her lightly against him as Paenther had and kissed her with surprising passion, sweeping his tongue inside her mouth. She kissed him back because she was supposed to, and because she liked him. But the kiss was mildly pleasant, nothing more.

Tighe pulled back and looked at his hands, then met her gaze with a lopsided grin. "I got a little carried away. That kiss you gave Lyon was . . . inspiring." He cupped her chin, briefly, then turned away.

Kara looked at Lyon, but his gaze was fixed firmly on the floor. What was going on? Lyon had told her this ceremony was only to choose the man who would help her ascend. But they were taking it far more seriously. With a sudden, horrible certainty, she knew it was more. Much more.

Vhyper strode toward her, his bald head gleaming, his silver earring shining with a fire all its own. "I keep waiting for someone to start the duck, duck, goose, but they're all so somber tonight."

Kara forced a smile, but couldn't hold on to it for more than a second. Her heart was starting to pound a deep thud. "What's the purpose of this ceremony?"

His gaze met hers, a spark of something sharp slicing through his eyes. "To find your mate," he said, then pulled her against him for his kiss.

Mate. *Mate?* As Vhyper's seeking mouth touched hers, she struggled against his hold. He released her so suddenly, she stumbled backward, off the pedestal. Strong arms caught her from behind and righted her before she hit the ground.

Vhyper thrust his hands in the air and turned in a circle like the champ of a prizefight. High above his head his fingertips glowed like blue Christmas tree bulbs. When he turned to face her, his eyes flashed with triumph.

"It looks like you're mine."

No. Kara leaped off the pedestal and ran to Lyon. But unlike before, he didn't open his arms to her. Instead, he clasped his hands behind his back and looked over her head, his shoulder-length golden hair framing a face made of granite as he refused to meet her gaze.

"You said this ritual was to choose the man who would help me ascend."

His jaw tightened, sending the bones of his face into harsh relief. "It was. It did."

"But that's not all it did, is it?" Tears burned her eyes as her hands fisted at her side. "You purposely misled me. What was the reason for this ritual, Lyon? What have you done to me by bringing me here?" She slammed her fists against the light furring of his hard chest, demanding he look at her, but he refused. "You've sold me." She beat on his chest. "You've *sold* me."

Lyon's hands shot around to clamp her wrists and still her fury. His gaze bore into hers, harsh, yet pained. "He's your destiny, Kara. The Pairing never fails."

"You expect me to *marry* him?"

"You will. He's your mate. The only one who can keep you from dying during your Ascension, the only one with whom you might ever have a child. He'll be the love of your life."

"You're *crazy*." Her vision blurred as the tears began to slip down her cheeks. "I'm not doing this." They couldn't make her marry against her will. *They couldn't.*

And who would stop them? They weren't human. Dear God, she wasn't human.

Lyon released her and whirled, striding away.

Kara ran after him. "Lyon!"

He turned, his face hard. "You don't have a choice." His voice was harsh. Angry. "You must ascend. And Vhyper is the only one who can help you do it."

Kara stared at him, feeling the ground beneath her feet drop away. In the past twenty-four hours, she'd lost her mother, her home, her world, even her very sense of who she was. Yet through it all, she'd had Lyon beside her, holding the terrifying sense of loss and chaos at bay. She'd trusted him.

And he'd betrayed her.

It was too much. She sank to her knees on the hard stone floor, wrapping her arms around herself as if she could keep from shattering into a million pieces. Her dress pooled around her like a lake of glistening tears.

"Kara . . ." In Lyon's voice she heard all the pain in her heart. "I'm sorry."

But when she looked up, he was already walking away.

Kara wasn't sure how long she'd sat there in the smoky room, in the ruins of the Pairing, the voices talking over her. Sounds of disbelief. Regret. Anger.

One hard voice cut through the others. "If Lyon touches her again, I'll kill him."

"You know Lyon better than that, Vhype. He'd never betray you."

"No. He won't." But the words sounded more like a threat than any affirmation of trust.

"I don't blame you for going crazy, my man. We're all hanging on to control by a thread. Lyon's no different."

"I said I'll fucking kill him!"

Kara shivered, feeling battered. Broken. She refused to listen to this anymore. She rose from the floor, wiped the tears from her cheeks, and started for the doorway.

Vhyper stepped into her path, blocking her escape. "You're going with me, Radiant. Nowhere else."

Kara stiffened, chilled as she stared into those cold eyes. "I need time. You have to give me time." A sob rose up to choke her. "This is all too much."

"Leave her alone tonight, Vhype." Tighe moved toward them, his eyes no longer yellow tiger's eyes, but green human eyes. "She wasn't prepared for this."

Vhyper cocked his head at Tighe, a smile forming on his mouth that quickly turned into a sneer. "I saw that tongue action, Stripes. You looking to make a little time with her yourself?"

Tighe snarled, his eyes flashing back to tiger, his fangs elongating.

But Vhyper ignored him and grabbed her, jerking her roughly against him. "She's *mine*."

It was too much! Whatever control she'd had dissolved in a cold wash of panic, her mind screaming as she struggled against the far stronger warrior, desperate to be free of this nightmare. She strained against his hold, kicked his leg with her bare foot, but Vhyper easily turned her against his side, pinning her.

"Let me go!"

"*Vhyper.*" Another Feral's voice. Wulfe's? "If your aim is to win her affections . . . *which it should be* . . . this is not the way to do it. She's going to hate you for this."

"Fuck off." Vhyper turned, dragging her toward the door.

"No!" Kara screamed.

Paenther stepped forward, blocking their exit. "Wait, Vhype." Amazingly, her captor stopped. "Kara." But she was too desperate to quit struggling. "Kara!"

She felt her jaw gripped in a firm hand and found herself staring into Paenther's black eyes. Eyes that were not unkind despite their hardness.

"I've known Vhyper most of my life. He's a good man." She made a sound of disbelief and tried to jerk away from his hold, but he held her fast. "He's jealous at the moment, and suffering from the lack of radiance, as we all are, but he'll make you a fine mate once you're ascended. Once you get to know one another."

Kara scowled. "I don't want a mate! I don't want to be your Radiant, I don't want to be immortal, I don't want any of this!"

Paenther released her and stepped back as she flailed against the arms that bound her. Finally, she managed to catch Vhyper in the shin with a good, hard swing of her heel.

"*You little bitch.*" Vhyper's hand closed around her throat, his thumb jamming hard beneath her ear.

Darkness fell.

"*Your blood, Radiant. I will have your blood.*"

She was dreaming. Kara knew she was dreaming, but the knowledge did nothing to ease the terror. Smoke stung her nostrils as firelight danced on dark walls. Like before. Like the Pairing. But this time, instead of standing on a pedestal in a beautiful gown, she hung from the ceiling. Naked. High above her head, ropes bit into her wrists, pulling her arms taut, nearly wrenching them from their sockets as her body swayed in the air. Warm liquid ran down her hips and legs, dripping from her toes.

"*Your blood, Radiant. I will bleed you slowly, stab by stab, until I have all I need.*" *The voice was neither high nor low. Neither masculine nor feminine. But pure evil. The voice's owner moved before her, cloaked head to foot in black, holding two long, sharp daggers dripping with blood. Her blood.*

"I shall bleed you until you die."

Kara jerked awake, pulse hammering, sweat soaking her nightgown. She sat up, then groaned at the terrible ache in her middle. The room was dark except for a sliver of hall light coming under her door. It was still night. The dream's terror swirled around her as she clutched her stomach, the devil stalking her with those bloody knives.

Light. She needed light.

Kara threw back the covers then sucked in a tight breath as her body protested. It wasn't just her stomach. She hurt . . . everywhere. *Why?*

Trembling, she reached for the lamp, gritting her teeth against the pain. What was the matter with her? Turning the switch, she cast the room into a soft golden glow. Her gaze darted around the empty room, diving into every corner, every cranny, but she could see nothing.

No fires. No robed devil with blood dripping from his blades.

She was completely alone.

With shaking hands, she grabbed for the hem of her nightgown and yanked it to her waist revealing nothing but a neat bellybutton surrounded by clear flesh. No wounds. No blood.

Already, the pain was ebbing away, but the fear remained sharp, pounding at her heart and making her mouth dry as dirt. The feeling of danger remained painfully clear.

It couldn't have been a dream. Dreams didn't cause pain. Not real pain. She hugged her knees to her chest as tremors wracked her, shaking the bed beneath her. It had to have been a dream.

Didn't it?

How could she possibly know what was real in this place?

Terror clung to her like a cloying mist, making it impossible to breathe. She couldn't do this. Couldn't stay here like this.

With Vhyper. And men who turned into animals.

She *wouldn't* stay here.

Pushing off the covers, she stumbled from the bed and dressed hurriedly in jeans and a sweatshirt, her hands shaking, her breath coming in tight gasps. *Get out of here, get out of here, get out of here.* The words pounded through her head as she slipped down the stairs and out the front door into the night.

Lyon woke with a start, his finder's senses ringing with alarm. Kara had left the house.

No one would take a Radiant into the night unless it was an emergency. His pulse started racing as he wrenched himself out of bed and strode to the window that overlooked the front drive. And saw nothing. No men racing with her to the car. No Ferals at all. Which told him everything he needed to know and sent his pulse into hyperdrive. The Radiant was out there alone.

Sweet goddess.

He yanked on a pair of jeans and flew out of the room, taking the two flights of stairs in three strides. Following his finder's sense, he ran through the house and out the back door. She was right where he'd known he'd find her, a good twenty yards away and moving in a crouched half run toward the woods.

Her emotion hit him like a sound blast, smothering him in her fear. Rabid, rampant fear.

Was she *trying* to get herself killed?

He ran for her on silent feet, catching her from behind and hauling her back against his chest. The moment he touched her, his senses exploded with the feel of her soft body against his, her sweet scent washing over him. The ache inside him twisted at the knowledge she would never be his.

Kara struggled against his hold. "Let me go!" Her raw terror squeezed something deep inside him.

"Easy, Kara. It's me. I'm taking you back inside before the draden find you."

She stilled abruptly as if he'd startled her back to wakefulness. Maybe he had.

"Have you stopped fighting me, little one?"

"Yes."

He released her, took her hand, and ran with her back to the house. When they were inside, and the door was locked against the creatures of the night, he turned her to face him, keeping tight hold on her hands as he tried to pull the raging fear from her. Moonlight lit her face, revealing the shadows of terror deep in her eyes.

"What happened?" he asked sharply.

The shudder that went through her reeked of fear, but as quickly as he pulled it from her, more rushed in to take its place.

"I don't know. A dream. Someone stabbed me." Her eyes tightened in confusion.

He started breathing again. It was as he'd suspected. "You had a nightmare."

"It felt so real."

His arms ached to pull her close and wrap around her, comforting her, but he didn't dare allow himself even that simple contact. Because he wanted it too much. And she wasn't his. She was Vhyper's now, and he had no business touching her at all.

"Tell me about your nightmare, Kara."

She shivered, remaining silent so long he wasn't certain she was going to respond. Finally, she sighed and relaxed into his hands as if giving herself up to his care, even as her fear kept coming.

Her mouth twisted. "It was just a B-movie horror flick. A dark-robed figure with a bloody knife coming after me. But I couldn't get away. I was tied."

"So you woke. And ran." He brushed his thumbs over the backs of her hands as he held her. Comforting her in the only way he dared.

"Did you hear me leave?"

"I'm the finder," he said simply. "I always know where you are." The feel of her soft hands, nestled tight in his, sent heat and need winding through his body. His gaze fell to the sweet fullness of her mouth, and he knew he was in trouble, or would be if he didn't put some distance between them now. Goddess but he craved another taste of her.

"I'm surprised Vhyper didn't hear you." His words turned hard-edged, acid spilling into his gut. Goddess, but the thought of her with that warrior, their bodies naked and sweaty . . .

His jaw clamped shut.

"Don't even say his name in front of me." The venom in her words had his protective instincts leaping.

He gripped her hands. "What did he do?"

She turned away, her mouth twisting with bitter unhappiness. "I don't know. After you left, he wanted me to go with him, and I refused. I told him I needed time and he went all caveman on me and knocked me out. I woke up in my own bed just a few minutes ago."

His fingers tightened, then relaxed. He knew Vhyper as well as he knew himself, and Vhyper would never hurt any Therian woman, especially the Radiant. Particularly, his mate. Even if he'd been sorely provoked. As he certainly had been.

Kara's gaze swung back to him, her eyes filled with as much fire as fear. "I hate him. *I hate it here.*" Tears sprang to her eyes, and she turned her face as if she wished to hide her weakness.

"I'm sorry, Kara. It shouldn't have been like this. Being chosen Radiant is the greatest of honors. Every Therian woman dreams of waking with the mark upon her breast. Every Therian woman who knows she's Therian," he amended. "This should have been a dream come true for you."

A tear glistened on her cheek, stabbing him through the chest. Her mouth twisted ruefully as she lifted her shoulder and wiped it away. "Yeah, I'm not exactly feeling like the luckiest girl alive." She turned sad eyes to him. "I just want to go home."

"I know. This will be your home, but I imagine it's hard to see that now. Believe it or not, I remember coming to Feral House for the first time. It wasn't this house, of course, but I'll never forget that feeling of being untethered, as if lost on an endless sea. Nothing familiar to hold on to. It didn't last. It never lasts. But it can be hugely unsettling while it does. You'll come to think of this as home, little one. Just give it time."

With a squeeze of his hands, he released her. "Let's get you back to bed so you can get some sleep."

At first, he thought she was going to refuse, but finally she released a noisy, unhappy sigh, and nodded.

"You shouldn't have lied to me," she said as she fell into step beside him.

"Would it have been easier if I'd told you, back in your house in Missouri, that I'm able to shift into a lion and intended to spirit you away to marry you off?"

Her soft burst of watery laughter eased his soul.

"No. I'd have run screaming into the night."

"That's what I figured. I gave you all the truth I thought you could handle, once I realized you believed yourself human." He lifted his hand, aching to touch her hair. Instead, he clasped his hands behind his back.

But his gaze he could not control. As he accompanied her back to her bedroom, his eyes drank their fill of the woman at his side. Though dressed casually in snug-fitting jeans, a white sweatshirt, and running shoes, the simple attire did little to hide the slender curves of her body or the unstudied grace of her walk. A grace that made him suspect a deer or gazelle in her deep Therian heritage. Soft golden hair brushed her cheeks and jaw, accentuating a decidedly pleasing, if strained, profile.

A strain he felt mirrored in every cell of his body as he struggled against the need to touch her, as he fought for self-control. How he'd formed such a powerful and inappropriate connection with her, he wasn't sure. But he had to find a way to close it off before he permanently damaged her relationship with the man with whom she was destined to fall in love.

He'd created one hell of a mess and had to figure out a way to fix it. Eventually, she'd turn to Vhyper. She must, not only for her own happiness, but for the well-being of the entire race. The problem was, she had to do it soon. Once she accepted Vhyper, everything would fall into place. Which meant he had to break this unholy bond between them even if it killed him.

As they reached her door, Kara turned to him, gripping her elbows, trembling. Fear shimmered in her eyes and continued to wash off her as strongly as when he'd first grabbed her from behind and halted her flight.

"That dream still has you in its grip, doesn't it?" He took her hand, unable to let her suffer when he could help her. As he pulled the fear out of her, he peered at her closely. "Or is it something else, little one? Has something frightened you?"

"It's the dream." Slowly, she calmed beneath his touch. "But it felt real, Lyon. I can't shake the feeling that someone's going to hurt me."

He relaxed. "If you can get yourself to fall back asleep, your dreams will be better. You'll have forgotten this one by morning." He opened the door for her. She'd left the light on, and it illuminated the room softly. "Come on. I'll make sure there's nothing here before I go."

He checked the bathroom and peered beneath the bed, finding nothing, as he'd known he would. Radiants tended to be weak of mind or spirit, as if nature sought to balance the physical power she gifted them with, but he'd thought Kara was different. She'd seemed stronger to him. Too strong to be quaking over a dream long gone. Then again, she'd had one hell of a couple of days.

What she needed was comforting. If he'd had his choice, he'd have crawled into bed with her and held her tight until the dream was a distant memory. Then he would have slowly peeled away her clothes and made love to her until he had her shaking for an entirely different reason.

She'll be okay, he told himself. But the eyes she turned to him, so full of unhappiness, made him ache.

"I'm not going to let anyone harm you, Kara. I promise you that."

She pressed her lips tight and nodded, that strength he'd seen in her before, sparking to life through the apprehension that swam in her eyes. Yes, she'd be okay.

Slowly, she stepped back, allowing him room to leave.

Goddess, but he wanted to stay. He forced his feet to move past her and closed the door behind him.

Then he stood there, staring at the door he'd closed, his beast whimpering to go back, his chest aching with her misery and his own loss. But the goddess always knew best. Vhyper would make her the better mate.

Even though he knew it, the knowledge made him bitter. Because with Kara, for the first time in his long life, he'd glimpsed something sweet. Something fine. A pull between them that went both ways. An attraction that was more than the physical. As badly as he ached to drive himself into her, he wanted to hold her almost as much. Hold her, talk to her, listen to her quick mind as he watched the emotions fly across her face and feel them caress his skin. He was attuned to her as he'd never been to another.

He'd never wanted the responsibility of a mate. He didn't want that now. Yet he wanted Kara.

He pressed his palm lightly to the wood as if he could touch her one last time.

Then turned and walked away.

Lyon paused on the second-floor landing the next morning, his gaze drawn to Kara's door. His finder's senses, so attuned to her, told him she was still in bed. His fingers clenched the rail beneath his hand. Goddess, but the pull of her was strong. All night he'd lain awake thinking about her, longing to return to her room. And now that he was here, so close, it was all he could do not to go in there, climb into her bed, and pull her soft, sleep-warmed body against his.

The wood beneath his hand groaned in protest, and he released the old banister before he broke it.

Kara needed to sleep. And even if she didn't, she was no longer his responsibility. She was not his to waken.

His beast howled, but he clenched his jaw and forced himself to continue down the stairs and head for his office as he did every morning to tend to the business of the Ferals over the breakfast Pink brought to him. But at the door to his empty office, he stopped. He didn't feel like eating alone this morning.

Maybe he'd eat in the dining room today.

Five of his men were already seated, eating heartily, when he entered the spacious room.

Jag looked up, his eyes hard and mocking. "So

our fearless leader deigns to grace us with his presence."

Wulfe, Foxx, Paenther, and Kougar all turned to face him, their expressions alert, questioning. As if the only reason he'd be walking into the dining room during breakfast was to issue orders or demand answers.

Had it been that long since he'd eaten with them? Maybe it had. Hell, he hadn't joined them in years. But that was to be expected. Chiefs kept to themselves.

Except he knew that was a lie. The previous Feral chiefs had always joined the men for meals, sitting at the head of the table as was their right.

Lyon never had because . . . he wasn't even sure why. Because he'd never wanted to. Never needed to.

And he didn't need to now.

This was Kara's fault, dammit.

He almost turned and left, but doing so would only make him feel like more of a fool.

"Is there a problem, Roar?" Paenther asked.

Lyon scowled. "Yeah, there's a problem. I'm hungry."

Jag snorted. "Since when do you eat with us?"

"I'm Chief of the Ferals. I can eat anywhere I damned please."

Paenther stood and thrust out his arm in greeting. "Glad to have you join us, Roar."

Each of his men rose and greeted him in kind, though Jag's greeting was last and decidedly unenthusiastic.

Wulfe smacked Jag in the head. "Show some respect!"

Jag went feral with a growl, then sheathed his claws and slunk back into his chair.

Lyon ignored the surly warrior. Jag had become a Feral long after Lyon became chief. From the day he'd arrived at Feral House, Jag had pitted himself against every man here. Lyon had tried everything from serious talks to harsh punishment, and nothing had ever changed. For a reason Lyon couldn't fathom, Jag seemed to thrive on the enmity of his companions. The more they hated him and punished him, the more it pleased him.

Lyon had long ago given up trying to change him and ignored him instead. For as long as his patience held out.

He grabbed an empty plate and sat at the end of the table, where he could watch the door. In case Kara came down.

As if he could ever *not* know where she was.

Wulfe shoved two platters his way. "Anyone else sleep like hell last night? It's got to be the lack of radiance. I haven't gotten a decent sleep in nights."

Lyon didn't bother to answer. He'd slept little last night, but he knew the reason. He began loading pork chops and roast beef onto his plate. His stomach was demanding food, and he sure as hell meant to feed it.

"Where's Vhyper?" Lyon asked when the worst of his hunger pangs had been quelled.

"Haven't seen him," Jag muttered. He eyed Lyon from beneath needling brows. "Wondering what kind of a lay the new Radiant is?"

Lyon's hand spasmed around the serving fork, his claws erupting to clink against the handle. Kougar's hand weighted his shoulder, pulling him back to his sanity.

Jag just smirked.

Teeth grinding, Lyon forced himself to loose his grip on the serving fork, pushing back the beast that longed to escape his rigid control. Dammit to hell, Kara wasn't his. He had no right to feel this outrage, this possessiveness. Taking deep breaths, he forced himself to calm down.

He looked to Paenther. "Get Vhyper."

The warrior nodded and left. Slowly, the conversation started again. Pink brought out more platters, and the meal was relatively pleasant, though Kara never stirred.

Lyon was nearly finished when Wulfe gave a deep growl and cleared his plate, Foxx's, and Jag's from the table with a single, furious sweep of his arm.

Jag snarled, but Foxx leaped at Wulfe, taking him crashing to the ground in a flurry of fangs and claws.

Lyon let them go for a good minute or two. Getting their anger out was often the only way for them to get back in their skins. Then he rose to put a stop to it.

"Enough!"

Foxx broke away from the fight, but Wulfe tackled the younger warrior and the battle resumed full force.

"Wulfe!" But the man didn't seem to hear him. *Bloody hell.*

It took both Kougar and Jag to tear the huge warrior off Foxx, but Wulfe continued to try to fight them.

Lyon stepped in and pinned Wulfe to the ground. "*Get back in your skin.*"

Slowly, slowly, the fight went out of Wulfe, and he sheathed his claws, his fangs retracting.

Lyon stared into the now-human eyes of one of his best fighters. "What happened?"

Wulfe shook his head hard, as if trying to clear it, then threw off Jag's and Kougar's hands. Lyon stepped back and let him rise to his feet.

"I don't know." His scarred face tightened with a frown. "I lost it."

"You can say that again," Jag muttered.

"Are you back in control?" Lyon demanded.

"Yes."

Lyon put his hand on Wulfe's shoulder, surprising himself. Surprising the warrior.

"Get some rest, Wulfe. You need it."

The warrior nodded and hooked his arm around Foxx's shoulders. "Sorry, cub."

"Don't call me cub." But Foxx slung his arm around Wulfe's shoulders in return. As the pair started for the door, Paenther returned.

"What happened to you?" Foxx asked.

"Nothing." Paenther looked as bad as Wulfe and Foxx, though his cuts were well on their way to healed.

Lyon scowled. "Well?"

Paenther glanced at the door, not turning back until Wulfe and Foxx were out of sight.

"I found Vhyper in bed with Zaphene and reminded him he had a mate," Paenther said quietly, rubbing his hand over one of the cuts on his face. "Didn't seem to like that."

"Damn him. He disrespects Kara. Steals from Foxx." Despite his anger, a small, jealous part of him was pleased that Vhyper had sought out a woman other than Kara. He'd kill the snake if he ever hurt Kara, but she had yet to want him. Foxx, on the other hand, would care very much that Vhyper had turned to Zaphene instead of his mate. "If Foxx finds out . . ."

He was used to fights, sometimes vicious fights between his warriors. They were, after all, half-animal. But generally, there was a reason for the scuffle. And if he demanded control, they found it. Always.

With the lack of radiance, that appeared to be a thing of the past.

How much worse was this going to get before they got Kara ascended? This kind of loss of control, and inability to get it back, was dangerous. To the Ferals and anyone near them.

Including their Radiant.

"Where's Vhyper now?"

"Nursing a concussion," the warrior said with a hard grin.

Lyon pulled out his cell phone and punched the snake's number. "In my office, *now*," he barked when Vhyper answered.

He snapped the phone closed and turned to his second. "We've got to get Kara ascended, and I don't want Vhyper near her."

"He's her mate," Paenther said simply.

"He's out of control. I won't have her harmed."

The prepping didn't have to be by the Radiant's mate, but usually worked better if it was. If for no other reason than it built a trust between them they'd need when it came to the Ascension itself. But those two had a long way to go to establish *any* trust. And there was no way he was putting Kara in any danger.

"I need you to prep her, B.P."

Paenther shook his head. "I'm not sure I'm in any better shape than Vhyper. He jumped me, but I went feral first. My control is razor-thin at the best of times. And these are not the best of times. I'm not the one you want with the Radiant right now, Roar. How about Hawke? Or Stripes?"

"Not Tighe." He'd seen the way Tighe watched her. Lyon was certain he wouldn't hurt her, but his jealousy stirred, thick and hot. "Has Hawke shown any signs of losing control?"

"Not yet."

"Then send him."

"What about you? You've got a good connection to her."

Lyon's jaw clenched. "That connection needs to break." He had to stay away from her. Because his own control was close to snapping in an entirely different way. A way that would dishonor them both, and that was a thing he refused to do.

Kara stood beneath the hot spray of the shower, shaking. Her heart hadn't quit thudding all night except for the minutes when Lyon had touched her. Her chest ached. Her stomach hurt as if the threat of stabbing from both nightmares had horribly come true. And there had been a second nightmare.

After Lyon brought her back to her room during the night, she'd sat by the door for more than an hour before she'd finally forced herself to get in bed and try to go to sleep. And she had, eventually, only to suffer through another horrible dream, almost identical to the first. Like before, she'd been hanging, naked, from the ceiling. This time though, instead of one robed figure closing in on her with a bloody knife, there'd been many of them. Eight. Maybe ten. Coming at her from all sides. She'd tried to scream and only woken herself up again.

And, like before, the fear hadn't fallen away with the end of the dream. It was as if she were somehow locked in the nightmare, caught halfway between that world and this. Awake in this one, but fully aware that the other waited for her,

ready to suck her back the moment she closed her
eyes.

Kara shook even as the hot water turned her
skin red with heat. Something was wrong. This
wasn't natural. Something was making her feel
this way, and she'd be damned if she was going
to hang around until she fell into that horror-
movie world for good. Yet Lyon wasn't going to
let her go.

When she was through with her shower, she
dried her hair and pulled on jeans. She was shoving
her arms into a green cotton sweater when a knock
sounded at her door.

Hope lifted, then plummeted as an unfamiliar
voice spoke.

"It's Hawke, Radiant. Are you up?"

She'd thought it was Lyon.

"I'm up," she called, and went to open the door.

Hawke stepped back from the door, his stance
casual and unthreatening. A smile lit his features,
softening them. "I'm glad to see I didn't wake you.
Lyon's asked me to teach you to pull the energies
from the earth."

Kara blinked. "Teach me what?"

Hawke's smile turned wry. "It's the first thing
you have to learn to do before you can ascend.
We'll go out to the river to work on it."

The river. Her pulse leaped. She knew there
was some kind of water around here, or the place
wouldn't be called Great Falls. Surely, going to the
river meant leaving the house. And that was all she
wanted to hear.

"I'm ready whenever you are. I just have to put on my shoes."

"Why don't you get some breakfast first?"

Kara shook her head. "I'm not hungry. I'd rather get started." She was too wound up to eat. Besides, she had no desire for a repeat of last night's dinner. The flamingo woman. Zaphene looking at her like she was a bug that had just crawled out from under a rock. No thanks.

Hawke nodded with approval. "Good, then. Let's go. You'll want a jacket. The wind's kicking up."

Kara grabbed the windbreaker she'd worn on the plane the night before last, her fingers clenching nervously around the rubbery fabric. This might be her only chance to escape this nightmare once and for all.

"Sit down, Vhyper," Lyon said, as the bald warrior appeared in his door.

Vhyper crossed his arms over his leather vest and propped his shoulder against the doorframe. "I'll stand." His demeanor was calmer than usual, his eyes cold, reminding Lyon of his own culpability in this untenable situation. Vhyper had watched him kiss Kara, bringing her to full orgasm in his arms, moments before the goddess chose Vhyper to be her mate.

If the situation were reversed, he'd be tempted to rip the snake's throat out. He had to remember that.

"What happened during the Pairing wasn't Kara's fault," Lyon told his warrior. He rose and moved around to the front of his desk, to prop his hip on the corner. "I was too heavy-handed when I ripped her from her life. With nothing familiar, she turned to me. She just needs time to get acclimated here. She needs you to be patient with her."

Vhyper raised a single dark brow. "Is that why she came when you kissed her?"

Lyon scowled, then released a frustrated breath. "I may have screwed up the Pairing. My only excuse is that my finder's senses went on overload with her. It doesn't happen often." Hell, he wasn't sure it had ever happened. Not like this. "I . . . got into it. Kissed her. The passion I was calling in her accidentally turned toward me."

He looked at the other man sharply. "That doesn't excuse the way you treated her last night."

Vhyper shrugged. "She's mine."

Lyon felt his fingertips tingle, and he rose slowly, clenching his fists against the feral anger sparking inside. "She's ours. Our Radiant. You hurt her, and you won't be alive for her to *be* yours."

Vhyper's jaw clenched, his eyes turning colder before he broke eye contact and glanced toward the window. "I didn't rape her, if that's what you're worried about. I knocked her out when she fought me, but all I did was lay her on my bed with the intention of trying to start over with her when she woke. I decided I didn't have the patience for it, yet, and took her back to her own room."

"And stole Zaphene from Foxx."

Vhyper turned back to him with a cool shrug. "*Stole* is a powerful word, Chief. She was interested, I was frustrated. It seemed like a good idea at the time."

"And you attacked Paenther when he pointed out that you had a mate."

"It was none of his business."

"How can you say that?" Lyon's patience snapped. "You're out of control, Snake. The goddess has blessed you with the most beautiful Radiant we've ever had."

"Sounds like you're jealous, Chief."

Hell yeah. Lyon scowled. "Start acting worthy of her. It won't take much to win her over if you use some kindness and your usual brand of humor. No more barbarian tactics."

"A little hard to win her over when you're pushing her off on other men. I saw Kara leave with Hawke."

"He's going to prep her for the Ascension."

A sharp light entered Vhyper's eyes. Something a little cruel. "You don't think she'd welcome my help right now?"

"No. I don't. And stay away from Zaphene. I don't want a war starting between you and Foxx. I've seen enough fangs the past couple of days. Find your control, Vhyper, and hang on to it."

Vhyper stared at him. "And what about your

control, Chief? The control that slipped so badly you couldn't keep your hands off the woman you were preparing to find her mate? Are you staying away from her yourself?"

Lyon's fingers tingled. He clenched his fists harder and nodded. "I am."

Chapter Nine

Kara stared down at the rushing water far below as the Potomac River pounded over the rocks that littered its path. The falls, they called it. Great Falls. She'd envisioned Niagara or some other vertical drop of water. Instead, these falls were horizontal, a rip-roaring rapids ride for any soul brave enough to try.

Great Falls was, she knew now, in the Washington, D.C. suburbs, in heavily populated Fairfax County. Yet out on the rocks like this, she felt nearly isolated but for the smattering of multi-million-dollar homes dotting the woods nearby. The place had a wild, untamed quality to it she wouldn't have expected to find so close to the nation's capital.

The drive from Feral House had taken little more than five minutes along winding, hilly, two-lane roads through dense woods, roads crowded with expensive cars, minivans, and high-dollar SUVs. Hawke had parked his car on an upscale residential street a short walk through the woods from this spot.

Oddly, or maybe not so oddly, her paralyzing fear had slowly ebbed as they'd driven farther from the house. The fear wasn't entirely gone, but had dulled to the level of dread she'd experienced yesterday, leaving her with an inner certainty something was wrong, even if she no longer felt she was in imminent danger.

Something or someone in that house meant her harm.

Lyon insisted otherwise. He said she was perfectly safe, but she wasn't. She hated Feral House. Hated feeling so scared all the time.

Lyon said she had to stay, but she couldn't. And Lyon wasn't here to stop her this time.

Hawke sat cross-legged on the wide, flat rock high above the rushing water he'd led her down to and held out his hand to her.

"Sit, Kara. It's important the Earth learn you."

"Learn me?"

He took her hand and pulled her down to sit facing him. Their knees almost touched. "You are the focal point, if you will, of the Earth's energies. The Radiant is the one through whom the Earth's power flows, the power that strengthens all Therians, particularly the Ferals."

"Are you talking about literal power or something more spiritual?" Her gaze caught on a bald eagle flying high over the water, his white head and tail flashing in the sunlight.

"Literal. You'll be the conduit, once we get you ascended."

But they wouldn't get her ascended. Not if she had any say in it. They were going to have to find another way this time. They were strong. Virtually immortal. There had to be another way.

"You're trembling, Kara."

If he thought this was trembling, he should have seen her last night. But clearly she wasn't as calm as she thought. It was best if he didn't know why.

"I . . . um . . . will the Ascension hurt?" As good a reason for her jitters as any, she supposed. At least she hoped he thought so.

"Not much. All our rituals require a little bloodletting from each of us, and the Ascension is no different. But the cuts will be shallow. You'll be fully healed before the ritual is over."

She gave him a wry look. "Easy for you to say." A memory surfaced from one of her nightmares, then disappeared, but not before she felt the stabbing pain of a knife piercing her abdomen. A hard shudder went through her.

Hawke put his hand on her arm. "It won't be bad, Kara. I promise. We'll all be cut right along with you. One of the hazards of being marked by the goddess." Hawke smiled and shrugged. "To tell you the truth, this will be my first Ascension, too. I was marked about the same time as Beatrice, but I didn't find my way to Feral House until after she was ascended."

The cool wind breezed over Kara's face, pulling a lock of hair loose from her ponytail. She tucked it behind her ear. "Then why did Lyon choose you to prepare me if you've never done this before?"

Hawke smiled, but his smile seemed directed inward. "I understand what has to be done. Until Foxx was marked, I was the youngest of the Ferals. I've spent a lot of time learning everything I can about our race, our powers, our rituals. I sometimes think I know more than any of them, even though they've been around much longer. I know what to do." He shrugged, a self-deprecating smile forming on his mouth. "I'm a natural student. I used to be a teacher."

He'd finally caught Kara's full attention. "Me, too. Did you teach children?"

"Yes, but Therian children are rare, so I never had more than one pupil at a time."

"When was that?"

"Soon after the humans' Civil War."

Kara stared at him. She knew they were immortal. But understanding was coming more slowly. The man didn't look a day over thirty. "How old are you?"

"One hundred fifty something." He thought about it for a moment. "Fifty-seven."

And he was next to the youngest. "What about the others?"

With his finger he tapped her hand. "Lay your palms on the rock."

"Why? So the rock can learn me, too?"

He grinned. "Something like that."

"How old is Lyon?"

"Close to seven hundred, I think."

"Seven hundred?"

Hawke nodded, his expression wry. "He's not the oldest."

"Who is?"

"Kougar, though no one knows how old he is."

"He won't tell you?"

"Kougar isn't exactly the sharing kind." Hawke leaned forward and covered her hands with his, pressing her palms more firmly to the rock. His touch was warm, but impersonal.

"You aren't as touchy-feely as the others." She grimaced, realizing she'd spoken the thought out loud.

But Hawke didn't seem to take offense. "As my name implies, I'm a hawk when I shift. We're naturally less physical than the cats and dogs. In ancient times, the various lines of shape-shifters lived separately. The felines and canines lived in prides and packs. The packs may be gone, but the Ferals are still physical beings for the most part. The snake and I less so. And Lyon, almost not at all."

"But Lyon should be, shouldn't he? He's a cat."

"He should be. Why he's not, no one really knows. Personally, I think it's the way he was raised. No one knows the full circumstances, but it's said he grew up on the streets without family. He may have been Therian, but he was still a child. And kids need family."

"Has he ever been married?"

"Mated? No. Few Ferals mate except for the one chosen for the Radiant. Few Therians mate, for that matter."

"Why is that?"

"Mating is for life. And when you live as long as we can, that's a promise few are willing to make. I, like most, will mate only if I find a woman I can't live without. And that's never happened. I have relationships. I enjoy them until I tire of them, then I move on. It's the way of the species. Bonding for life is rare."

"But you're not lonely?"

Hawke shrugged. "It's hard to get lonely when you live with ten others." He tapped her fingers. "Do you feel anything beneath your hands?"

"The rock's getting warm, but I suppose that's to be expected."

"Actually, this rock doesn't heat like that. It's warming to you, which means it's time to get started." He lifted his hands from hers and placed them palm down on the rock at his sides. "Do what I'm doing. Then close your eyes."

"O-kay." She was having a hard time believing this was accomplishing anything. Then again, she had no idea what they were supposed to be doing.

Kara mimicked Hawke's move and was startled when the rock at her sides felt just as warm to her palms as the rock she'd been touching while they talked.

"Keep your eyes closed, Kara, and think about

pulling the warmth from the rock into your body."

"How did you know it was warm?"

She heard the low sound of his amusement. "I told you it was warming to you. Now, I'm going to put my hands over yours and call to the goddess."

Her eyes snapped open. "The goddess?" How many more creatures didn't she know about?

Hawke's hands slid lightly over hers. "Easy, Radiant. By the goddess, I only mean Mother Earth. Nature. She's not a living, breathing being, but the world in its purest state. The wind, the sea, the sky. The lifeblood of every living creature. And the power and energy that flows through all. An energy only a few can tap into, and only one directly."

"The Radiant?"

"Yes."

She took a deep breath. Calling to Mother Nature was kind of like calling to God, wasn't it? *Oh, man, this is all too weird.*

"Close your eyes, Kara."

She nodded and let her lids drift shut.

Hawke's hands covered hers more firmly, and he began to say something under his breath, something she could barely hear, let alone understand. With a start, she realized something was happening. Her palms were beginning to tingle.

Strange sensations rippled under the skin of her hands, climbing into her wrists, crawling like worms beneath the skin of her arms. The worms turned to geysers and shot up her arms, into her chest.

With a startled shriek, Kara jerked her hands back and stared at her normal-looking hands.

Her gaze flew to Hawke's. "What just happened?"

"Did it hurt you?" Hawke asked worriedly.

"No. It just felt . . . bizarre. Like if I didn't quit, it was going to short out my heart." She rubbed her upper arms, trying to dispel the lingering crawling sensation.

"You're strong," Hawke said, a note of admiration in his voice. "Especially considering you came to us only yesterday without an ounce of Therian energy. I hadn't expected the Earth to respond to you for at least another day, yet it leaped, didn't it?"

She nodded slowly. "That was supposed to happen?"

Hawke grinned. "That and more. At this rate, we're going to be able to ascend you early. Ready to try again?"

"No, I . . ." God, she didn't like this. Any of it. She was beginning to suspect the role of the Radiant was little more than electrical plug. Hook her up to the power source and watch her buzz.

Kara rubbed her upper arms, not having to pretend she was chilled. "I'm going to run back to the car and get my jacket, Hawke. Then I'll be ready to try it again." She stood and thrust out her hand, hoping Hawke didn't notice it was trembling. "Can I borrow the keys?"

To her dismay, he shook his head and rose. "Sit, Kara. You look a little pale. I'll get your jacket."

Damn, damn, damn. "No, I . . . feel like moving."

Hawke nodded. "I'll go with you, then." Kara saw no hint of suspicion in his eyes. No clue she meant to use this chance to run. The man was simply being annoyingly chivalrous. Or protective.

Getting the car would have been ideal, but the important thing was to be left alone. She sank back down to sit on the rock.

"I think I'll wait for you, after all. That power surge hasn't quite left my body."

Hawke nodded. "I'll be right back."

As Kara watched him climb the rocky path, her pulse began to hammer. This was it. She was finally alone. Away from Feral House. Away from Lyon.

She hated leaving him this way, but she didn't have a choice. He wouldn't let her go, and she had to get out of here. Even the thought of returning to Feral House had the fear leaping all on its own. She wasn't going back there. Even if it meant she would never see Lyon again. The thought rolled through her, harsh and miserable, as her gaze followed Hawke.

The moment he reached the top of the rocks and was out of sight, she took off in the opposite direction of his car and Feral House, climbing along the rocks, staying below the level of the woods so Hawke couldn't look back and accidentally spot her. She felt a pang of guilt for leaving him, knowing Lyon would probably be furious with him.

Hawke was a nice man. But if this worked, she wouldn't see him again. She wouldn't see any of them again. As long as she managed to stay ahead of Lyon and his finder's skills until he finally gave up on her.

When the rock face curved around a mansion built on the edge of the cliffs, she used the house to shield her and raced into the thick woods on the other side. Not too far was the road they'd traversed to get here, a busy two-lane that ran parallel to the river. With Lyon's ability to track her, her only hope of escape was to get to the road and try to flag down a ride. Preferably a ride heading out of state. Way out of state. Maybe halfway around the world.

A soft, illogical part of her hoped Lyon would eventually find her anyway. That he wouldn't give up on her.

How had the man become so important to her in such a short space of time? Too important, she admitted. Was it the man, or merely the circumstances? Would she have felt this same intense need to be in his arms if she'd met him casually at a wedding or at a church social? She tried to imagine him taking her to Bill Barton's Steakhouse, chatting with her neighbors in Spearsville, and utterly failed. There was something too wild about him, too untamed. She almost found it easier to imagine him shifting into an honest-to-God African lion.

Yes, she thought. She *would* feel this same need to be in his arms no matter how she'd met him. Even when she'd thought he was there to hurt her, he'd stirred her senses. But it was his combination of strength and gentleness that had her aching at the thought of never seeing him again.

She ran through woods dotted with houses as sound carried to her from every direction. The rumble of the falls behind her, the wind in the trees, and the dull roar of traffic ahead. Far behind her, she thought she heard her name. Her breath caught, and she quickened her pace. Hawke knew she was missing. He'd be after her, now. And though she was pretty sure he didn't have Lyon's finder's senses, it wouldn't take much for him to see her if he headed in this direction. And, really, where else could she have gone?

A bead of sweat ran between her breasts. Branches scraped her hands and cheeks and tangled in her hair, but she pressed on, desperation lending her speed she didn't usually have. Getting caught meant going back to that house of nightmares. And she wasn't doing that.

The sound of cars grew louder, nearly drowning out the thudding of her pulse. In the distance, a flash of light caught her eye, and another, the sun glinting off cars as they passed on the road. She was almost there. Just a little farther.

She felt something. A trembling beneath her feet. A light, pounding rhythm vibrating in her ears.

The sound of pursuit. Her pulse leaped.

I will not go back.

The chase excited Lyon's beast.

Hawke had called to say he'd lost Kara, wanting

to know which direction she'd gone, but Lyon told him to go back to the house. It was his fault she'd run. His mistake in thinking her attempt to leave last night was merely a result of a nightmare.

More importantly, no one was chasing Kara down but him. Because he knew what happened when predators gave chase. The blood pounded hot and wild through his veins as her scent coated his skin, a heady mixture of sweat and fear and woman.

As Lyon leaped over a fallen log, he caught sight of her through the trees, her green sweater catching the light, her blond ponytail swinging. His beast gave chase, tearing free of his control as he closed in on her, the wildness overtaking him.

Lyon sprang, tackling her to the ground in a tumbling roll, even as he locked her within the protective cage of his arms.

Mine, his beast roared as he claimed her mouth, his senses exploding. Her hair sprang free in a tumbled array as she struggled beneath him. Just as quickly, she began to kiss him back as she seemed to recognize who held her. Desperate fingers dug into his hair, her body straining against his as she met his passion with a fierceness that rivaled his own.

His beast gentled, his kiss turning hot and needy, recognizing the creature beneath him as his mate, not prey.

Her scent sank into his pores, the feel of her soft body beneath his, rocking with need sent him spinning out of control.

His tongue swept inside her mouth, drinking her sweetness, stroking her teeth, her tongue, the insides of her cheeks. He had to taste her everywhere. He was insane with wanting her.

Her pulse pounded, and his mouth followed the sound, raining kisses along her jaw until he found the pulse and licked the throbbing spot beneath her ear until she cried with pleasure, her hips rocking hard against him, her fingers digging desperately into his hair, making him growl with feral satisfaction.

Passion swirled around them like a sharp, wild mist, clouding his mind to all thoughts but one. *Mine.* He had to have her. Lost to the passion, to the demands of his beast, Lyon filled his hand with Kara's soft breast, kneading the perfect mound, then pinched the hard tip through her sweater and bra, making her moan with pleasure and arch into his touch.

It wasn't enough. He yanked up her sweater and pulled the sweet fleshy mound from the casing of the bra and took it into his mouth, pulling and suckling the silken skin, twirling his tongue around her taut nipple, over and over until she was crying out from her release.

While his mouth worshipped her breast, his hand found her hip, stroking her with ferocious need, his fingers digging into her soft buttocks. Her moan inflamed his need, hot flames devoured his patience. *Now.* He had to be inside her, *now.*

It was the sound of the zipper that startled the beast long enough for the man to regain control.

Lyon came back to himself in a rush of self-loathing.

With Herculean effort, he flung himself off Kara, away from the raw, brutal temptation of her. Lying on his back, his gaze to the tree canopy above, he struggled to regain his breath and his balance. The beast might be under control, but the beast was only half the problem. The man wanted her every bit as much.

To his surprise, Kara adjusted her clothes, then followed him, scooting against his side and laying her head on his shoulder. He fought an inner war, knowing he should push her away, yet he was desperate to pull her on top of him where he could thrust his tongue back in her mouth and press her hard against his thick arousal. Her emotion washed over him, her own desire crushed beneath the sheer weight of misery. And he could do neither.

Instead, he lifted his hand to her hair and stroked, recognizing her desperate need for comfort. "I'm sorry, little one. You ran and the animal within me rose to the chase. I lost control."

She only shuddered and pressed herself closer to his side.

"I would never hurt you," he murmured, painfully aware of the tangled emotions of the woman beside him.

"I know. I'm not afraid of you."

"Why did you run? Is it still the nightmares?"

"They're more than nightmares, Lyon. It's the house. Something in the house."

"There's nothing there that can hurt you, Kara. You just need to get used to it, and you'll be fine."

He'd meant the words to calm her, but he could feel her flare of temper and watched as she pushed herself up on her elbow to look down at him. Her lips were swollen from his rough kisses, leaves tangled in her hair, and he thought she'd never looked more beautiful. The shudder of longing that went through him was almost more than he could contain, followed quickly on its heels by one of harsh self-recrimination. How could he keep Vhyper away from her when he had no control over himself?

Goddess, but he wanted her.

"I don't want to get used to it. I hate it here. *Hate* it." She pushed away from him and stood up.

He rose to his feet and turned to look elsewhere, anywhere but at the woman who called to his basest instincts. Out of the corner of his eye, he watched her finger-comb her hair, dislodging the leaves clinging to the silken strands.

She met his gaze, her eyes desolate. "There's something wrong, Lyon. When I'm in that house, I'm constantly afraid, and I don't know why."

"But not out here. Not as bad."

"No."

"Maybe it's gone," he said hopefully.

Her lips made a rueful twist. "And what if it's not?" He felt her emotions burst with panic. "I don't want to go back there."

She worried him.

"Kara . . ." He took her arm, and she tried to jerk away from his grip.

"No. I'm not going back." She struggled against his hold, her emotions spiking with desperation. *"I'm not going back."*

His patience snapped, and he grabbed her roughly by the shoulders. "We must have an ascended Radiant, Kara, and we won't get another until you die. You cannot escape your fate."

"And what *is* my fate? Something in that house wants to hurt me. *I can feel it.*"

"Kara." He sighed, releasing her. "Nothing's going to hurt you. There's nothing wrong that won't be fixed by your Ascension."

She stared at him. "You think this is all in my imagination."

He opened his mouth to deny it, but saw the knowledge in her eyes and couldn't force the lie. "I don't know what else it could be."

"And no matter what I say, you're not going to let me go."

"No. I'm sorry, Kara, but no. You have no choice."

He watched the fight drain out of her, her eyes filling with hopelessness, and he hated the fates for what they'd done to her. For what they were doing to them both. With a flinch of her eyes, she stepped forward and began walking, accompanying him without further resistance. But on the drive back to the house, her tension began to fill the air until his knuckles were clenched and white on the steering wheel.

Was she suffering from some kind of paranoia? Was that it? Had her human upbringing damaged her mind? Or was this his doing? A result of ripping her from her world with too much violence and too little care.

Hell if he knew. And hell if he knew what he was going to do about it. Keeping her here was only half the battle. Ascending a Radiant required the full cooperation of the woman, both during the preparation and during the ritual itself. An unwilling Radiant would never ascend.

The thought chilled him. As Chief of the Ferals, the responsibility for ensuring they had an ascended Radiant lay squarely on his shoulders.

Though it had never happened before, he knew that if the day ever came that he couldn't ascend the Radiant chosen for them, he would be forced to clear the way for another.

Even the thought of it made his beast roar with anguish and bile rise in his throat. He couldn't do it. Goddess, help him, he couldn't take her life.

He must see her through this, which meant finding a way to calm her fears. A tall order considering the current state of her emotions. She'd nearly escaped him twice. Three times, if he counted the way she'd wrecked his car, then run back to her mother when he tried to take her the first time. The woman was strong. Determined. Stubborn.

All traits that would make her a good Radiant if he could just get her through this anxiety of hers. And if he couldn't?

He would have to destroy her.

No. The denial rushed up from his chest, filling his throat until it was all he could do not to yell the word into the car.

If it was the last thing he did, he would get this woman ascended even if he had to lead her through every step of the preparation himself.

With a groan, he realized that was exactly what he was going to have to do. He was the only Feral she couldn't escape.

Chapter
Ten

As Lyon drove into the long, circular drive of Feral House, Kara felt her heart picking up speed as if preparing for takeoff. Her stomach clenched, her hands turned damp, her mouth went dry.

Why?

Yes, she didn't like Feral House, hated that they were trying to force her to marry a man she didn't know and didn't like. But Lyon was sitting in the seat beside her. Lyon who was the biggest, most powerful male she'd ever known. The leader of nine such men, all determined to protect her.

Apprehension she could understand, but not this rising panic. It made no sense.

Lyon parked Tighe's car in the drive and got out. As Kara opened her own door, a full-fledged rush of terror ripped through her body, nearly driving her back in her seat. She gasped at the onslaught. This wasn't right. It wasn't natural.

Was she somehow doing this to herself?

As she pushed herself out of the car, Lyon took her hand. Almost as soon as his warm fingers curled around hers, the fear started to ebb.

His free hand slid beneath her ponytail, his palm clasping the back of her neck in a sensual, proprietary grip. She closed her eyes and leaned into his calming touch, relishing the feel of him, the strength, as he waged a battle against the emotions that kept rushing back.

As she leaned back against the car, his thumb slid up her neck, sending sweet chills racing over her skin, then retraced the path, sending a flutter of heat through her veins. What was it about this man? All he had to do was touch her, and she turned to putty in his hands. All he had to do was kiss her and she . . . mmm. Her body tightened down low in hot, welcome memory.

Her eyes fluttered open and she found him watching her, his own eyes filled with a heat to match her own as if he knew exactly what she'd been thinking.

"Your touch is magic," she murmured.

"No one reacts to it like you do." His voice was low, private, and intensely sexy, sending a rush of dampness to the juncture of her thighs.

Why couldn't he have been the one the Pairing chose for her?

She looked away as bitter unhappiness welled

inside her, wrapping around a longing so deep she could hardly fathom it. She'd known him little more than a day, yet more than anything in the world, she wanted to wrap her arms around him and never let him go.

Her gaze returned to his. "I wish you'd been the one chosen for me," she said softly.

For a second she thought she saw an unhappiness in his eyes almost as deep as her own, but then it was gone. He looked away.

"We need to go inside." Though his tone was brusque, his hand remained on the back of her neck as he led her up the brick walk to the front steps and opened the front door for her. "Let's get you some lunch. You'll feel better."

She wasn't at all sure about that, but she *was* hungry and didn't object when Lyon steered her down the hall toward the dining room and the voices raised in lively discussion. At the doorway, he released her and ushered her into the room.

To Kara's dismay, Zaphene was there again, though Vhyper, thankfully, was not.

The volume of the voices dropped slowly away as Lyon steered her to a single empty seat between Paenther and Jag. He held the chair out for her and she sat, wondering why he'd chosen not to sit beside her.

"Bring her to my office when she's finished eating."

Kara whirled in her seat, fighting down the need to beg him not to leave her, only to watch his long strides take him quickly from the room. Emotions pummeled her as she slowly turned around to face the table and the six men and one woman sitting there. Fear. Discomfort. And flat-out embarrassment as she eyed the beautifully groomed Zaphene, knowing she herself probably still had leaves sticking out of her hair.

Across the table, Tighe glanced up at her, and she mustered a smile for him. But no answering smile came her way. His green eyes, man eyes, were filled with disappointment as his gaze returned to his plate.

Her stomach clutched at the obvious cut, wondering why he was mad at her. The last time she'd seen him, right after the Pairing last night, he'd tried to come to her aid.

She forced herself to look at the others. The only one who met her gaze was Wulfe. And in his eyes she saw rank disapproval. Her stomach clenched, her scalp tingling as she wondered if her fear had a basis after all. Were they planning to turn on her, now?

At the other end of the table, she saw Hawke and felt a kick of guilt for running from him. And suddenly she understood what was going on. They knew she'd tried to run away. And they were angry.

"Next time you want to escape, sugar," Jag drawled, confirming her suspicions, "come find me. I'll take you places you never dreamed of."

"Shut up, Jag," Tighe said.

Paenther reached for an empty plate and handed it to her without meeting her gaze.

"Thank you," she murmured, but got no reply. She forced herself to take a slice of ham from the platter in front of her with hands that were once more shaking. The men's silent disapproval wore on her until she could barely force a bite in her mouth, let alone swallow. They clearly blamed her for trying to leave them, as if she were some kind of spoiled brat.

She wasn't. She was just . . . scared. Constantly. Exhaustingly. Inexplicably.

Maybe she *was* going insane.

A far door swung open to a flash of pink feathers. Kara tensed as Pink entered the dining room, carrying another platter of food.

She tried not to stare at the strange bird-woman, but couldn't keep from watching surreptitiously as the woman crossed the room in her odd, bird-like gait. Kara owed the woman an apology. There wasn't anything she could do to ease the men's anger at her, but this she might be able to fix. The bird-woman set the platter on the table and turned away, without ever glancing in Kara's direction. As she headed back to the kitchen, Kara tried to rise to follow. Paenther grabbed her wrist.

Kara met his fierce, black gaze. "I . . . I need to apologize to her."

He stared at her, the feral claw marks raking across one hard eye. A chill skittered along her flesh.

Finally, his fingers loosened, and he released her arm. "Don't try to leave. You won't get far."

Kara's breath left her on a trembling sigh. "Believe me, I know how short my leash is."

As she stood, so did Paenther and every man at the table. At first, she thought Paenther had changed his mind. They were all going to stop her. But they didn't move toward her, merely stood.

Manners.

From wild animals. *Who would have thought?*

"Sit. Please. I'll be right back." She hurried toward the kitchen before she lost her nerve. Just seeing the flamingo gave her goose bumps. How much harder would it be to try to talk to her?

As Kara pushed through the swinging kitchen door, Pink looked up from filling a water pitcher, then turned back to her task, ignoring her.

Kara swallowed. "Pink?"

"Yes, Radiant?" The bird-woman's voice sounded high-pitched, though basically human. She set down the water pitcher and turned to face Kara. Her eyes . . .

Kara's scalp crawled. Pink's eyes were round and wide. Not human. She forced herself to meet that unblinking gaze. "I'm sorry for the way I acted yesterday, when I first saw you. I wasn't prepared. Lyon forgot to tell me there was such a thing as shape-shifters."

If there was any warmth in Pink's gaze, Kara couldn't see it. She wasn't entirely sure the bird-woman even heard her.

Kara shrugged self-consciously. "I just wanted to tell you I'm sorry. If there's ever anything I can do to help you, I'd be happy to." She gave the woman a wry smile. "I'm not a bad cook."

Pink said nothing, in no way acknowledging her words. Self-pity tightened Kara's throat. All her life, she'd been surrounded by people who knew her. Who liked her. She might not have been the class president or the track star or the town brain, but she'd always been well thought of. Everyone in Spearsville loved Miss MacAllister.

Even at Feral House, the men had been friendly to her. Most of them, at least. But now she'd lost even that. She had no friends here except Lyon, and though she was certain he desired her, she wasn't entirely sure even he liked her.

Blinking back her misery, Kara turned to go.

"Radiant."

Kara pressed her finger and thumb to her closed eyes, then turned back to meet Pink's unnerving gaze.

"I forgive you for startling at the sight of me. Most do. I do not forgive you for betraying those who depend on you for life."

Kara met the woman's hard gaze, opening her mouth to deny she'd done anything of the sort, then closed it slowly and sighed.

"Thank you, Pink."

Kara turned to retrace her steps, Pink's words ringing in her ears. . . . *those who depend on you for life.* Was it true? *For life?* Lyon said they needed her ascended to be able to shift again, but they didn't really have to shift, did they? She'd never stopped to think what would happen to them if they couldn't. If she got away.

As she pushed back through the swinging door, the men rose, their manners so ingrained as to be automatic. But while the others remained with their chairs, Wulfe stepped forward, lunging toward her, his scarred face cold, his brown eyes slowly turning golden green as the irises grew to those of a feral wolf.

"You faithless little bitch!" he snarled, fangs slowly elongating top and bottom.

Kara reared back.

"Wulfe!" Tighe barked, but the warrior continued to stalk her.

"You'd leave us like this? Without our ability to shift? Don't you care that your people will weaken and die without the life-giving energy you provide? That once the Ferals are gone, there will be no one left to keep the Daemons from rising again? And that once they're freed, the world you think to run back to will crumble beneath the chaos and terror they bring?"

Kara stood rooted, shaking.

Claws snapped out from his fingers. A snarl vibrated in the bones of his face. *"You're unworthy of your calling."*

She was frozen as much by his words as from the menace in his eyes. Her mind screamed *run!* but she remembered what had happened when she'd run from Lyon. This man would tear her to shreds.

Both Paenther and Hawke leaped on Wulfe from behind, but the huge man didn't go down until Foxx swept his feet out from under him, sending the lot of them crashing to the floor.

Tighe grabbed her and pushed her behind him, his claws unsheathing as if he intended to protect her.

Lyon stormed into the dining room. *"What's going on?"*

Kara peered around Tighe's solid form to get a glimpse of the fury on Lyon's face. His gaze landed on her, and some of the tension seemed to leave him.

"The dog lost it," Jag muttered. "He was getting ready to shred our pretty little Radiant."

Lyon crossed to where the four men were struggling, Paenther and Hawke looked like they were trying to end the fighting, but Foxx looked nearly as out of control as Wulfe.

"Enough!" Lyon shouted, but nothing changed. Foxx and Wulfe were fighting and clawing one another as if they wanted to kill. "Jag, give me a hand."

Lyon and Jag wrenched Foxx free and held him back while Paenther and Hawke finally pinned a thrashing Wulfe to the ground.

"Get back in your skins! Both of you," Lyon snarled. "You *must* be able to regain control."

Kara eased farther to the side, where she could get a better view. Paenther and Hawke were already back to looking fully human. As she watched, Foxx's features slowly returned to normal. But Wulfe continued to thrash and fight.

"Jag's right," Tighe said. "He's lost it."

Lyon's brows narrowed. "We can't leave him like this. We'll have to open the prison until he's back in control."

Paenther nodded. "We're going to need some help getting him down there. Not Foxx."

Tighe and Jag stepped in, and the four men struggled to pull their feral companion from the room. When they were gone, Lyon turned to Kara.

"Are you all right?"

She nodded. Her heart was still thudding, but that was nothing new. "He didn't touch me."

"We've got to get you ascended," he said. His hand slid behind her neck, the fear instantly beginning to drain. "I need to get some lunch first."

He turned her toward the table, where Foxx was sitting beside the auburn-haired woman. "It's not safe for you here, Zaphene. I suggest you stay at one of the enclaves until things settle down."

Foxx scowled. "I can protect her."

"Can you?" Lyon asked pointedly. "You didn't look like you had it entirely under control yourself."

"I'm fine. Zaphene's fine. Aren't you, Zaph?"

The auburn-haired woman smiled. "I rather enjoy the sight of blood. It's so . . . wild."

Lyon steered Kara back to the table, where he moved her plate to one of the two empty places at the end.

"Are you staying?" she asked hopefully, looking up into his strong face.

His amber gaze met hers. "I'm staying." He grabbed a plate from the stack in the middle and began filling both his and hers from the nearby platters.

"I can't eat all that."

"Try. It doesn't look like you've eaten anything at all."

And she hadn't. She forced herself to cut a piece of meat. As she set down her knife and picked up her fork with her right hand, Lyon's palm covered her left. Immediately, the rising fear began to ebb away.

"You have prisons in the basement?" she asked him. She didn't remember seeing anything like that when they were down there for the Pairing.

"If we ever get searched by human authorities, they'll find a basement with our ritual room and our workout gym. But the chambers below the house are far more extensive, flowing out beyond the footprint of the house. There are actually two levels of subterranean chambers, though the lowest level has never been used. The prisons are in a hidden section of the upper level, beyond the gym. We haven't had to use them since the last Mage war, soon after the house was built."

He grunted as he speared a piece of ham. "At the rate we're going, we may have those prisons filled again in no time."

As they ate in silence, her mind returned to Wulfe's accusations. And Pink's. Were they right?

Was she really that important . . . *to the world?* She'd kind of assumed they wanted to be able to shift again because, well, it was fun. And if they'd implied that it was more important than that . . . much more important . . . she hadn't wanted to hear it. She hadn't been ready to hear it. She still wasn't sure she was ready, but Wulfe hadn't given her the choice any longer. And this time she'd heard him loud and clear.

Finally, four of the men returned, their clothes changed, the blood gone. Wulfe wasn't with them.

Tighe smiled at Lyon as he took his seat across from Kara. "Glad to have you join us, Roar."

Lyon nodded, his expression serious. "Any improvement in Wulfe?"

"No. He's still feral." Tighe looked at Lyon with worry in his eyes. "He's like a wild animal. It's as if his beast has completely taken over. There's no sign of the man at all in there."

Paenther sat on the other side of Kara. "How soon can we get Kara ascended?"

"Soon. I'm going to take over the prepping myself. If she's as strong as Hawke predicts, it may not take a full week."

"Thank the goddess," Paenther said.

As the men dug back into the meal, Kara picked at her food as she struggled to process her role as she now understood it.

She was some kind of power plug for the Feral Warriors. And if Wulfe was right, if she failed, even Spearsville could be in trouble. Shame filled her at the realization. She'd been so worried about saving herself, she'd given very little thought to what her leaving would do to everyone else.

Dear God, she couldn't continue to live with her heart constantly trying to pound its way out of her chest, though. But maybe there was a reason for it, a reason Lyon would find and eliminate. Or maybe once she ascended, she'd be able to see it for herself, if it didn't go away.

Either way, it didn't matter. She had to stay.

As bizarre as it might seem, the world was depending on her.

Miss MacAllister. Preschool teacher. Radiant.

The source of power for the guardians of the world.

Chapter
Eleven

"You can feel my fear, can't you?"

Kara gripped the interior car door handle as Lyon drove back to the falls after lunch, taking the hills and sharp turns like a roller-coaster car.

He took his eyes off the road ahead for one moment to meet her gaze. "I can, yes."

"Have you felt the way it's been dropping as we've gotten farther and farther from the house?"

"The mind is a powerful thing, Kara. You're probably associating bad feelings with that place. Your grief the night your mother died. The nightmares."

Kara frowned at him. "You think I'm insane."

He met her gaze with a rueful lift of his lips. "Not insane."

"Deluded, then."

"Maybe a little unsettled by the shock of everything."

"Even though, as soon as I leave the house, I'm suddenly better?"

Lyon shrugged, his thick, golden hair brushing the broad shoulders of the rust-colored silk shirt he'd changed into after lunch. "Once we get you ascended, everything will be fine. You'll see."

"Fine?" Somehow she couldn't imagine life with Vhyper would ever be *fine*. But she didn't want to think about him right now.

She was still trying to wrap her mind around the fact that she was so blasted important to the world. If she was going to stay in this world of immortals and shape-shifters, she supposed she'd better start trying to understand it.

"Tell me more about the Therians, Lyon. Why were you at war with the Mage?"

"Most recently, because they'd killed three of my warriors and captured their replacements. Vhyper and Paenther escaped, but the newly marked jaguar died at the hands of his Mage captors."

"So the spirit of the jaguar somehow found Jag? That's how this works, right?"

"Yes. Upon the death of the man, the animal spirit flies to the strongest Therian with the blood of his line still running through his veins. Jag was the strongest."

"Was he a child?"

"No. Children are rarely the strongest. Jag was over seventy at the time."

"Why did the Mage kill the previous jaguar?"

His jaw hardened. "They wanted the Daemon blade. They've always felt they should be the ones to guard it, and we've always disagreed. More than once the question of its guardianship has caused war between us."

"I can't believe anyone would willing go to war with you and your men."

"The Mage have just enough magic to even the odds. Their magic and their damned superior attitude."

"What do you mean?"

"Most of them consider all other creatures inferior to them. Greatly inferior. In their eyes, Therians are little better than the animals we can, or could, shift into. Humans are no account at all."

"Are there only the three immortal races? The Therians, Mage, and Daemons?"

"There were others, but we're the only ones who survived."

"Are the Mage as strong as you are?"

"Physically, no. But they have their weapons. Mostly they're just pains in our butts. Unfortunately, we have to be very careful not to kill them with the freedom we might like. While we tap into the Earth's energy through our Radiant, the Mage are part of nature itself. At least they used to be. Before the mortgaging of their power to imprison the Daemons, the Mage could affect, and often control, many of nature's functions. The weather, the growth of plants and trees, the reproduction of many of the Earth's species."

"They sound like gods."

Lyon grunted as he turned onto the same residential street Hawke had earlier. "They think they are. But since the loss of their power, they've been reduced to doing little more than small spells and charms. The greatest danger they pose to us is their ability to mess with our minds."

"What do you mean?"

"Beguilement. Bewitchment. It's generally how they get the upper hand before we know they've declared war on us again. They can't maintain the beguilement long and generally have to be touching the Therian to do so. If a Therian goes missing, we always assume a Mage attack." He made a sound deep in his throat. "We quickly end the wars they start." There was something dark in his tone that told her the Mage involved generally didn't survive.

Lyon parked the Land Rover, and they both got out. The day was fully overcast, now, the clouds darker and the wind stronger than before. Kara zipped her jacket and joined Lyon as they started toward the woods they had to walk through to reach the falls.

"So they've enchanted Ferals to try to steal the Daemon blade?" she asked, glancing at him. The breeze had blown his tawny hair back, revealing the strong lines of his ruggedly handsome face.

"That's usually their goal."

"Why do they want it?"

"Because we're the only ones who can free the High Daemon and his horde."

"I have to admit, I can see their logic."

He scowled at her. "We would never free him. And we're not giving up control of that knife."

"What danger is there in letting the Mage have it if they can't free the Daemons?"

"The Mage have always been more vulnerable to Daemon manipulation than we are. And while the High Daemon is safely locked in the blade, there is evil still in the world that craves his return. We who cannot be turned to evil keep the blade."

"Do Mage look like us? Like humans?"

"For the most part. The only real difference is their eyes. True Mage have copper rings around their irises. Distinctive." He glanced at her sharply. "If you ever see someone with eyes like that, get away from them and tell one of the Ferals immediately."

"Would you kill them?"

"Depends. If they threaten you, then yes. I'll kill them."

Kara shoved her hands into her jacket pockets, lifting her shoulders against the chill of his words. There was something both heady and horrifying about his simply stated declaration. A vow she had no doubt he meant. Once again, she was reminded of how important she was to them.

The Radiant.

As they entered the woods, Lyon lifted a low-hanging branch for her to pass beneath. "In the old days, there was a second way to tell a Mage. The cantric. Occasionally you'll still find someone with one, so you should know what they look like, as well."

"What's a cantric?"

"A braided copper circle that takes a Mage's natural magic and magnifies it. All Mage are implanted with a cantric upon maturity. Without them, they'd have almost no magic at all anymore."

"So both the Mages' eyes and their power magnifiers are copper circles?"

"Not a coincidence. Copper is one of their elements."

"Where do they implant the cantrics?"

"Beneath the skin. Where depends on the person and the century in which he or she was born. In the old days, Mage wore the cantrics in their faces, usually on the cheek. You could see the outline of it clearly beneath the cheekbone, and they often tattooed the skin over it so none would miss it. Humans knew to be wary of these creatures whom they considered witches. The hysteria against witches in the seventeenth century put an end to visible cantrics after half a dozen Mages were captured and burned at the stake. Most of the Mage cut the cantrics out of their faces and implanted them in other parts of their bodies. Unseen places."

The rocks became more numerous, until the path through the trees became little more than a rocky climb. The wind flipped her ponytail against her cheek, and she raked it back. "There's a painting in my room of a lion with a head beneath its paw. The face has a circle on the cheek. A shiny copper circle."

Lyon nodded. "It was painted by a Therian artist to commemorate my victory over the Elemental in 1738. The Elemental is the supreme leader of the Mage."

She gaped at him, holding her ponytail so it wouldn't flick her in the face again. "So it's a painting of you?"

He met her gaze, a hint of pride gleaming in his eyes. "It is."

Seventeen thirty-eight. A painting of a victory of a lion over a man who was essentially king of the witches. It was real. Not only real, but the victor, the *lion,* walked beside her now. A man. How was she ever going to get used to this stuff?

"Have you really been alive seven hundred years?"

"I have."

Together, they started down the rocky path to the goddess stone, Lyon's long strides making her hurry to keep up. He grabbed her hand, his warm fingers curling around hers, and tugged her with him. "Are you ready to pull the power again?"

"Out of the rock?"

"Out of the Earth, yes. It's coming from far more than just the rock."

"Then why do we have to come here? Why not do this in the backyard?" A car alarm went off in the distance, a bizarre counterpoint to her strange new reality.

"The goddess stone is sacred. A place where the Earth's energies are focused most strongly. It's where you will connect to the Earth. Once you've connected, you'll potentially be able to access the energy anywhere you can access the Earth. Every Radiant is different."

"Isn't the Earth everywhere?"

"Let me put it another way. Anywhere you can touch dirt or rock."

"Oh. No pulling the energies in the house, then."

"No. Not usually. I knew of one Radiant who was able to pull through other materials in an emergency, but she was old and powerful. It's been known to happen, but it's rare."

Lyon squeezed her hand, his touch almost affectionate, then released her.

Answering affection welled inside her. Strong and confident, he was as gentle and patient with her as anyone had ever been. And his simplest touch consumed her with fire. A fire she was almost certain he shared.

She was falling for him. In a big way. Which, unfortunately, was not a good thing. Not when the Pairing had chosen another for her. As if some game of kiss-the-immortal-shape-shifters could honestly choose her husband. How ridiculous. And awful. Yet she couldn't deny the blue glowing from Vhyper's fingertips. There'd definitely been something mystical at work. But whatever that mysticism was, it hadn't been her friend. If it had been, she'd be marrying Lyon, with only a token grumble at having the choice taken away from her.

The way things stood now, as soon as he got her

ascended, he'd walk away. But really, what made her think he wouldn't have anyway if there hadn't been a Pairing? If her husband wasn't some preordained mystic thing? A man like Lyon could have any woman he wanted. He would never, in a million years, need to settle for average.

Kara crossed her arms, shielding herself from the brisk wind as much as the disheartening thoughts.

Lyon jumped down onto the goddess stone, then held out his hand to her again. "I'll invoke the Feral Circle, then we'll get started."

She tucked her hand in his and let him help her down. "What's the Feral Circle?"

"A blind of sorts. If any humans pass by, they won't see us. If anything happens, they won't hear."

She gave him a skeptical look. "What's going to happen that's going to make that kind of noise?"

The look he gave her was almost amused. "Nothing bad. Come have a seat."

He led her to the center of the stone where she'd sat facing Hawke that morning. While she sat cross-legged in the middle of the stone, Lyon raised his hands and face to the sky, looking as wild and exciting as the wind tossing his mane of golden hair. A rush of pleasure pressed against the insides of her chest as she watched him. He was gorgeous. Thrilling.

But the pleasure slowly turned bittersweet. If only he could be hers. Even just for a little while.

After a few moments of murmuring incantations, he lowered his arms.

"Why didn't Hawke do that earlier?" she asked.

"It's not needed the first time, when all you're doing is letting the Earth learn you. It's usually not needed for the first two to three days, but Hawke said he was able to pull a surprising surge through your hands earlier, and I don't want to take any chances."

"Chances of what?"

"Your raising fire when a human's watching."

"Oh."

He squatted in front of her. "I want you to try to pull the energy yourself this time."

"I don't know the words."

"The Radiant needs no words. You are the conduit, the channel for the energies. They'll seek you and be ready at your command once they become accustomed to you."

"And that's what we're doing?"

"Yes. Close your eyes and think about the power rushing into you through your hands. In your mind, imagine you're pulling the power from the Earth."

"Like a vacuum cleaner?"

A flicker of amusement softened his features. "Like a vacuum cleaner. Try it, Kara."

She closed her eyes and tried to imagine she was sucking the rock up through her hands. But imagining had nothing to do with reality. Except, she wasn't human, was she? And she needed to start opening her mind to the possibility she could do things humans couldn't. Other than heal quickly.

Concentrate, she told herself. Be *the vacuum.*

The rock began to tremble under her, heating beneath her hands. Her eyes snapped open, her gaze jerking to Lyon's. "Is this supposed to be happening?"

"Yes." But he was clearly surprised. "Keep going. Keep pulling."

"O-kay." She closed her eyes and concentrated harder. This time she imagined herself a bigger vacuum. Industrial-strength. The trembling increased until she started to worry that the rock would break apart and tumble them into the raging river far below.

"Lyon?" she asked, keeping her eyes closed.

"Keep going, Kara." His voiced was laced with excitement. "You're doing well."

The rock beneath her hands began to feel hot, nearly too hot to touch, but she didn't move, telling herself to just keep vacuuming. If she sucked too hard, could she turn the world inside out?

And suddenly it wasn't heat going into her palms, but a jolt of hard-charging electricity that rushed into her body. Kara yelped and jerked her hands back, staring at Lyon with disbelief.

"Are you okay?" He grabbed her hands, turning them over in his. A different kind of energy surged through her at his touch. His voice roughened as if he felt it, too. "New power can hurt until you get used to it."

"It only hurt for a second. It just . . . startled me."

Lyon inspected her palms, running his thumbs

over her flesh, as if he didn't believe her. Each stroke sent shivers rippling over her skin.

"Did it burn you?" he asked.

"Kind of. Could you feel the heat?"

He nodded. "I was having trouble crediting it. That's what I was hoping would happen eventually, but I didn't expect you to be able to do it for a few days at least. And not without help." Approval lit his eyes, warming her from the inside out. "Good job, little Radiant."

Kara smiled, the buzz of happiness so rare these past few days, she almost didn't recognize it. "Thanks. That was actually kind of fun in an *oh-my-God-what's-happening* way. Not nearly as creepy as this morning."

A smile glimmered in his eyes. "What happened this morning?"

"The power felt like worms under my skin."

"I've heard of that before. It'll get easier as you get stronger."

"Just how much stronger can I get? It felt like I caused an earthquake."

His lips tilted. "You didn't. With the Feral Circle in place, the quaking never extended beyond the rock."

"That's good. I'd hate to be responsible for a natural disaster."

The smile that had slowly been forming on his face finally found its way out and spread, widening his strong mouth, blossoming inside her, filling her with a pleasure so raw, so pure, it nearly brought tears to her eyes.

And made something move in his own. Their gazes locked in a way they never quite had before, and she felt herself falling. Tumbling into those warm, liquid-amber depths. Only the grip of his strong hands on hers kept her tethered to the ground.

Inside her chest, her heartbeat changed, shifting to a pulse that was deeper, stronger, as if they'd somehow, in that moment of connection, become one. Her heart was no longer hers alone.

And she knew.

She'd fallen in love with Lyon.

Lyon dropped Kara's hands and rose, feeling suddenly strange. Off-balance. His chest heavy, like he wasn't sure he remembered how to breathe. Was this another problem due to the lack of radiance? Or something else? Something caused by the woman herself?

The moment he pulled away, Kara's gaze fled to the falls. She stared out at them now, her hair a golden glow around her. The pulse throbbing in her neck.

What just happened? She'd smiled, and he'd fallen. He'd felt as if his feet had been jerked right out from under him. As if his equilibrium had been suddenly stripped away.

Goddess, but she was a temptation he couldn't

afford. What was he thinking bringing her out here alone? He should have at least brought one of the others with them. Hawke could have prepped her while he kept watch. Or Vhyper. He should have invited her mate. He could have watched to make sure he didn't go feral. But the thought of that snake's hands on her sent hot jealousy rushing through his bloodstream.

Damn, but he needed to get control.

Kara turned back to Lyon, feeling off-kilter. As if the sands had shifted beneath her feet. She loved him.

How screwed up was *that*?

She took a deep breath and struggled to settle down. What she felt for Lyon wasn't going to matter so long as he was convinced she had to marry Vhyper. Maybe there was a loophole somewhere. Dear God, there had to be a loophole somewhere.

Maybe for now, she simply needed to learn all she could about this world and her role in it.

She looked at Lyon, watching the wind toss his thick hair as he watched her in return with enigmatic amber eyes.

"What's the purpose of this energy pull?" She linked her fingers together in front of her. "What can I do with it?"

"You have to pull the power in order to ascend."

"You keep using the word *ascend*. I'm not actually going anywhere am I?"

He turned away. "No. You'll call the power from the Earth, and we'll all share it."

"How?"

"There's nothing for you to fear."

Warning bells clanged in her head and she stood, staring at his strong profile.

"Oh, no you don't. The moment you tell me I shouldn't be afraid, I know I'd better start worrying. Spill it, Lyon. All of it."

"Later." His tone hardened with impatience. "You need to get back to work." But he wasn't meeting her gaze. She'd been down this path before and wasn't going there again.

"No way. You sent me into the Pairing without telling me I was getting a husband, and look how well that turned out. Don't you dare send me into another one unprepared."

His jaw clenched, and he remained mute.

Kara crossed her arms over her chest. "In case you hadn't noticed, this is *not* the way to calm my fears."

He glanced at her with a scowl. "You aren't going to like it."

"Tell me anyway. It's better if I'm prepared."

With a huff of frustration, he turned away and began pacing with tight agitation. "When the Ascension is over, you'll feel a rush of power like nothing you've ever experienced. We all will. And we'll be able to shift again."

"That's nice. Tell me the rest, Lyon."

He looked out over the river, then back at the

path. Anywhere but her. Finally, his jaw set, and he met her gaze.

"The Ascension requires blood. And sex."

Kara's eyes widened as the word did a strange number on her pulse. "Sex? *During* the ritual?"

Lyon shrugged. "It's necessary. Only at the moment of sexual release is the body and mind fully opened. It's only at that moment that you'll be able to raise the powers of the Earth and make them yours."

She thought of the Pairing. How they'd been prepared to make her kiss them all. Them *all*.

"Sex with whom? *How many times?*"

"For goddess sake, Kara, we're not *complete* animals. One time. With your mate."

"With Vhyper." She went cold, imagining him forcing himself on her, *into her,* with the others there. *With Lyon there.* "I'm not having sex in front of eight men!"

"The rest of us won't watch."

"But you'll be there?"

"Of course. We have to be touching you when you raise the Earth's power in order to be renewed ourselves."

"*Touching me?*" Dear God, this was getting worse by the second. "Touching me *where?*"

"You'll be clothed, Kara," Lyon replied, his voice tight with strained patience. "In a ritual gown. Standing. We'll be kneeling, touching your feet or calves, heads bowed. *Not watching.* Your mate will enter you from behind."

Kara groaned. "You're making this up." They'd be right there, touching her legs, listening to every groan, every slap of flesh on flesh while she was mounted like some kind of . . . some kind of . . . *animal*. Her scalp crawled at the thought of Vhyper's hands on her, his penis pushing against her, forcing itself inside her tight dryness, because she would never be ready for him. Never.

Lyon threw up his hands in frustration. "This is why I didn't want to tell you. I knew you wouldn't take it well."

"It's like some kind of frat-boy fantasy! You'll hear everything!"

Lyon scowled. "You wouldn't find it barbaric if you'd been raised Therian. We're shape-shifters, Kara. Part animal. Not a bunch of computer salesmen."

She flung her hands outward, mirroring his own frustration, and whirled away from him. "I can't believe this."

"Don't go anywhere."

She tossed him a heated glare and turned her back on him as she looked out over the river.

Lyon wished he could take back his words. He shouldn't have told her about the sexual nature of the Ascension, not this soon. She was far too human-minded for such truth. At the very least, he should have waited until after they were through with their work today.

They'd barely started, and already Kara stood at the far end of the stone, silhouetted against the brooding sky as she stared down at the Potomac, her back to him. The wind toyed with her hair, rippling the blue jacket that shielded taut shoulders.

For all her innate power and her Therian blood, she wasn't one of them, yet. The human world and morals had molded her thoughts and expectations. She needed time to accept the Therian ways, but time was the one thing they didn't have.

He stood, watching her, and raked his windtossed hair from his face. His timing might have been off, but she was right. The Ascension couldn't happen without a fully cooperative Radiant, and springing the sexual aspect of the ritual on her as they tried to ascend her would have been disastrous. At least this way she might get used to the idea by the time they got to it.

If she were his, he'd get her used to the idea. Goddess, but he'd enjoy getting her used to it. Bending her over, sliding inside her hot, wet sheath. *Think of me. Only of me.*

Blood rushed to his groin even as his stomach clenched with pain at the thought of kneeling at Kara's feet while Vhyper took her. How would he stand hearing Vhyper's groans and Kara's sexy whimpers as the passion rose between them? Listening to her cries as she came. Cries he'd come to love.

Goddess spare me.

He would survive it because he must, and thank the heavens and Earth he only had to be present for their coupling the one time. He'd find a way to be absent from their actual mating ritual, if it killed him.

"You aren't a bunch of shape-shifters," Kara muttered from behind the barrier of her stiff back. "You're a bunch of perverts."

Lyon had had enough. He went to her, took her by the shoulders, and forced her to face him. "You. Are. Not. Human. The sooner you stop thinking like one, the better for all of us, Kara. Yourself included."

The temper in her eyes drained away.

He softened his grip on her shoulders. "It sounds strange to you, I know, but it won't be. You'll be so caught up in the power, you won't think about being self-conscious. I promise."

The look in her eyes turned almost bleak. "I don't want it to be Vhyper."

His hands spasmed. His beast howled with a bleakness to match her own. What had he done? What grief had he pulled down on all their heads by giving in to his need for her when he'd prepped her for the Pairing? If she were his mate instead of Vhyper's, he was certain he'd be able to lead her through the ritual with relative ease because she trusted him. With the right encouragement, he could make her want him even under circumstances that might be embarrassing for her.

But Vhyper was still a stranger to her. Her acceptance of him under those trying circumstances was questionable. Even doubtful. And she must accept him.

* * *

Lyon's eyes were shuttered, his jaw tight as he squeezed her shoulders and released her. "Let's get started again. Sit down, Kara. We're going to try something a little different."

Kara wanted to argue. He was asking too much. At every turn he demanded she accept the strange ways of this world and forsake everything she'd ever known. Forsake everything she was for a role that meant next to nothing to her. A role she'd give anything to give to someone else.

But at lunch she'd begun to accept that while the role might not mean anything to her, it meant everything to them. And she was stuck with it, whether she liked it or not.

Her teeth worried her lower lip as it occurred to her she was railing against the fates for giving her no choice. Yet those very fates had delivered her to a mansion where she was expected to live in comfort, do no work that she was aware of, and be paired with a man who would supposedly be the love of her life. Oh, and by the way, the fates had tossed in a body that never aged and healed, as it always had, miraculously fast.

All over the world, men and women, alike, were living the lives forced on them by birth and circumstance. Many of them were miserable lives, filled with hardship, abuse, and disease.

She wanted life on her terms. But that *was* spoiled, when so many depended on her for their power. And possibly even their lives. It was time she got over herself and concentrated on getting herself ascended. Then, maybe, she'd be in a better position to assess what kind of control she'd be able to steal in her life.

"Okay, I'm through sulking." Kara followed Lyon back to the center of the rock. "What now?"

He glanced at her, a look in his eyes that might have been relief. Or approval. "I want you to pull the power as before, but this time visualize it turning to flame in your hands."

"Why flame?"

"Because you're going to try to call fire this time. Fire is the physical form of your power."

Every time she thought she'd accepted this stuff, it turned more freaky on her.

"You're not talking about *real* fire, are you?"

Lyon motioned her to sit, then sat in front of her, crossing his legs as she did hers.

"The mystic fire I want you to pull looks real, but contains no heat. It won't burn you."

A thought occurred to her. "Will it hurt other people? Can I use it as a form of self-defense?" Maybe if she had some real way to protect herself, she wouldn't have to feel so afraid.

Lyon's brow quirked up, his mouth softening into a promise of a smile. "Are you seeking a way to defend yourself against me, little Radiant?"

"I was thinking more of finding a way to protect myself."

"I won't let anything harm you, Kara."

She frowned at him. "You're not with me a hundred percent of the time. You can't make promises like that." She hooked her arms around her knees.

"Humor me, Lyon. I'd feel better if I thought I had a way to protect myself."

Lyon shrugged. "Once ascended, some Radiants are able to throw fire. Real fire," he told her. "I've only seen it happen once, but I know some can do it. From what I've seen so far, I wouldn't be surprised if you were able to develop that kind of strength."

"But what about now? Can I do anything before I ascend?"

"I don't suppose you've studied karate?" It sounded like a joke, but there was no humor in his expression.

She made a face at him, then released a long-suffering sigh. "Show me how to pull the fire, Lyon. I want to know how."

He nodded once. "We'll start the same way as before, with your hands on the rock. When you feel the jolt of power this time, try to stay with it. Let it come. It could take a hundred tries before you can capture it, but it's critical you do."

Kara shrugged. "My calendar's free." She placed her hands on the rock between them, palms down, closed her eyes, and lifted her face to the wind.

She felt the rock warm beneath her palms. *Be the vacuum,* she thought, and pulled hard, willing it into her body. The power shot up her arms like before, and she yelped and jerked her hands back. But it hadn't hurt this time. Did he really expect her to hold on to this?

"Once you're able to hold that surge of power, I'll help you take it to the next level."

Kara licked her lips and nodded, placing her hands back on the rock, feeling a razor-sharp sense of anticipation. Holding her breath, she pulled.

Again the power caught her. Again she jerked back, this time with a laugh. She looked up to find Lyon watching her intently, a smile hovering at the edges of his mouth. If only they could stay out here like this. Sealed away from the rest of the world. Alone.

A sharp longing pierced her breastbone, and she closed her eyes against his too-perceptive gaze.

Power. Draw the power. This time she would catch it, no matter what.

The stone began to rumble beneath her, but she ignored it. She was the vacuum. The chosen one. The Earth would give up her energy to Kara alone.

The power leaped. She gasped as it raced up her arms and dove into her body, but she held on this time. It was too much. Too strong. She felt like she'd taken a bolt of lightning inside that was ripping her innards apart. Her jaw clenched, her mouth compressing with pain. But she held on.

Slowly, the pain dimmed, as if the bolt of lightning had quieted and no longer tried to escape. She could feel it inside, highly charged, but warm. Exciting. And she was finally able to breathe again.

A smile tilted her mouth even as her eyes remained closed. "I caught it, Lyon," she said, pleased with herself. "What do I do with it?"

"I'm going to cover your hands, little one. Don't move. Hold the power."

But the moment his hands slid over the backs of hers, pure lust shot into her, as if the natural attraction they shared had found a powerful conduit. Her body came roaring to life, her breasts suddenly full and heavy, her skin tingling as if Lyon's fingers were touching her everywhere. Between her legs, she felt a series of small contractions and a rush of dampness as her body opened and readied itself for his penetration.

"*Lyon.*" She opened her eyes and found his eyes closed, his head thrown back in an expression that was part pain, part ecstasy.

"Sweet goddess." His voice sounded as strained as hers had. "Don't lose the power, Kara. Hold it. Just . . . give me a minute."

"You feel it, too."

"Oh, yeah." He gave a strangled laugh. "Never expected that to happen."

His hands held on to hers, the power flowing between them. The desire raging. When his head tilted down, and his eyes opened, she gasped all over again at the blazing need in his eyes.

"Lyon."

His hands gripped hers harder.

"Kara, *concentrate*. Hold the power." He groaned. "I suddenly understand why it's traditional for the Radiant's mate to be the one doing this."

Kara's breaths came in tight, shallow pulls as desire swirled around them and through them.

Lyon clenched his jaw. "We need to continue."

"How?"

"Grip it, Kara. I'm going to lift your hands, but I want you to keep hold of the fire. The real fire."

She gave a strangled laugh. "Okay." It wasn't like that other fire, the one that was melting her from the inside out, was going away anytime soon. Not as long as Lyon was with her. Because, while the Earth's energy had definitely shot her desire for him into orbit, it had been there from the start. And, she was afraid, always would be.

With a shaky breath, she closed her eyes and forced herself to concentrate on the power flowing through their joint hands. Lyon turned hers until they formed a bowl.

"Keep the power in your hands, Kara. Focus."

"It's still there?"

"Yes."

"You're helping." She could feel him, now, pulling at the power, too.

He held on to her, cupping his hand beneath hers, as the desire between them slowly descended from the stratosphere, and she could breathe again.

"All right, Kara. Now I want you to visualize the flame. Imagine it erupting in the middle of the bowl of your hands. A simple, cool flame that can't hurt you."

She did as he directed, and within seconds, to her amazement, their hands began to vibrate.

"Something's happening," she gasped.

"That's it!"

Kara's eyes snapped open, her jaw dropping as she gaped at the tiny blue heatless flame they held between them. A second later, it flickered out.

"I lost it." Kara looked up at Lyon with disappointment, but saw none in his own expression. He was watching her with a heat and intensity that had her libido leaping a second time.

"That was an excellent start."

"It was?"

He nodded slowly, his gaze dropping to her mouth.

The moment stretched, the heat of his gaze tingling along the surface of her lips until she could almost feel him. She wanted him to kiss her. Wanted the pressure and strength of his mouth on hers, his tongue sliding between her lips.

She wanted until she was shaking with it.

But he didn't move. He sat there as if carved in granite, need vibrating off him in waves.

"Lyon," she said softly, and reached for his hand.

But her movement broke him out of his trance and he shot to his feet and moved away.

Lyon stared out over the rough Potomac, the cool wind in his face doing nothing to ease the painful need surging through his body.

Goddess, but he wanted Kara.

He'd been a fool to think he could prep her. Even before the surge of power had burst over him, inflaming every nerve ending, leaving him hard and ready and wanting, he'd known it had been a mistake.

Watching her out here, away from the house and the constant fear that had been riding her, he'd gotten a taste of the woman she'd been before. Before her mother died, before he'd wrenched her from everything she'd known and thrust her into the immortal world of the Ferals.

And he'd become intrigued by her more than ever. Enchanted.

How was he ever going to get over her?

There was an elemental quality to her out here, a wildness, that called to his beast. And a sweetness and strength, despite everything, that drew the man. He would be perfectly content to sit out here for hours every day, watching her. The play of light along her fine bones, the emotions flitting across her face.

He heard her approach and knew the moment she came to stand by him. For a long time she said nothing, simply stood at his side as if that was the very place she belonged. By sheer dint of will, he kept his hands to himself and didn't pull her closer. He didn't touch her at all. But that in no way meant he wasn't excruciatingly aware of her.

"When were you born exactly?" she asked finally. Her face was turned to the wind, the breeze tugging wisps of hair free from her ponytail to tease her cheek. A cheek he knew to be soft as silk.

"I was born somewhere around 1314. Maybe 1315. Dates were unimportant back then, and no one ever marked my birthday."

She turned to glance at him, her brows drawing together. "Even your mom didn't know?"

Lyon turned back to the river. "My mother was human. She died when I was born."

"I'm sorry. Who raised you?"

"Me."

"You had no one?"

"I had a father. A Therian. But I wouldn't go so far as to say he raised me. He'd been kicked out of the enclaves years before for excessive drinking. He was basically an immortal drunk. He'd have committed suicide a dozen times over if he hadn't been such a coward, and if it hadn't been so damned hard to do. He hated his life. Hated his wife for dying on him."

"And hated his son for killing her?"

He met her too-perceptive gaze, his gut clenching as a vivid memory rose from the distant reaches of his mind.

His dad dumping him, headfirst, into the rain barrel and holding him there until his lungs were full of water and exploding with pain. The summer solstice. The day his mother had died. It had happened every year on the summer solstice, until Lyon finally stopped going back.

He'd never told anyone. "Why would you say that?" he asked sharply.

Kara shrugged and turned back to the water. "One of my preschoolers, last year . . . It was his birthday. When we sang 'Happy Birthday' to him, he burst into tears. I took him aside and he told me he wasn't allowed to celebrate his birthday because it was the day he'd killed his mom. His dad had told him that. The next morning, he came to school with a black eye and bruises on his back and stomach. I reported it, and his father was arrested for child abuse."

She turned back to meet his gaze, warm sympathy in her eyes. "I'm sorry that was you, Lyon.

Even if he never actually hit you, blaming a child for something that was so clearly not his fault is a terrible thing to do."

"Yeah, well, it was a long time ago." And not a memory he'd ever wanted to keep.

"When you say a long time ago, you're not kidding," Kara said softly. "Hawke did tell me no one knows who your father was. Have you ever seen him since you became a Feral?"

"No. I left him when I was ten or eleven. I'd gotten pretty good at avoiding the fists and boots of the other drunks on the street, and had been feeding myself and fending for myself for years. He beat me once too often. I left and never went back."

Kara's soft hand touched his shoulder. "I'm sorry."

Lyon shrugged. What he'd said was true. It was a very long time ago. The memories should have faded long ago.

"Where was this?" she asked.

"The slums of London."

"Were you always called Lyon?"

He gave a soft snort. "I grew up as a scrawny kid by the name of Arthur Bannister. A Feral isn't named until after his first shift, when he discovers which animal has chosen him."

Her sweet face turned to him, her eyes bright with curiosity. "That must have been amazing. To discover you could become a lion."

"It was . . . strange. And, yeah. Amazing. And one hell of a relief."

A smile trembled on her lips. "Why a relief?"

"Because, back in those days, the moment a new Feral arrived at Feral House, the others started calling him Mouse. It was a long-running joke, but of course, I didn't know that. They swore up and down that the Feral who'd recently died, the one I'd been marked to replace, had been a mouse." He shrugged. "I was sixteen. They had me totally convinced."

"But you turned into a lion."

"I did. It was the proudest day of my life." Her eyes shone as she gazed at him, making something tighten and ache deep in his chest. He cleared his throat, suddenly uncomfortable. "I'm not sure why I told you all this. I've never told anyone."

"I'm glad you did."

The urge to reach for her nearly overwhelmed him, and he shoved his hands into his back pockets. She was too close. Too tempting. Again, he considered calling one of the others to finish for him. They knew she was a flight risk, now. They'd never let her out of their sight.

But then he'd miss the look on her face the first time she turned radiant. Goddess, but he was turning into a glutton for torture.

He turned away, putting what distance he could between them. "Let's try again, Kara."

Without a word, she returned to her place on the stone and sat. Could he possibly touch her again without giving in to the need riding him to pull her against him?

The answer to that was a resounding *hell if I know.*

"Why don't you try it yourself this time," he suggested, and sat a distance from her this time, leaning against the rock wall that formed the backdrop of the goddess stone.

Kara nodded, placed her hands on the stone, and closed her eyes. Lyon stretched his legs out in front of him, settling back as he watched her go through the steps on her own. Concentrating, pulling, over and over until finally she succeeded in pulling the small blue flame. But each time it flickered out. Again and again.

Finally, she held it.

Lyon tensed with excitement, leaning forward. "That's it, Kara." He watched as the flame sank into her hands, flowing out beneath her skin like a faint, iridescent glow that lit her from within wherever it touched.

Kara's gaze flew to his, and she gasped. "What's happening?"

Lyon grinned. "You did it."

Chills tingled along his skin as he watched the glow spread up her neck and illuminate her face in a beautiful wash of light and color.

Her jaw dropped. "I'm glowing."

"You're radiant," he murmured. *Beautiful.* The sight of her like this, the fire beneath her skin, the amazement sparkling in her eyes, was the most incredible he'd ever seen.

"Can I move? Will I lose it?"

"You can move. You won't lose it until you let it go."

With an uncertain half smile, she rose to her feet,

her gaze on her hands. Slowly, she lifted her hands up to the sky, watching them. Laughter bubbled out of her throat, and she turned, her eyes glowing as she met his gaze.

"It feels . . . amazing. *Powerful*." She twirled around, her head tilted to the cloudy sky, and laughed. "I feel like I could fly. Like I could lift this rock with you on it and carry you both to the moon."

Her joy and awe of her power made something warm and painful move in his chest. She was so alive, so achingly lovely. More than anything in the world, he wanted to grab her up and twirl her around. Without even realizing he'd done so, he'd risen to his feet, but he forced himself to stay where he was.

Kara stopped spinning, her face truly aglow. "Is this why I'm called the Radiant? Because I can light up like a campfire?"

Her description, her sheer delight, pulled a chuckle from him. A surprising burst of happiness. "Yes."

As he watched, she twirled again, spinning, coming to a halt directly in front of him. Eyes gleaming as brightly as her skin, she started to reach for him, then snatched her hand back.

"Can I hurt you?"

He smiled at her, totally under her spell. "No."

As soon as the word was out, the moment that single soft finger traced the line of his cheekbone, he recognized his mistake. Her power leaped at him, tumbling him into a sea of erotic fire.

"Does it hurt?" she asked.

Had he groaned? "No." It didn't hurt. Not precisely.

She lifted her other hand and traced his opposite cheek, but her gaze fell to his mouth. His body tightened down low.

"What are you doing?" His voice sounded strangled to his own ears.

Her sweet mouth lifted into a small, womanly smile. "Reveling in my power."

"By touching me?"

Her blue eyes lifted to caress him. "Do you feel anything when I touch you?"

"Always." He had to clench his hands at his sides to keep from reaching for her, to keep from cupping her slender waist and sliding his hands up over her rib cage, over her breasts.

"What does it feel like?" Her palms pressed flat against his cheeks as her gaze dropped again to his mouth. He saw the intent in her eyes plain as day and knew he had to stop her. But, heaven help him, he wanted to kiss her. He was dying to kiss her.

She tried to lower his head, but he shook her off, lifting his chin.

"No, Kara." He knew he should push her away, but he didn't have the strength.

"What does it feel like?" she persisted. "Do you feel the buzz of power like I do?"

"Yes." The word came out choked, as one glowing thumb slid against his lower lip. He was frozen in a battle between his beast and his honor, one trying to break free to claim her, the other fighting to push her away. Neither won, and he stood immobile, letting her touch him even as he managed . . . barely . . . to keep from touching her.

Until she slid her thumb into his mouth. His beast leaped free of his restraint. He felt his fingers and mouth ache in warning. For one terrible moment, Lyon thought he was going feral.

His control was too thin. Kara was playing with fire in two ways, one of which could get her killed if he lost control as completely as his men had.

He grabbed her wrists, yanking her arms over her head and turned her, pushing her face first against the rock wall and pressing himself tight against her, pinning her.

"Don't move."

"What are you doing?" Her pulse raced beneath his hands, her breathing fast and labored.

"*Don't move.*"

Instinctively he'd known he couldn't push her away or try to escape her himself. His beast would have fought to reach her. Now he had her. He had her. His body pressed against her. But with her back to him, he couldn't kiss her. And clothed he couldn't take her. Not unless he lost all control and ripped her clothes from her.

Pressing against her like this eased his inner torment, his beast's desperate need to touch her, to feel her against him, her hair brushing his cheek, her soft buttocks nestling the part of his anatomy that craved the feel of her most.

He pulled the air into his lungs, breathing the scent of her with each hard breath, drowning in the feel of her even as he struggled for control.

Little by little, his beast calmed until he was certain he was in control again. He released Kara's wrists, pushed away from her, and stepped back before she tempted him again.

She turned toward him slowly, warily, her radiance fading and disappearing as he watched.

"What happened, Lyon?"

He couldn't tell her how her beauty had nearly driven him to the point where he could have harmed her, without wanting her all over again.

"Nothing."

"Lyon . . ."

He silenced her with a wave of his hand. "I'll tell you later." He turned his back on the confusion in her eyes and started for the walk. "Let's go, Kara." What he'd told her earlier held true. He wasn't letting her out of his sight again. But he'd been a fool to allow himself to be alone with her. His control was shot. Another Feral might help him keep the wildness at bay.

Or protect Kara if he failed.

Damn, but he needed to get away from her altogether.

As they walked to the car, he pressed his fist against the ache in his chest. She made him want things. Things he'd known little of and never cared about before. Smiles. Laughter.

But the goddess had known what she was doing when she gave Kara to Vhyper. Vhyper, once he was himself again, would make her laugh. He'd make her smile. He'd make her happy in a way Lyon never could.

The sooner he remembered that, accepted it, and quit wishing for things that could never be, the better. Because if he didn't, this obsession he was developing for Kara was going to make his life a living hell.

Chapter Fourteen

The drive back to Feral House was short and silent. Kara could feel the fear rising inside her as if someone had opened her up and was pouring it in. With each rotation of tires, her pulse increased. Her mouth went dry. Her stomach clenched with misery both real and forced as she held on to the hope that Lyon would figure out what was doing this to her.

Before she found out in the dark one night. Alone.

Tears burned her eyes at the horrible return of fear and the loss of the brief hours of pleasure she'd known on the rock. The freedom. Lyon's company. His smile.

He sat beside her, silent and brooding, as he

drove them back to the place she least wanted to go. If only they could have stayed out there in the wind, beneath the open sky, with the sound of the rushing water filling her ears instead of the thudding of her heart.

If only she could have stayed out there with Lyon.

But after that last incident, he'd been hell-bent on getting away from her. Her cheeks heated as she remembered the way she'd touched him after he'd told her no. He hadn't stopped her, but neither had he encouraged her to continue. Yet she had. Until he turned her and pressed her against the wall.

He'd been close to losing control. She'd felt it, felt the hardness of the erection he'd ground against her backside.

God, she'd wanted him. As he'd pressed against her, she'd longed for whatever he'd wanted to give her. With the rush of power had come an incredible joy, the combination turning into a raging need. For Lyon.

A need he'd shared. He'd given her no doubt about that. But he'd refused to give in to it.

Because she belonged to somebody else.

As they drove into the drive, Lyon could feel Kara's fear rising exactly as it had earlier. He frowned. What if she was right? What if this wasn't natural?

"Kara, we're going to do a little experiment."

She looked at him dubiously. "What kind of experiment?"

"Close your eyes. Tightly."

She glanced at him for a moment longer before he watched her golden lashes sweep down over her eyes.

"Now what?"

"Nothing. Just keep them closed for me while I drive around for a few minutes."

He felt her relax against the seat, but her fear didn't ebb. Until he drove out of the driveway. But that didn't necessarily prove anything.

Lyon drove to the end of the street, then turned around and drove into a drive two houses down from Feral House with a drive he knew to be of similar length to their own. As he curved around in front of the house, her emotions remained level and unaffected. Then suddenly began to spike, but with worry, not fear.

"Are your eyes closed?" he demanded.

"Yes."

"What are you worried about?"

"We're in front of Feral House, aren't we? Yet when I can't see it, I'm not afraid."

"Keep your eyes closed. We'll try it again."

This time when he drove to the end of the street and back again, he drove into his own drive. And her fear quickly began to rise.

"You can open your eyes, Kara." He flipped open his cell phone and called Paenther. "Meet me in my office in five."

"What's the matter?" Kara blinked at him.

"The second time, I didn't pull in here. I pulled into a neighbor's drive. That's the time you didn't react."

"You believe me," she breathed.

Her relief was so acute, he reached for her and squeezed her shoulder. "We've probably got a dark charm in the house. It happens from time to time."

"What's a dark charm?"

"A Mage spell attached to some item that finds its way into our house. It'll cause us problems for a couple of days before we find it and destroy it, or until the magic peters out. This one's strong, though, to be causing you this much anxiety when you're not even wearing it. But it makes sense why the fear disappears when you're away from the house."

"Could the dark charm have caused Wulfe's problem?"

"Good question, but no. Unascended as you are, your natural defenses against magic are virtually nonexistent. Not so ours. No dark charm has the power to rip a Feral loose from his humanity. The Mage simply don't have that kind of power anymore."

He parked the car and turned off the ignition, then reached for Kara's hand, beating back the rush of fear from her body. "Once we find the dark charm, you'll be fine."

His own relief was huge. She wasn't weak of

mind or spirit but simply a victim of a minor Mage attack. One he could easily counter.

Lyon released her, then went around the car to Kara's side. The moment he opened the door for her, a blast of fear rolled off her, slamming into him like a sound wave. She shrank back into the seat, then grabbed his hand like a lifeline when he reached for her.

"Please tell me you felt that."

He nodded. "I did. Definitely magic-born." His hand tightened on hers as he fought to help her battle the vicious emotion.

Lyon steered her up the front walk and down the front hall to his office, his hand at the back of her neck, siphoning her fear. As he pulled the emotion from her, she calmed, her body relaxing beneath his touch.

Kara looked around as he ushered her into his private sanctum. "Nice. Now this is more like it."

"In what way?"

"It looks like a man's room."

"It is. Beatrice stayed out of here." He really looked at the room for the first time in a long time. It was, and always had been, his favorite room in the house with its floor-to-ceiling bookshelves, the large hearth, his mahogany desk, and the dark-painted walls.

"It feels like you."

"It's my sanctuary." A sanctuary that would never be the same, he realized, as she slipped from his hold to peruse his collection of books. His gaze drank of her beauty, mesmerized by the blond, wind-tossed wisps that curled around her face where they'd escaped the confines of the elastic. Her scent would linger here, in his memory if not in truth. Nowhere would he be safe from thoughts of her once she'd turned to Vhyper.

The fear began to rise in her again. As he felt it, she was already moving back to his side. He ran his palm beneath her ponytail and over the silky skin of her neck.

Her face tilted up to him, her blue eyes concerned. "What does it do to you when you help me like this? Does it hurt you when you take my emotions?"

His gaze caressed her features one by one, the dark gold lashes sweeping up from her eyes, the curve of her brows, the high soft line of her cheekbones.

"It doesn't hurt."

"Do you feel them yourself when you take them from me?"

"No. Not as you feel them. There's an energy in emotions, especially strong, negative ones. I feel it like a low current. Not pleasant, but not painful." His thumb traced her jaw beneath her ear. "Knowing that I ease your discomfort gives me pleasure."

Her gaze softened, her lips lifting in a small, sweet smile that set up an ache deep in his chest. "Thank you."

At the sound of a throat clearing behind him, Lyon turned, dismayed to realize he hadn't even heard Paenther's approach. The black-haired warrior stood in the doorway now, his gaze flickering between him and Kara, his mouth tight with a disapproval he gave no voice to.

"There's a dark charm in the house that's been affecting Kara, B.P. Organize a full search."

If Paenther was surprised, he didn't show it. He nodded and turned to leave. "Vhype."

Paenther's greeting had Lyon's head snapping up just as Vhyper froze in the doorway.

Cold eyes watched him caress Kara's neck. "Get the hell away from my mate."

Lyon released Kara slowly, a deep growl escaping his throat as his beast rose. Lyon fought back the wildness. "She needs my help, Vhyper."

"I'll just bet she does. The same kind of *help* you gave her during the Pairing?" The snake's eyes began to turn feral red.

"Stay in your skin, Vhyper."

"Go to hell, Chief." Wicked, curved, snake's fangs sprouted from his mouth. "*Give her to me.*"

As Vhyper closed the distance between them, Lyon shoved Kara behind him, his beast leaping in protective fury, snarling beneath his skin.

His fingers burned, but he fought the feral anger, balled up his human fist, and smashed it beneath Vhyper's jaw in a hard uppercut.

The snake's head snapped back, two trails of blood trickling down his mouth from where his fangs pierced his lower lip.

"Back down now, Snake," Lyon snarled. "Get back in your skin, or you're joining Wulfe in the prison."

Vhyper hissed at him, his red eyes spitting with anger.

"You wouldn't."

Lyon leaned forward until he was fully in Vhyper's face. "Watch me. If you're not in control, you threaten the safety of the Radiant, which endangers us all."

"So this is how you stay away from her, Chief?" His voice was low and hard. "With your hands all over her? And you condemn me for losing control? Not a man in this house would blame me for taking you down for this insult." A low sound rumbled from his throat. "You have no right to touch her, no right to keep me from touching her."

His beast roared in protest. She was his to protect. *His.*

But, dammit. What Vhyper said was true.

It didn't matter. He wasn't letting her go. His teeth clenched and unclenched in a low, rhythmic violence as his innate fairness battled with his beast's hyperprotectiveness and the primitive instinct that told him not to let her out of his sight.

His instincts won.

"Tomorrow night we ascend her. Then she's yours. Until then, as the finder and chief, she's my responsibility." His voice brooked no argument.

Vhyper's fangs slowly retracted, a show of more control than Lyon himself had. "She's your responsibility? Or is she yours? To touch. To fondle. To fuck?"

Lyon's hands balled into fists, and it was all he could do not to smash them through Vhyper's face. *"Watch your language, Snake."*

"Watch your hands, Roar. I saw you touching her. Holding her. You've said yourself you lost control during the preparation for the Pairing. And every Feral watched you lose control during the Pairing itself. Why in the hell should I trust you with her now?"

He shouldn't. Goddess knew, Lyon didn't trust himself. What in the hell was he doing?

Yet he couldn't back down. Kara needed him. All he knew for certain was she needed him.

He rarely explained himself to his men. He sure as hell didn't feel like explaining himself now. But he didn't have a choice. At the very least, he had to convince himself he was doing the right thing. That he hadn't, in fact, lost complete control.

He straightened and crossed his arms across his chest, pinning the other man with his hardest look. "Until she's ascended, you're not touching her. And I'm not letting her out of my sight."

With a hiss of anger, Vhyper whirled and stormed from the room.

As his beast roared with approval, Lyon wondered what in the hell he'd just done.

"I'll be right outside your door," Lyon told Kara that evening as he stood with her in front of her bedroom. This was the first time he'd been alone with her since they'd returned from the falls. Dinner had been a tense affair, with Vhyper glaring at him and Foxx snarling at every man at the table. Kougar and Jag had gotten into it over something trivial, but both managed to regain control when he'd demanded. Not once had he left Kara's side, but neither had he trusted himself to be alone with her.

He rested his hands on either side of her neck, now, draining the emotions, hoping she'd be able to fall asleep before they became unbearable again. Because the one place he didn't dare follow her was into her room while she slept.

His control wasn't that strong.

"Are you going to stay out here all night?" Her blue eyes watched him.

"All night." His thumbs brushed the underside of her chin. If not for Vhyper, he might have attempted the torture of staying with her to keep the emotions at bay. But Vhyper's accusations were too close to the truth. He wanted this woman with a need that was like fire in his blood. The temptation of her was just too much.

Kara lifted her hands to cover his. Warmth flowed into his bloodstream.

"I'm glad." She sighed, her lips parting, drawing his gaze. He tried to look away, but it was no use. Her scent teased his nostrils, her hair gleamed beneath the golden glow of the lamplight. Her mouth beckoned until his hands shook from the effort of not giving in to the need to taste her again.

He should leave. Now. Before he did something he'd regret.

But the thought of putting so much as a door between them had his beast howling with unhappiness. His fingers brushed her neck. With one hand, he stroked her hair.

"Have they found the dark charm, yet?" she asked.

"Not yet. But they will. And if they don't, I'll call the Shaman. He has a unique ability to sense magic. He'll find it for sure."

Something warm glowed in her eyes. "I almost wish you'd wait and call the Shaman later."

He lifted a brow in surprise. "Why?"

"Because once the fear goes away, you won't have any reason to touch me."

Lyon tossed back his head and groaned even as he pulled her against his chest and dug his fingers into her hair.

Her slender arms went around his waist. "I wish it were you." Her voice was so low he wasn't certain those words had been meant for his ears, but he heard. Goddess help him, he heard.

His hand slid down her back, hard, shaking with a need he couldn't slake. The blood pooled between his legs, heavy, his erection pressing against her abdomen.

If only he could slake his desire for her. Maybe it would be over, then. He'd be able to forget her.

But he couldn't. Ever.

He needed to get the hell away from her.

Lyon gripped her shoulders and pulled her gently back. "Go to bed, Kara. Before I do something I'm going to regret."

The look she gave him was almost a smile. A sad one, but a smile.

"Good night, Lyon."

He locked his hands behind his back to keep from reaching for her. "Sleep, little one. Dream-free." Then she turned and left, closing the door behind her.

Lyon settled on the floor, propping himself against the wall. It promised to be a damned long night, but he wouldn't be able to sleep in his own bed for wondering if she was okay. At least this way, he'd hear her if she became distressed during the night. And more importantly, he'd be here if Vhyper got it into his head to claim his mate.

He could hear the sound of a basketball game on the television in the media room punctuated by the yells of his men as one team or another scored. More than two hours had passed when Paenther came upstairs.

"No sign of any kind of charm. I called the Shaman, but he's in New York visiting one of the enclaves. He's going to drive back tonight and will come over after dawn."

"Good. Any change in Wulfe?" Lyon asked, as the other warrior leaned one wide shoulder against the wall.

"None."

"What about the others?"

"Foxx is holding on to his control by a thread. As is Vhyper." His black eyes met Lyon's with the hard glint of truth. "And you."

Lyon couldn't deny it. He was definitely teetering on the edge.

"Jag's more volatile than usual, but that may just be because his digs are getting more reaction than he's used to. The others seem fine. They're taking turns watching Wulfe. Pink's annoyed as hell at all the blood spilling but showing no signs of trouble. Hawke and Jag have been mopping up the messes for her."

"And you?"

"I've been balancing on the edge of control for centuries. Nothing's changed." His gaze flicked to Kara's door. "How's she doing?"

"Well enough."

"Are you going to stay here all night?"

"I am. It's either that or lock up Vhyper."

Paenther eyed him soberly. "You really think he'd hurt her?"

"I think he's mad enough to want to. And I'm not sure his control is currently strong enough to refrain if he gets the chance. I'm not risking it."

Paenther's mouth compressed, but he said nothing as he met Lyon's gaze. Finally, he nodded, said good night, and went down the hall to his room.

Lyon tipped his head back, resting it against the wall behind him, his senses tuned to Kara. She was sleeping, he was almost sure of it. He was too far away to feel her emotions clearly, but low levels of fear were reaching him in regular waves. Unless he was touching her, she was never free of the rancid emotion. He wondered how she stood it.

His beast refused to settle down, whimpering continuously to go to her. To touch her, to ease that fear. To simply be near her.

What had she done to him? Just thinking about her made him ache in a way he barely understood, filling him with a need that was more of the spirit than of the body, though that ache was an ever-present torment as well. As soon as she was ascended, this ache would leave him. He'd go back to being as he'd always been.

He didn't need anyone. He'd never needed anyone.

Until Kara.

And it had to end.

She hung from the ceiling, her arms stretched until she thought they would break, her body hot from the ritual fires that surrounded her, sweat running down her temples and forehead, dripping into her eyes.

Eight robed figures circled her, daggers tight in their hands. Through the fog of dream and fear, she saw the flash of metal, then felt a pain worse than fire. And screamed.

Lyon wasn't sure when he'd fallen asleep, but he woke suddenly to Kara's low cry of distress, her fear washing over him.

He was on his feet in an instant, through her door a heartbeat later. As he rushed to her side, he found her on her back, thrashing in the bed as small cries escaped her throat.

"*Kara*. Kara, wake up." Easing onto the bed beside her, he stroked her damp brow. "Kara, sweetheart, wake up. You're having a bad dream."

She jerked beneath his hand, then went still, trembling like a leaf in the rain. Slowly, she opened her eyes. But instead of being comforted by his presence, raw terror flooded her eyes, and she jerked away from his touch.

He moved back, giving her room as he attempted to gentle her with his voice. "Kara, it's me. You had a dream."

She was shaking hard enough to rock the bed. Her hands came up to clutch her skull as tears slid down her cheeks. "God, I *hate* this."

She didn't protest this time when he pulled her against him and onto his lap. Her arms wrapped around him, her damp face buried in his neck. Her pulse thundered so hard he could feel it pounding against his chest.

Lyon stroked her back, her hair, murmuring words of comfort. "You're safe, Kara. It was just a dream."

Slowly, Kara quieted in his arms as he pulled the fear out of her.

His palm splayed over the soft fabric of her nightgown, rubbing gentle circles on her back. "The Shaman will be here in the morning. He'll help us figure out what's going on."

Kara turned her head, pressing her ear to his shoulder.

He held her, stroking her until she fell asleep in his arms, then eased her back onto the bed. But when he straightened, intending to return to his post outside her door, his beast snapped at him. His deep, primitive instincts prowled, restless, sensing that something was wrong. Demanding he protect what was his.

She wasn't his, of course. But his beast would not be denied. He would protect her.

Lyon lifted the silk sheet and climbed in beside her, pulling her tight against his body. Kara gave a soft, satisfied sound and curled against him.

Both beast and man purred.

But less than an hour later, Lyon was the one in pain.

He didn't know what Kara was dreaming, but instead of her fear leaking into him, all he could feel was the steady rise of her arousal. Was he the one she was dreaming of? She was sure as hell dreaming about someone. A twinge of jealousy broke into the passion that was rising inside him. Goddess, but he wanted it to be dreams of him that had her hand clutching his shirt and had her making those soft, mewling noises deep in her throat.

With every one of her soft moans, his cock grew harder, more painfully engorged until it was all he could do not to flip her on her back and bury himself deep inside her.

He'd never been so acutely aware of a woman. The scent of her hair, the feel of her breath on his neck, the warmth of her body lying tight against his side.

He tried to keep his hands still, tried to keep

from touching her, and failed. So he rubbed her back, his hand shaking.

Kara's low moans increased, and she lifted her leg over his, her knee just millimeters from his swollen erection. Instinctively, his hand shot out and captured that slender thigh. His fingers curled around the soft flesh, driving his need a hundred times higher. He wasn't even sure why he'd caught it. To push it down, or pull it closer? Or, perhaps, to reach for what lay beneath.

With a groan, he tipped his head back, fighting to stay in control. The only sane thing to do was to get up and leave her.

He'd left sanity behind the moment he'd pulled her into his arms.

Kara made a soft sound of need and pressed her leg tighter against his, pushing her hips into him as if seeking relief.

"*Lyon.*" The soft, breathiness of her voice nearly undid him.

"You're awake."

"I was dreaming about you." She sounded like she was still half-dreaming, her voice sexy as hell.

His fingers spasmed, digging into her thigh.

"This was a good dream." Her hips pressed against his side. Heaven help him, she was rubbing herself against him. "An amazing dream."

"Kara." His hand slid up the long, smooth length of her thigh. Shaking. Needing. His fingers moved closer to her heat. One reached, stroking her own engorged flesh, brushing her wetness.

She sucked in a breath. "*Lyon.*"

Beneath that scrap of nightgown, she was bare and wet, and wanting. Needing him.

And he could not take her.

But neither could he find the strength to move away.

Her fingers splayed across his chest, digging into his shirt, shaking as badly as his hands were.

"Put your fingers in me."

"I can't."

"You can. So close." The air was so heavy with her arousal it nearly sent him over the edge.

He gave in to the moment's weakness and stroked her wet folds again, drawing a gasp of such longing from her he knew he had to stop now, or he was going to finish. His entire body was shaking with the need to take her, to pin her to the mattress and drive himself into that wet heat.

"Lyon, please."

"No, Kara."

But her own control had been lost somewhere in her dreams. He felt her hips rise off the bed, felt her leg lift to straddle him. If he let her continue, let her press that wet heat against his erection, it was all over.

With Herculean effort, he forced himself to push her leg away, pressing her to the bed to keep her from trying to ride him again.

"Lyon."

"No, Kara." A funny ridge of bone deep within the fleshy part of her hip teased his fingertips. His finger moved, tracing the ridge. A perfect circle.

Shock vibrated through his body.

A circle. Embedded in her hip.
A Mage cantric.
His lungs collapsed. His heart shattered.
Kara was Mage.
Kara was Mage.
Kara was Mage.

Chapter Fifteen

"*No.*"

Kara froze at the low sound of agony that tore from Lyon's throat.

She felt his body go taut, felt a deep rumble rise from his chest in a sound that held the jagged edge of rage.

"You *bitch*."

"Lyon?" Kara's arousal cooled, her head ringing with confusion. "What's the matter?"

He moved so quickly, it was almost unnatural. One moment he was lying beside her, the next he was on his knees, one hand pressing against her back, holding her down, while the fingers of his other hand dug into her rear, hard, in the same place he'd traced seconds before.

"Lyon, what are you doing? That hurts."

But he didn't let up, as if he didn't care. As if he meant to hurt her.

Her heart began to race with uncertainty. With fear.

"Did you think we wouldn't know?" His words were hard as gravel. "Did you think we wouldn't figure it out?" His knee replaced his hand, digging painfully into her back. "How could you, Kara? *Damn you.*"

"Lyon . . . I don't know what you're talking about. What are you doing?"

"You're Mage."

"No." She gasped. "How could you even . . . ?"

His hand closed around hers and he yanked it back, forcing her fingers to her own backside.

"Feel this."

He pushed her fingers hard into the flesh of her buttocks. Deep beneath the muscle she felt something hard. Bone. It was just her bone!

But as Lyon moved her finger, digging into her flesh she felt the narrow ridge and realized it was circular. *No.* It wasn't there before. She'd have known, wouldn't she? *Would she?*

"What game have you been playing?" There was so much anger in his voice. So much pain she wanted to cry.

"Lyon, no. I'm not . . ." But, Dear God, did she know that? Did she know she wasn't a Mage? Did she know anything about herself?

His knee pressed harder until she could barely breathe. "Lyon . . ." He killed Mages. He told her he'd killed them. "Lyon, I didn't . . . I'm not hurting your men. I'm not doing any of this. It's not me."

The sudden shock of pain made her cry out. Her eyes burned with tears as fire followed the circle he'd forced her fingers to trace moments before. A trickle of warm liquid ran down her hip. Blood.

"Lyon. Please."

His hand clamped around her wrist and he hauled her to her knees, pulling her around to face him. Anguish and fury riddled his eyes as he shoved his hand in front of her. In the curve of his palm lay a bloody mass, a woven metal circle. Copper, covered in blood and bits of flesh.

Bile rose and she swallowed it down. That thing had been inside her.

For how long? All her life? Would she have known?

A low rumble started deep in Lyon's chest rising to a full-scale roar. The dim light in the room grew as Lyon's eyes began to glow. Inhuman eyes. Lion eyes.

The glow reflected off the fangs now visible beneath his lips.

The blood rushed from her face. "Lyon," she gasped. "Don't."

She'd just begun to feel the scratch of his claws on her wrist when he threw the bloody copper ring against the wall and whirled away from her, leaping from the bed. In a haze of tears and bitter pain, she scrambled off the bed, backing toward the wall, shaking. A shadow sailed across the room ending with the sound of crunching wood and breaking glass. The scrape of wood on wood told her he was lifting the chest from the end of the bed. A moment later, the dresser disintegrated in a burst of raw destruction.

Kara pressed back against the wall, easing toward the door, the terror pounding in her chest for once all too real.

She was Mage. And Lyon was going to kill her.

The door flew open, flooding the destroyed room with light. Paenther and Tighe stood silhouetted in the entrance for an instant before Paenther lunged toward Lyon and Tighe held out his hand to her.

"Get out the room, Kara." He ushered her into the empty hallway and closed the door against the rage of the lion.

Tears blinded her as she ran down the stairs, her hip bleeding and burning, her heart shattered. On a broken sob, Kara wrenched open the front door, and fled into the night.

"Roar. *Roar!*"

The feral haze slowly began to clear as Lyon stared up into the bloody and fanged faces of Paenther and Tighe. He was flat on his back on the hard floor, destruction all around him. Kara's room.

Kara.

He struggled for control, feeling his claws retract. "Let me up!" The pair released him, and he leaped to his feet. "Where is she?"

"I got her out of here before you hurt her," Tighe told him.

Lyon's gaze spotted the damning piece of bloody copper lying on the floor beside the crushed bed. He scooped it up and tossed it to Paenther.

The panther snarled. "A cantric." His black gaze looked up in surprise. "Kara?"

"Yes." Lyon closed his eyes, searching for her with his senses.

"Are you going to destroy her yourself, or can I?" Violence laced the panther's words.

Lyon's claws sprang and he lunged until he was in Paenther's face. "*You won't touch her.* She's mine."

Suddenly, his finder's senses caught her. Outside. Away from the house. *Hell.*

Lyon ran for the door, heedless of the blood coating his quickly mending flesh. He leaped down the stairs in two strides and tore through the front door, taking a second to secure it behind him before he raced into the night.

She's Mage, his logical mind cried. *Let the draden take her.* But the draden rarely bothered with Mage. They wouldn't take her. And he needed to know how she'd fooled them into thinking she was their Radiant.

He had to know!

Deep inside, his beast growled at him. She was Kara. *Kara.*

But he knew better. She was Mage.

His enemy.

Branches whipped across Kara's cheeks and tangled in her hair as she followed the sound of the river, but she kept running. Away from Lyon's knife. Away from the terrible pain of having the only man she'd ever loved, a man who'd promised to protect her, turn on her.

Damn him. *Damn him.*

All she could see as she ran was the fury in his eyes.

The wound on her hip hurt, the air tearing at her lungs, as she ran into the night. With no destination. No plan. Nowhere to go.

In a bloody nightgown. Now wouldn't that be a sight any homeowner would love to see on her doorstep in the middle of the night? Not likely.

It didn't matter. There was nowhere she could run that Lyon wouldn't find her. She'd learned that over and over again. She was fooling herself to think she could get away. He always knew where she was, and he'd come for her again. With his knife, ready to cut out her heart.

No, not that. He'd already done that.

The sky was clear, the moon full, lighting her way through the trees as she followed the rumble of the falls. A hard breeze blew, freezing the sweat on her skin, chilling her to the marrow of her bones, but still she ran. Because she didn't know what else to do. She couldn't go back.

She didn't know how long she'd run, or how far, when she finally pulled up at the edge of the trees and sank back against the rough bark of one, her arm tight across her middle as she fought for breath. Her lungs ached and her bare feet felt torn and shredded from the branches and rocks as she stared out at the glistening Potomac River.

She pressed her palm to her forehead. What was she going to do? Did she dare try to get help? Human help? What would Lyon do if someone tried to protect her?

Her heart clenched with pain. She'd thought she'd known him. But she hadn't. She hadn't known him at all.

No, she did know him. She knew one thing for certain.

He'd never let her go.

A dark shape soared over the river, catching her eye. A bird of some kind. But not. Her brows creased. The thing seemed to be moving too quickly. And behind it . . . a dark cloud, little more than a shadow against the night sky. If she didn't know better, she'd think a swarm of locusts was about to descend on the D.C. area.

Not locusts.

Realization slammed into her like a wall of ice water, freezing her blood on contact.

Draden.

Oh *shit*.

She hadn't seen one since the night her mother died, and she'd forgotten.

She straightened, her body tensing to run, but as she watched the cloud draw nearer, she knew there would be no outrunning them. And nowhere to go if she did.

This would be her last mistake. Game over.

An unnatural calm settled over her.

"Lyon," she whispered, her heart crying out for him in these final moments. Not the man who'd looked at her with rage flaring from his lion's eyes but the one who'd smiled at her on the goddess rock, looking at her as if she were the only person in the world. The one who'd promised he'd never let anything harm her. The one she'd trusted. The man with whom she'd foolishly fallen in love.

The draden were almost on her, their hunger feeling like ants crawling over her skin.

As tears began to track down her cheeks, she covered her face against the impending attack. The man who'd sworn to protect her wasn't here. And there was nothing left to do but try to face her fate with the same grace and courage her mother had.

As she waited for death to descend on a cloud of demons.

Chapter Sixteen

Lyon's heart stopped in his chest as he saw the swarm of draden diving for Kara in a deadly descent. She stood still as granite against the tree overlooking the river, awaiting the impending attack.

"Kara! Run!"

But if she heard him, she ignored him. Did she welcome death?

Did he offer her anything better?

Hell. He didn't know. She was Mage.

She was Kara.

"Kara!" He ran through the trees toward her, logic flying in the wake of his desperation to reach her before the draden stole her away. He closed the distance between them as the first of the draden attacked. With his knife, he stabbed the two that had latched onto her and hauled her against his body, curving himself around her, making it as hard as possible for the draden to reach her.

"Try to go radiant, Kara. If you go radiant, they can't hurt you." But he knew she was too new, too untried to pull the power in the midst of such an attack. He had to get her to the goddess stone, where he could call a Feral Circle to protect her.

She said nothing, running, climbing over the rocks with him. He could feel the power spitting inside her and tried to help her, but it was harder away from the ritual stone, and harder still when her feet weren't staying planted on the ground. The only place he could help her was the goddess stone. And as he urged her faster, the cloud descended on them. Half a dozen of the bloody fiends latched onto him, but it was Kara they wanted. Kara he fought them for. He tucked her tight to his side as he used his knife on the Daemon dregs, fighting them off her as fast as they latched on.

She didn't scream. Didn't cry. At least not that he could hear. But whenever one of the little sons of bitches flew at her face, she ripped its heart out.

The rock wasn't far. Out of instinct or luck, she'd run this way. But twenty yards under a full-scale draden attack felt like twenty miles. Finally, they reached the path he sought and leaped down onto the flat stone.

Lyon pulled Kara to the ground and covered her with his body. "Go radiant, Kara! *Try.*" The draden covered them, but he only felt a few bites.

It was Kara they wanted and all he could do was fight them off, stabbing those within reach of his right hand and ripping out the hearts of those on his left while he chanted the words in a heated rush that would raise the circle around them.

Beneath him, he felt Kara's power spitting and dying as if the strength she'd had earlier was all but gone. Or had come not from her Radiant's power, but from the cantric buried deep in her hip.

He threw all his concentration into raising the circle and felt the mystic energies rise and finally pop into place. A high-pitched cry of fury tore at his eardrums as the draden were forced back, away from their prey. He looked over his shoulder, watching until the cloud slowly rose and disappeared into the night.

Lyon's heart thudded as his chest rose and fell in harsh agitation. So close. *Too* close. He rolled off Kara and stood, his gaze taking in the bloody bites on her limbs. And the dark bloodstain soaking the hem of her gown, reminding him why she had run.

She was Mage. Everything he'd felt for her, everything he'd dreamed was a lie. Her strength, her sweetness, her vulnerability. All lies.

He might be able to forgive her for those, all was fair in love and war, after all, except for one thing. She'd made him feel. She'd cast a spell over him that had ripped open his heart and laid it bare, exposing the emptiness where he could see it. Where he could feel it like salt on a wound.

And it had all been a lie.

She pushed herself up and stood facing him, her arms and legs streaked with rivulets of blood. Her stance was wary, her arms away from her body like a boxer risen for another round. In her eyes he saw the heart of a cornered animal prepared to fight for her life.

Was that what she was? Cornered? He didn't know.

All he'd known was he had to catch her. He'd had to save her from the draden. But as his fingers stung with warning, as his fangs elongated in his mouth, he wasn't entirely sure he wouldn't kill her himself.

"I hate you." Kara lunged toward Lyon, fury blazing through her. Then stopped abruptly as she saw the light spark in his eyes, his irises expanding until they were glowing amber fury.

Real fear mixed with her anger.

He grabbed her shoulders, his claws pressing against her flesh. "What was your plan, Kara? To try to control us?"

"No! I haven't been working against you."

"To break down our defenses until you could . . . what?" He shook her. "What have you done?"

She tried to knee him in the groin, but his reflexes were too quick. His knee knocked hers away, deflecting the blow. Outrage threatened to choke her. The injustice of his accusations. The betrayal of everything she'd believed he was.

"I thought I was human. *Human. You* were the one who ripped me from my life, who insisted I was

Therian, who told me I was the Radiant and was doomed to be your power plug for the rest of my life. *I don't know what I am.* I've never pretended to know." She kicked at his jeans-clad shins, hurting her bare toes, but her fury needed an outlet. She had to hurt him somewhere. Somewhere. Because, dear God, his betrayal was killing her.

"You said you'd protect me, and I trusted you. *I trusted you.*"

He growled and pushed her hard against the rock wall at her back, getting in her face, his fangs glistening. "What spells have you cast over me, *witch*? You made me want you. You drove me to my knees with lust for you. I've never cared whose legs spread for me, but you changed that, didn't you? You made me want *you.*"

"I didn't do anything! Or if I did, I didn't do it on purpose."

"*Tell me what you've done.*"

"Go to hell," she shrieked at him. "You don't believe me. You're not even listening to me."

"You made me want you. Now you're going to live with it." His face loomed close, his fangs disappearing a heartbeat before his mouth was on hers, grinding against hers until she couldn't breathe.

She'd wanted him to kiss her. How many times had she wanted him to kiss her? But not like this.

Kara wrenched her mouth away. "I thought you refused to touch me."

"I thought your mate had been chosen for you. Now I know you bewitched me, then made me think I couldn't have you. To torture me."

She laughed, but the sound was bitter, then gone when his mouth captured hers again.

Kara pushed against his shoulders, but she might as well have been trying to push away a tank. No matter how hard she beat at him, he didn't budge, just ground his mouth harder against hers until she tasted blood.

Her eyes burned with tears. She'd loved him. How could she have been so wrong?

His hands covered her breasts, squeezing, kneading, raising a fire she didn't want, and pulling a moan from her throat. The kiss changed, no longer punishing, but hot. Desperate.

His tongue stroked her lips until she let him in, that single stroke melting her body, melting her resistance. With a groan, his tongue swept inside her mouth, staking its claim, stroking her own until she was spinning out of control. The first release ripped through her, scattering her to the winds.

She came back to herself clinging to him, her fingers buried in his hair, her body rocking hard against his.

Lyon growled and pulled her hard against him. "You want me."

"Yes." Her affirmation was little more than a gasp, but there was no denying it. She didn't want to want him, but her body was on fire, burning from the inside out.

He pushed her back, then sheathed his claws and stripped out of his clothes, tossing them onto the rock. He stood before her, bathed in moonlight, wild and untamed, more beautiful than any man ever made. On his arm, the armband gleamed and shone, the jeweled eyes of its lion's head shining as brightly as Lyon's own. His shoulders wide and strong, his chest ripped with muscle, tapering to a hard abdomen, he was glorious.

Between his legs, his erection curved toward her, thick and long and ready.

His eyes met hers, their golden glow hard. Hot. "Take off your gown, witch, or I'll rip it off you."

She stared at him, her breath lost somewhere between her lungs and her throat, the pulse pounding in her neck. Her legs had gone weak, a dampness forming between her thighs. With trembling fingers, she lifted the hem of her short nightgown and pulled it over her head, tossing it aside.

Lyon's eyes grew impossibly hotter as his gaze traveled slowly down her body, stopping at the juncture of her thighs. The melting inside her intensified, the heat between her legs growing until she thought her entire body would go up in flames.

He closed the distance between them and grabbed her arm. She gasped with pain as his hand closed over one of the draden bites. She'd forgotten the bites, the nipping pain spiraling into the greater haze of sensation as he turned her around and pushed her against the rock face.

"I've got to have you, Kara. I can't wait." As his hands grabbed her wrists, pinning her hands to the rock above her head, his leg parted her thighs. His thick erection slid down the curve of her rear, sliding through the crease. In one hard thrust, he entered her from behind, filling her, stretching her almost to the point of pain. He gave a guttural cry of pleasure, pulled nearly all the way out, then slammed home again, pressing her hard against the rock.

At the exquisite feel of his domination, Kara felt a wild stirring inside that made her almost believe her ancestors, millennia back, were shape-shifters, too. Animals. In the distance, a dog barked as if sensing the wildness.

Lyon's mouth came down on her arm, his tongue stroking one of the draden bites, stealing the pain. Each stroke of his tongue sent heat shooting to her core, making her wetter, easing the thrusts of his erection.

Her body tightened, rising higher, to a crescendo she knew instinctively would surpass everything that had come before.

Four strokes, five, and she was gasping, shattering, her inner muscles squeezing him as she came. Still he rammed into her, his mouth moving to a different wound until she fell apart again. Over and over, seven times, eight, he brought her to climax before he finally roared his own release.

For long moments, he pressed against her, filling her, his ragged breath stirring her hair. Then he pulled out of her and turned her to face him, still pinning her hands above her head.

"I'm not through with you."

She tilted her head back to look up into his eyes, eyes shining with a fierce brightness that mocked the dark. "Good."

His teeth flashed for one instant before he swept

her up and deposited her on her back on the cold rock, then knelt at her feet and lifted her ankle to his mouth where another of the little fiends had bitten her. She remembered how the rock had warmed to her when she'd tried to pull the power that morning, and later when she'd finally gone radiant. Pressing her palms to the cold stone, she pulled.

Almost at once, the rock began to warm, easing the chill of the air on her damp flesh.

"Do it," Lyon growled.

"Do what?"

"Pull the flame. See if you can go Radiant. It'll help heal these wounds." His tongue stroked her ankle, stealing her thought as her pulsing womb tightened all over again. He brought her to climax four times before she could concentrate enough to pull the flame. She'd just pulled it when his tongue stroke sent her into a fifth raging climax. Without realizing what she was doing, she pulled the flame inside and felt it burst within her, filling her with light and warmth even as she cried out with the pleasure of the release.

And then Lyon was on top of her, shoving deep inside her, his mouth drinking from hers, his body hard and demanding as he drove her up yet again.

But this time, when she broke, the pleasure nearly sent her out of her body, and Lyon was there with her. They cried out as one. Fell as one.

Kara cradled his weight, loving the feel of him on top of her, inside her, as she struggled to catch her breath and knew he did the same.

Of their own accord, her hands stroked his damp back, reveling in the play of muscles along its width. She hated what he'd done to her. Hated that he didn't believe her. But she didn't hate him. She couldn't hate him. Even when he thought she was his enemy, he'd saved her from certain death. Even when he was stealing his pleasure from her body, he'd returned it a hundred times over. And he'd taken the time, made the effort, to heal her wounds.

Her emotions were a confused mess, too tangled to figure out. She still loved him. That was the only thing she was sure of. But she was beginning to understand the importance of the Radiant. And she didn't know if she could convince them she could do the job even if she wasn't the Therian they'd thought her. She didn't know *how* to convince them. She barely understood the difference between the races herself.

Her life, her fate, were out of her hands. From the moment she'd first seen Lyon in her kitchen at home, her fate had ceased to be her own. Maybe it had never been her own. Even though she hadn't known it, she'd always belonged to this world. Of Ferals and Mage, of magic and radiance and terror.

As she held Lyon, a strange and profound peace settled over her. A rightness. As if this place, this moment, this man, were what she'd been waiting for all her life.

All she could do was hope this wasn't the end.

* * *

Lyon wasn't sure how long he'd lain within the cradle of Kara's arms and the tight welcome of her body. All he knew was, he never wanted to leave. Was this, too, bewitchment? Or something more? Something all Kara.

He pulled out of her and rolled away, to lie on his back beside her.

He turned his head to look at her, his breath catching at her shining beauty. "You're radiant."

Her head rolled toward him until she met his gaze. There was something warm within the wariness and confusion in her eyes. "How can I go radiant if I'm a Mage?"

"I don't know. Why don't you have the Mage eyes? You're probably only half-Mage."

"Can you have a Radiant who's half-Mage?"

He turned his face to the stars, unable to voice the truth. But Kara was too sharp to need it spelled out for her.

"You'll kill me to make way for my replacement." Her words were simply said, without emotion. But he felt her pain, the pain of betrayal. "Why didn't you just let the draden have me? Why did you save me and heal me if you're only going to kill me again?"

"I don't know. It's probably the spell you put on me. I still feel protective of you."

"I didn't put a spell on you, Lyon." She rolled onto her stomach, rising on her arms to look down at him. Her body still glowed, but in her eyes, he saw a hurt and a bleakness that raked at his soul. "You've been sensing and pulling my emotions since you found me in Spearsville. Wouldn't you know if I've been lying?"

He tucked his hand behind his head as he looked up at her. "Yesterday, I'd have said yes. Absolutely. I believed everything you told me. Tonight, I'm not so sure." But searching her eyes he saw no cunning lurking in those blue depths. No slyness. In the emotion that rolled out of her he felt an anguish of the spirit that had his beast whimpering in pain. With his free hand he reached for her, needing to touch her, to comfort them both.

He stroked her cheek. "Goddess help me, but I want to believe you."

She turned her face and kissed his palm. "If I've done anything to hurt you or yours, it was an accident, Lyon. I would never hurt you on purpose." The truth of her words swam in her eyes and sank into his heart, making him ache.

With his thumb, he traced her cheekbone. "Even after I cut you?" The thought of what he'd done to her made him ill. He reached for her and pulled her on top of him, cradling her head beneath his chin.

He shouldn't care. *She's Mage,* his mind railed. *She's Kara,* his heart replied.

All he knew was she was hurting, and it was his fault.

"I'm sorry, little one. What I did was inexcusable." Barbaric. He'd felt that cantric and all he could think was that she'd betrayed him. That she'd opened him up, made him feel, and it was all a lie. *She* was a lie. He'd attacked her. Turned on her without asking a single question. Judge, jury, and executioner in one brutal act.

His hands slid over her back, comforting. Begging forgiveness. "You had to have felt that cantric before."

"I didn't. As deep as it was buried, how would I have felt it? I'm not in the habit of exploring the bones in my rear. You only found it because you were pressing so hard."

What she said might be true, he supposed. "When I felt it, I went a little berserk."

Her cheek brushed his collarbone, her soft hair sliding against his chin. "I noticed. Is there anything left of my room?"

"Not much. I don't think I hurt the bed, but I can't entirely remember." His hand slid carefully over the place where he'd cut her. "Are you okay?"

"It's healed."

Physically. The emotional pain he'd caused her would take far longer. He marveled that she trusted him to hold her after that. He felt no hate coming from her, though he thought he just might hate himself.

He stroked her hip and buttocks where he'd hurt her, his fingers exploring the sweetness of her curves. His body responded and rose to the feel of her along his length, her naked breasts soft against his chest, the sweet scent of her hair. His senses swam and goddess, but he wanted her. He had to have her again.

His fingers dug into her buttocks, kneading,

pressing her against the arousal growing thick and heavy between their bodies. He reached lower, sliding to the crevice of her rear, and down, past the tight pucker of her anus, to the soft, wet folds he sought.

As he stroked her, dipping his finger into her heat, Kara moaned, rocking against his hand.

His mouth brushed her hair. "Do you want me again?"

"Yes. *Always.*" She lifted her face for his kiss, and he didn't disappoint her. He pulled her head down, cradling it as his tongue drove into her mouth. A groan broke free of his throat while between their bodies his erection surged and bucked, demanding attention.

He kissed her hard and long, then released her head to reach for her hips. She propped herself up on his chest, and he lifted her and drove himself deep inside, her hot, slick walls expanding to fit him. He lifted her hips, pulling nearly out of her, then pushed home again, his hips rushing up to meet hers. Over and over again, he took her, watching the passion drench her radiant face. But it wasn't enough.

He rolled her beneath him and covered her mouth with his kiss, needing to erase the distance between them. His body craved the feel of her, everywhere. Inside, outside. No space. In that moment, if he could have crawled inside her, he'd have done so. Or better, yet, tucked her inside him. Where he could keep her safe. His.

As he captured her mouth and stroked her tongue,

he sent her crying out with a release that clutched him hard enough to send him spinning after her.

His body warm and sated, he dropped his head to her shoulder even as his mind railed at his body's betrayal. *She's Mage. The enemy.*

Unable to stop himself, he opened fully to her, feeling her emotions, knowing her heart.

And his mind was finally forced to accept what his heart had known all along. No matter what Kara was, she was innocent of malice and subterfuge.

She might be Mage, but she wasn't his enemy.

Unfortunately, he wasn't sure it mattered.

As Chief of the Ferals, his first duty was to his men and his race.

No matter what his heart wanted, or what his beast demanded, he would do what he must.

Even if it meant destroying the only light that had ever warmed the dark caverns of his soul.

Chapter Seventeen

Kara felt them before she saw them. That odd energy like ants crawling over her skin. Her eyes flew open at the exact moment Lyon tensed and rolled off her.

"Draden," they said together. The little demons were back, hovering barely ten feet above their heads.

Lyon lunged for his pants and his knives. "The circle's weakening."

"Can you call it again?" Kara scrambled up and grabbed her nightgown. Safety was a fleeting thing around here.

"Not until it dissolves, but by then, it may be too late." He pulled two switchblades and a cell phone from his pockets and snapped open the phone.

"Goddess stone. We've got a draden swarm. Bring the smallest ritual robe and three men to guard her."

He flipped the phone shut and dressed. "Stay radiant, Kara. If this magic fails, they'll be all over you again if you don't."

"What about you?" She pulled on the little nightie, wishing she'd worn something thicker to bed. Like a suit of armor. "Don't they bite you, too?"

"They do, but when you're around, they tend to do little more than nip before they realize I'm not the one they want. The tiny nips will usually heal on their own."

"Why am I the one they want?"

"Because your energy, now that it's been tapped, is the purest. It's the only energy the sires can feed from."

"The sires?"

Dressed and armed, he stood beside her, his gaze fixed on the enemy above. "The easiest way to understand draden is to think of a bee colony. The sires are like the queens, the only ones capable of reproducing, though they reproduce through energy. Each sire has its own swarm."

She stared at him. "I thought the term *sire* was male. And queen is definitely female."

His gaze dropped to her with a quick roll of his eyes. "These are mindless, soulless energy creatures, so just go with me on this one."

"The sires can only feed from me? So they can only survive by attacking me?"

"They don't have to attack, though they will if they get the chance. They can survive by simply being near you and feeding off your energy from a distance, though not too great a one. They also get energy secondhand through the swarm. Whatever energy any of the draden swarm picks up from you goes back to the sire."

She watched them above her, the glow from her own body illuminating the hideous faces and jagged, terrifying teeth. A hard shudder tore through her. As one swooped toward her, stopping only a few feet in front of her face, she pressed back against the rock behind her.

"They're getting closer."

Lyon stepped in front of her, backing up until he pressed her against the rock. "The circle's failing. If they break through, cover your face and stay radiant. I'll kill as many of them as I can until my men arrive."

"I thought I was safe as long as I stayed radiant."

"You are. But the moment you lose it, they'll be on you. I don't want to take any chances."

"What about you? If they can't attack me, they'll feed from you." Her fingers gripped his waist as the awful realization hit her hard. "They'll kill you."

"Just stay radiant, Kara. Stay radiant to keep the draden off you and to prove to my men when they arrive that you're more than Mage. Or you're dead either way."

Her arms slid around him. "Let me stand in front, Lyon. As long as I'm radiant, let me shield you."

She felt his hand grasp hers and squeeze gently. "No."

"Then at least give me one of your knives. I can help keep them off you as you did for me."

He didn't respond immediately, then he moved, reached for something. And a deadly blade glinted in her own glow as he handed it back to her.

"Though you might have cause, after what I did to you tonight, I'd appreciate it if you'd refrain from stabbing me. At least until we get home. If you weaken me any further, this circle is going to fail entirely."

"I'm not going to stab you. On purpose, at least. I've never used a knife before on anything that moved."

"I'll consider myself warned."

"How long do you think we have?"

"I don't know how long the circle's going to last. But my men will be here in a couple of minutes."

"Won't the draden just swarm them, too?"

"Right now, because they sense you, they're far more interested in you. By the time they pay the other Ferals much notice, they'll be inside the circle, helping me shore it up. Once the draden take off again, we'll leave."

If his men got here in time.

Kara pressed her forehead against Lyon's warm back, her heart beginning to pound in her chest as it had so many times since she'd arrived here. But this fear felt different. It *was* different. Because she knew the source. It came from her mind and senses and the knowledge that if the circle failed, they would almost certainly both die.

"How did you ever survive as a child? Weren't there draden in London back then?"

"There were, from time to time, but they were rare. London wasn't the home of the Radiant at that time. Since the sires follow the Radiant and swarms follows the sires, there are few draden elsewhere, though there are always rogues."

"So most of the world's draden right now are here."

"Yes. Which works for us since, in our animal forms, we're well designed to hunt and destroy them."

"But you never get them all."

"No. We can usually keep them under control, but nine Ferals can only do so much."

"I don't understand how they're like bees if they were somehow left over from the Daemons."

"They're not like bees except for the fact that they swarm and, like bees, have only one member of a swarm who can reproduce. Otherwise, they're totally different. The Daemons may have possessed separate consciousnesses, but they were all linked to the High Daemon, Satanan."

"Satanan? *Satan?*"

"Hard to say if they're one and the same, though the legends of the humans' Satan may well be based on Satanan. Goddess knows, they had reason to fear him. But he never lived in a place called Hell. Satanan was very much a creature of the Earth, as we all are.

"When Satanan was imprisoned in the blade, so too were the souls of the others. An entire race. Since Daemons are energy creatures instead of blood and water, the life forces that were left behind were only wraiths of the original. Draden. Without minds, without souls, they live by sucking energy from Therians, especially the Radiant. Like all nature's creatures, they learned to reproduce or they would have died off."

"What would happen if the Daemons were ever freed from the blade?"

"They'll flow back to the draden, reanimating them to their original form. But since the Daemons in their true form are cunning, sentient beings, they'll return to feeding the way they did millennia ago, on the pain and fear of the creatures they captured."

"Animals?"

"Humans. Most often children. By the thousands."

Kara shivered. "They won't be freed, will they?"

"No. Only through the will of all the Ferals and the blood of their Radiant will that scourge be released upon the Earth again. And none of us will ever let it happen."

The draden seemed to be pressing lower.

"Get down, Kara."

She slid down the rock, pulling her knees tight to her chest as Lyon squatted in front of her.

"What's happening?" she asked. "The circle seems to be getting smaller."

"It is. I can feel the edges of it. The dome usually covers the entire rock, but we're down to about six feet by six. I'm shoving at it as hard as I can, but my power's drained too far. Until we get you ascended . . ."

He didn't finish the sentence. He didn't have to. They both knew her Ascension was suddenly in serious doubt.

A dog barked in the distance. To her surprise, Lyon answered, mimicking the sound rather amazingly.

"They're coming."

"That was one of your men?"

"A dog bark is a natural sound around here and draws less attention than shouting. Especially at this hour."

"Yeah, I guess a roar would stand out."

He reached behind him, his hand gripping her knee. "Whatever happens, I want you to know I'm proud of you."

"Why?"

"Because I know how scared you are. It throbs around me like a pulse beneath my skin. Yet you're solid. Demanding a weapon. Trying to guard me."

His words warmed her.

"You'd have made us a damned fine Radiant."

Would have. If she hadn't been Mage. The warmth died in a wash of cold.

"Here come my men," Lyon said as he crowded her against the wall.

In a pounding rush, a swing of knives, and a shout of magic incantation, the Feral Circle burst wide again, and the draden were flung away. Lyon rose and pulled her to her feet beside him. In the dradens' stead, stood three Ferals, watching her.

In Tighe's eyes, she saw deep disappointment, in Jag's, wary curiosity. And in Paenther's nothing less than raw hatred. Any hope she'd harbored that the men might come to her defense died with that blast of enmity.

"How's she radiant if she's Mage?" Jag wanted to know.

"Black magic," Paenther growled.

Lyon shook his head. "I think she's part Mage. And I don't think she knew it. But that discussion will keep until we get home."

"Leave her for the draden," Paenther urged. "We'll never ascend her."

Kara recoiled from the hatred in his voice.

"I said we'll discuss her fate when we get back to the house," Lyon snapped. "For now, she's your Radiant, and you will protect her with your life. Whether you like it or not."

Tension pulsed between them, but Lyon was fully in charge. His hand landed on her shoulder. "I want you to stay radiant as long as you can, but you've got to stay covered. If any humans see you, it'll cause problems."

Jag tossed a black bundle to Lyon, and he shook it out, revealing a hooded robe, like the ones in her nightmares. A shudder went through her, but she let him put it over her, hiding her light, casting them all back into the night's shadows.

The robe had obviously been made for a Feral. The hem pooled on the ground at her feet, the sleeves hanging below her fingertips. Running in this thing wasn't going to be fun.

"Roar," Tighe said. "Her radiance will only draw the draden back faster."

"*She will be protected.* No more discussion. We're going." He pulled the hood over her head until she could barely see out.

She grabbed up the robe, holding it high enough that she wouldn't trip over it with one hand, while Lyon took hold of her free hand.

"We're going back through the woods, the same way we came when I drove you over here this afternoon. Keep your head down and run."

Paenther led the way, Jag close behind him. Tighe took up the rear as they ran up the steep, rocky path and into the woods. Lyon held her tight, pulling her nearly off her feet, but she flew beside him, knowing he was her only hope of survival, in so many ways.

As the tree limbs tore at her hood, desolation clawed at her courage. They didn't want her. They didn't trust her. Yet they couldn't get another Radiant until she died. Even Lyon, who said he believed her, couldn't promise he'd protect her. Because his goal, his own desperate need, was to get a Radiant ascended.

He didn't want to destroy her. She felt that in everything he did. But he was too determined a leader to shy away from whatever must be done.

They reached Jag's Hummer just as the first of the draden were about to descend.

"The cars are warded against draden attack," Lyon told her, as Jag put the car in gear and took off. "They can't even sense you in here, so they shouldn't follow us."

She hadn't asked, though her question had been there. Had he felt it, that question? Was he that attuned to her now?

"That's good," she murmured. "I lost the radiance."

"You've lost contact with the Earth."

She was wedged tight between Lyon and Paenther, the two huge males taking up far more than their share of the seat. But Lyon's arm was around her and stayed that way for the drive back to Feral House.

Jag drove right up to the front door, and they ran into the house without incident. As Lyon predicted, the draden hadn't followed them.

If she'd thought she was returning to a house as dark as the one she'd left, she was mistaken. Kougar, Hawke, and Vhyper stood in the various doorways of the fully lit foyer, watching her with dark, menacing eyes. Mage meant enemy to them and, dear God, she couldn't think of any group she less wanted as her enemy.

She sidled closer to Lyon and he snatched her hand, pulling her against him.

Vhyper pushed away from the wall where he'd been waiting, fury in every line of his body as he entered the foyer, stopping inches from Lyon's face.

"You mated with her, you bastard. I can smell it. She's mine!"

Lyon growled, deep in his throat. "She's Mage. She's no one's."

"Like hell. The Pairing was true. But you couldn't keep your hands off her. You took her for yourself. And now you're trying to make excuses. *She's mine.*"

Lyon snarled. "No one touches her but me until we get this sorted out. No one!" He looked at Paenther. "How soon until the Shaman gets here?"

"A couple of more hours."

Lyon wrapped his arm around her waist and pulled her hard against him, tugging her with him as he pushed past Vhyper. "Everyone in the war room. *Now.* I'll meet you there in five."

"Where are you taking her?" Vhyper demanded.

"I'm locking her up where she can't escape again. And where she'll be safe until we make a decision." Sliding his arm from around her waist, he took her hand and led her down the same narrow set of stairs he had on their way to the Pairing. The basement of the house.

But they passed the ritual room and crossed the wide gym to a mirror on the far side. With a press of his hand, the mirror opened to reveal a long, dimly lit hallway, both the walls and the floor, paved in stone.

The ceiling was high enough for Lyon to stand easily, but the passage itself was barely wide enough for the two of them to walk side by side. It reminded her of the dungeons of a castle.

Deep inside, she heard the growling and thrashing of an animal.

The passage opened onto a wide room filled, as

Lyon had warned, with cages built into the walls. Cages separated by two feet of solid stone walls, each with a door made of thick massive steel bars.

Real torches hung on the walls outside the cages, the smoke darkening the air.

Wulfe's glowing eyes peered out from one of the doors, his fangs visible as he snarled.

A chill of foreboding snaked down her spine. "You're going to lock me up with him?"

"With him? No. But I'm putting you in one of the cages."

"Lyon . . ." She didn't like it down here.

"It's for your safety, Kara. The discussion upstairs is going to get heated. With everyone already on the edge of control, more than one may go feral. Especially if you're in the room. I'm not sure I can protect you from them all, especially if I, too, lose control."

He opened one of the cages, ushered her inside, then followed her. He took her into his arms and kissed her thoroughly until she was soft and melting against him.

"I won't let them hurt you, little one." His eyes were earnest.

Kara shook her head. "Don't make me any more promises, Lyon."

His jaw tightened, but he nodded. He brushed her cheek with his knuckles, then retreated, locking her into a tiny cage, barely large enough for her to lie down in. He'd just turned away when the sounds of a commotion reached her ears.

"Dammit to hell," Lyon muttered.

She watched as Tighe and Paenther carried a struggling Vhyper between them, Hawke walking close behind.

"He lost it, Roar," Tighe said. "I don't think he's getting it back this time."

Lyon nodded. "Lock him up." He disappeared from her line of sight as they got a snarling, spitting Vhyper into the cage. The door slammed shut on him with a clang.

As he reappeared, Lyon met her gaze briefly, the weight of the world in his own amber depths. Then he turned away and followed the other three Ferals down the long hall that would lead them back into the house.

Anything could happen to her down here, and he'd never hear it. Never know.

In the cage next to hers she heard Wulfe thrashing and growling like a wild animal. She shivered, glad for the robe that covered her from head to foot but knowing it wouldn't do a thing for the fear that was freezing her soul. The fear that her own strange heritage was going to wind up dooming her. As she glanced down, preparing to sit as she waited for her sentence, a movement outside her cage caught her eye, then was gone before she could be certain she'd seen something.

When she heard the clink of metal and the squeak of thick door hinges, she knew she hadn't been mistaken.

Her heart began to hammer. One of the Ferals was loose.

It took no time for her to wonder who. A moment later, Vhyper stood before her own cage, a smile playing around his mouth. A chilling smile.

"Convenient how all I had to do was pretend to go a little crazy and they brought me right to you, little mate of mine."

Kara shrank back, until the wall pressed at her back. "What are you doing, Vhyper?"

"Why, Kara, what do you think? Lyon said you're not mine, but he was wrong. You are mine. All mine. And those dreams you've been having?" He smiled coldly. "They're about to come true."

A figure stepped beside him, draped in the dark robe that matched her own, the robe of her nightmares. From the darkness of the figure's hood, strange, copper-ringed eyes shone.

Mage eyes.

The gate of her cage swung open and Vhyper filled the doorway. A cruel smile twisted his mouth.

"Come, Kara."

"Lyon!"

Vhyper lunged for her, twisting her back against him as his hand slammed over her mouth. "Shut up, bitch. He'll find you soon enough, but with any luck, it will be too late."

Kara struggled against him, but his hold was like iron, and he was too strong. When she tried to kick at his shins, he lifted her like she weighed nothing, immobilizing her.

Carrying a single torch, the Mage led them deeper into the tunnels.

Kara could hardly breathe for the hand blocking

her mouth and covering half her nose. Her heart thundered in her chest, her mind shimmering with a fear greater than any she'd known since she arrived here. Because deep in her soul, she knew this was the danger she'd feared all along.

They stopped before a wooden door that appeared to be nailed closed, but the Mage pulled lightly, and the door swung open.

The musty smell of damp earth slammed into her as Vhyper carried her down the long, narrow steps into what looked to be little more than an underground cave. The steps and walls were formed by stone. The floor was dirt. Smoke from the torch filled the fetid air.

As the light filled the shadowed spaces, she saw the place wasn't as empty as she'd believed. Fire pits formed a small circle, in the middle of which hung a long length of thick rope hanging from a pulley attached to the ceiling.

But it was the gleaming metal that caught her eye and sent the blood rushing from her head in a cold wash of terror.

Knives. Long, wicked-looking daggers lay in a perfect row along one wall.

Her nightmares.

Dear God, no.

Vhyper released her suddenly, dropping her to the ground like a bag of mulch. Kara caught herself with one hand, wincing at the pain that shot up her wrist. Before she could lever herself up, a yank of her robe had her tumbling back down. Unceremoniously, the robe was pulled off her.

Kara scrambled to her feet and tried to run, but Vhyper's hard arm caught around her middle and lifted her off her feet.

"Lyon!"

"He can't hear you, Radiant. And I'll not have you escaping. This is your night, you know. The fulfillment of your destiny. Maybe not the destiny Lyon's been filling your head with, but your destiny all the same."

He lifted her off her feet and carried her to the center of the circle, where he once more dumped her on her face and followed her down with a knee crushing her back.

Tears sprang to her eyes. Even when Lyon was at his most furious, he'd treated her with some amount of care. But Vhyper showed her none. He wrenched her hands above her head and tied them together with the end of the rope lying on the ground.

The vivid horror of hanging from the ceiling in her nightmares came back to her in a rush. Terror stole her breath. The moment Vhyper's knee released her back, she leaped to her feet, desperate to keep that nightmare from coming true, but there was nowhere to run. Even as she tried, the rope went taut, jerking her to the middle of the circle.

Slowly the rope pulled at her hands and arms, lifting them until she was on her toes, stretching to the point of pain. And then the ground fell away beneath her until she was swinging freely in the air.

Sweat ran down her temples, her skin at once flushed and freezing as panic ripped at her pulse.

Her body swayed and turned until she could see the robed figure bending at the wall, lifting two daggers in its hands. Terror exploded behind Kara's eyes.

"Vhyper, please. Please don't do this."

"Ah, but I must, Radiant." His voice was calm and pleasant, without remorse. He slid a wide plastic vat beneath her swaying feet. "The good news is, we probably won't kill you." He smiled in a way that had her heart clawing to crawl out of her throat. "The bad news is, by the time we're finished with you, you'll wish death had been our only intent."

Vhyper took one of the knives from his assistant and came to stand before Kara, his eyes gleaming with a cold brightness that spoke of true evil.

"Vhyper, don't. Lyon will kill you for this."

Vhyper chuckled. "Perhaps. But you *are* the Mage, right? And I *have* been suffering from a lack of radiance." He shrugged. "Time will tell what our fearless leader makes of all this." His face turned hard. "But it changes nothing."

He lifted the pointed tip of his dagger and pressed it against her chest, piercing her flesh just above the neck of her nightgown.

She gasped at the lick of fiery pain. But before she could catch her breath from that first tiny, assault, he slid the blade downward in a single mind-ripping swipe, slicing a shallow furrow from her sternum to the top of her pubic bone.

A scream escaped her throat.

Vhyper laughed, then turned her around and drew a second line of pain down her back.

Warm blood began to trickle down her thighs.

"Vhyper," she gasped. "*Don't.*"

"Oh, but Radiant. I've barely begun." Two more scores across her shoulders, and the shreds of her nightgown fell away.

Her terror spiked.

"Get the others," Vhyper said. "Quickly."

Kara barely heard the sound of footsteps in the dirt above the pounding in her ears. But the sound of metal clanking together stopped her heart.

Tears trickled down her cheeks. Her fear spiraled.

Into her line of vision came the robed figures of her nightmares. Four stood where she could see them, but her ears told her there were more behind her. The hoods hid their faces from her frightened eyes.

"Vhyper, don't," she begged. "Please don't."

"Ah, but I must, Radiant. I must. Now!" he shouted suddenly.

All around her blades flashed. In a single, mind-shattering blaze of hot, white pain, they pierced her abdomen, clanking inside her as they pierced her like the spokes of a brutal wheel.

Her mind went blank, and all she could do was scream.

"We can't ascend a witch!" Paenther snarled, pacing the war room.

Lyon stood by the door, his back against the wall, arms crossed over his chest. Other than the two already in cages, all his men were in this room. And all were staying here. He would take no chance on one deciding to take Kara's fate into his own hands.

"She's the Radiant," Tighe argued. "You saw her as clearly as I did, B.P. We need to ascend her. It could take months for another to come forth, and we don't have that kind of time. We'll all be as crazy as Wulfe and Vhyper by then."

"Tighe's right," Hawke said, seated at the oval conference table, his eyes thoughtful. "We've got to ascend her. But we've also got to protect ourselves from whatever power she acquires as a result. If she already has magic, goddess knows how strong she'll get."

Lyon had listened to the arguments for more than twenty minutes and still had no clearer picture of what he was going to do. Though everything inside him told him Kara was innocent of any malicious intent, he wasn't a fool. He couldn't discount the possibility that she had, utterly, bewitched him. Which meant his belief in her innocence could well have been manipulated.

Deep inside him, his beast growled and snarled, demanding he protect her. "We'll wait until the Shaman gets here." He pushed away from the wall and met Tighe's gaze. "I'll be downstairs."

Tighe nodded.

Paenther fell into step beside him. "I'll go with you."

Lyon glanced at his second. "Afraid I might free her?"

Paenther made a move of his head that was almost a shake, but not quite. "I just figure you could use some company."

Lyon gave a bark of what passed for laughter and gripped the other man's shoulder. Something he almost never did. But it felt right, somehow.

"I'm not going to let you kill her, B.P. If she has to be destroyed, I'll do it myself."

Paenther's head dipped once. "Agreed."

They descended the stairs to the lower chambers in silence. Not until they opened the mirrored wall in the workout gym did the sounds of Wulfe's snarls reach his ears.

The prisons had long ago been soundproofed in case any enterprising humans tried to search the premises. Humans the Ferals preferred not to kill.

Another sound reached his ears. The sound of a distant scream.

His blood went cold and he took off running. Rounding the final corner, his gaze flew to Kara's cell. *Please don't let those screams be hers.* But her door was open, her cell empty.

In that single moment, he died a thousand deaths.

"Vhyper's gone," Paenther said.

The scream continued, a continuous siren of agony that killed him over and over. He forced himself to still and closed his eyes, sending his senses outward. *Kara.* He felt her close by. And yet not.

His heart thundered.

"The witch and Vhyper have escaped," Paenther said into his cell phone. "Leave Kougar on guard upstairs," Paenther snapped into the phone behind him. "Everyone else down here."

Below. He felt her below. *Damnation.* "He's broken into the dungeons!" He ran for the far passage and the long-sealed door.

The passage was long and winding and took an eternity to traverse as Kara's screams ended, then resumed at fevered pitch. What in the name of the goddess was he doing to her? He'd kill him. Kill him.

Finally, he came to the door. The wood sealing it shut appeared to still be in place. But when he gave a tug, the door moved easily in his hand.

The moment the door cracked open, he was blasted with a wall of such pain it nearly drove him to his knees.

He lunged forward, down the dark, dank stair-well that he'd believed sealed for centuries. Kara screamed again, the sound ripping through his gut and twisting his heart.

Dead snake. Dead snake. Dead snake.

A hundred scenarios danced through his head, a hundred horrors that Vhyper might have been visiting on her.

As he rounded the bend into the room, his mind froze. The bile tore to get out.

None of his imaginings came anywhere close.

She was hanging from a rope, naked and bleeding from no fewer than eight daggers protruding from her waist like a cruel, macabre belt. The blood ran down, coating her hips and legs, to pool in the dirt at her feet.

Standing behind her was Vhyper, his eyes glowing feral red, his snake's fangs elongated, a ninth blade in his hand.

Lyon lunged for him. *"What have you done?"*

"She's a Mage witch!"

Lyon felt his claws slash outward. If he'd been able to do it, he'd have shifted and torn out the other man's throat. With a lunge, he tackled Vhyper, grabbing his knife hand and slamming it to the dirt floor as he shredded the man's throat with his claws. But Vhyper was damned near as strong as he was and, crazed or not, wasn't about to go down without a fight.

"Lyon!" Paenther's voice shouted behind him. "It's not Vhyper's fault. It's the lack of radiance."

Lyon heard the words, but his beast was beyond heeding them. He didn't care why Vhyper had attacked her. The only thing that mattered was that he *had*.

Never in his life had he fought to kill another Feral, but all he could see was death. His beast smelled it. He wanted it.

Interfering hands tore him away from his victim and he turned on them, attacking, slashing until the voices finally tore through his head.

"Lyon, get back in your skin!" Tighe's voice. "Kara needs you."

Kara.

The fight left him in a cold rush as if he'd been doused with ice water. He jerked free of Tighe and Paenther's hold and whirled, lunging for her. Then stopped.

Kara.

He wanted to cut her down and gather her close, but the knives.

Sweet goddess. He didn't know where to start.

Her pain was almost more than he could bear. But the terror he'd felt when he first opened that door was gone. She was safe. She knew she was safe.

"*Lyon.*"

Vhyper had her hanging just above eye level. He stepped into the puddle of her blood and cupped her face with his hands, holding her shattered gaze. "I'm going to get you down, little one, but it's going to hurt. So I'm going to knock you out."

"Do it."

He slipped his finger to the base of her ear and pressed until she went limp. Then he pressed his left palm against her rib cage, grabbed the hilt of one of the knives with his right, and pulled. Even unconscious her body jerked, and the pain leaped until he feared the weight of it would crush him. One by one, he pulled the knives from her, praying over and over that the damage wasn't too great. That her body would heal from this brutal attack. It wasn't until the last knife slid free, that he realized the other wounds were continuing to bleed.

"She should be healing. She's not healing," he said to no one in particular.

Tighe stepped beside him and grabbed one of the knives off the floor. "Hold her while I cut her down."

Lyon gathered her against him, then swept her into his arms as the rope came free.

"The others are taking Vhyper back to the prison."

"Search him. He must have had a key on him when they put him in there. And add a chain this time."

Lyon stepped back from the puddle and knelt in the dirt, lifting Kara's torn waist to his mouth. She should have healed. If she couldn't do it herself, he had to do it for her. He closed his lips around the nearest wound and stroked the gash with his tongue. The taste of warm blood pleased his beast, but he knew better than to swallow much of it in his human form.

The blood kept coming. Denial flashed through his head and he leaped to his feet, cradling Kara against him. "I've got to get her help. She's not healing."

"Maybe she's not as immortal as we thought."

The thought made him go cold.

As he rushed up the stairs, he shouted orders. "Tell Hawke to keep someone down here on guard duty. Then meet me in the foyer and bring Jag and Paenther with you. We're taking Kara to the healer."

"You don't want me to have the healer come here?" Tighe asked.

"No. We can get her there faster. But I'm going to need help with the draden. Find out where Esmeria is, then call the Shaman and tell him to meet us there. I want to know what the hell is going on with Kara, and I want to know now."

Even an immortal couldn't bleed forever without her body eventually shutting down. And he didn't know what the hell Kara really was.

All he knew for certain was she needed help. And she needed it now.

Chapter
Eighteen

"It's not working. Even the stitches aren't hold-ing," Esmeria said wretchedly, more than an hour later. The short-haired brunette sat on the lip of the large, tiled bathtub where Lyon held Kara, her hands and white shirt soaked with Kara's blood. "It's almost as if she's under some kind of bleeding spell."

"Then treat it like a bleeding spell," Lyon snapped. "There's got to be a way to break it." His own blood had long ago turned to ice, the moment he'd seen Kara hanging from that rope. A moment that was permanently carved into his brain. But the fact that the finest Therian healer that had ever lived couldn't knit these wounds was scaring the hell out of him.

He wouldn't lose her. *He wouldn't lose her.*

"She's part Mage. Untrained, I think," he told the healer. "Maybe she accidentally did this to herself. Or maybe this is my fault. I cut out her cantric."

Esmeria winced at his confession, but said nothing as she went back to work, shoving her hands beneath the blankets to lay her hands on Kara's wounds once more.

They'd made it to the Georgetown enclave without the draden finding them, but Kara wasn't healing, and her body was losing blood fast. Faster than her quickly healing body could make more. If this continued, her organs would start shutting down.

Lyon held Kara still as Esmeria worked. She lay tucked against him, beneath a warm layer of woolen blankets soaked with her blood, her skin white as death. He'd climbed into the dry tub with her the moment they'd arrived, not wanting to ruin any more carpets or furniture than necessary. Kara had to be losing a good pint every minute. Despite the blankets, she was shivering in his arms, and he was terrified that the spell, if that was what it was, would take her. That he'd caught Vhyper too late.

"How's she doing?"

Lyon looked up to find Tighe standing in the doorway. "We can't get this bleeding to stop."

Concern clouded his expression. "I'm sorry. Maybe the Shaman can help figure out what's wrong. He's just arrived, by the way."

As if on cue, Paenther stepped through the door, followed by the Shaman. Jag brought up the rear. One of the oldest of the Therians, the Shaman had been the victim of a Mage attack in his youth, and while he'd continued to age for a few more years, he'd ceased to grow or fully, physically, mature. He was taller than Kara, but not by much, and far shorter than other Therian males.

He wore his dark hair long and tied at his nape and still dressed in an old-world manner, with his black pants and ruffled white shirts. His thin face remained youthful, never having quite developed a full beard, nor the hard angles of a full-grown male. But the man had long since accepted what he was and often said a few inches of height was a small price to pay for the ability he'd acquired as a result. A talent for magic.

Though the man had a name, it was ancient and hard to pronounce. He'd long ago asked to simply be called *the Shaman*.

The three Ferals took up posts around the outer walls of the oversized bathroom while the Shaman came to sit on the side of the tub, opposite from where Esmeria continued to struggle against the constant flow of Kara's blood. His eyes were wary and guarded, reminding Lyon this man had as much reason to hate the Mage as Paenther did.

But as the Shaman stared at Kara, something shifted in his eyes, filling them with confusion. He reached out and placed his hand on her head, then slowly shook his own.

"She's not Mage." His eyes flicked up. "Why did you think she was Mage?"

It was moments before his words finally penetrated Lyon's stunned mind. "She had a cantric buried in her hip."

The Shaman's dark brows shot up. "A cantric." He closed his eyes and began to nod his head. "She's got echoes of a load of magic garbage inside her. Including a bleeding spell. Has she been around any Mage in the past few days?"

"She's been nowhere but Feral House."

"Any symptoms other than the bleeding?"

Lyon nodded. "She's been afraid. Terrified. And it's been getting worse. How long has she had that cantric?"

"Impossible to say. Maybe years. But the magic's new."

The Shaman watched her thoughtfully, then shot out a hand and laid it on top of Lyon's own head.

Lyon stifled the rumble in his throat and let the man work.

The Shaman stood and went to each of his warriors, one after the other, touching them thoughtfully.

"You're off. All of you."

"What do you mean . . . *off*?" Lyon demanded.

"Not bewitched, or anything like that, but off somehow. I suspect you have a dark charm in the house. A strong one. It would account for the oddness I'm feeling in you and for the strange fear your Radiant's been experiencing. That cantric acted as a magic catcher. Probably didn't bother her at all until she arrived at Feral House and came in contact with the charm. Whatever the dark charm was designed to do is probably going crazy inside her and may have triggered any number of old spells that cantric may have come in contact with long before it was ever put inside her. I don't feel it in her now. Did you take it out?"

"I did."

"Good." He looked thoughtful. "If she's been acting afraid, that might be the purpose of the dark charm. Have any of your men been experiencing similar symptoms?"

"Fear, no. But they've been going increasingly feral. I've had to lock up two of them."

"Definitely a dark charm, then. Probably with some kind of chaos spell. I see them from time to time, though I haven't heard of one strong enough to bother a houseful of Ferals in a long, long time." He rose. "I'll drive out there first thing in the morning and find that charm. Once I've taken a look at it, I'll be able to tell you more. In the meantime, I suggest you and your warriors each find a willing female and clear yourself of magic." He nodded at Kara. "Once she's healed, she's going to need a good sexual release, too." His eyes narrowed. "Full penetration. Nothing less is going to clean out that mess of magic inside her."

"There!" Esmeria cried. "I think . . . *no*." The healer pulled her bloody hands out from under the blanket and sat back with a sound of deep frustration. "I thought I'd stopped it."

"Don't give up, healer," Lyon growled. "I will not lose her!"

"I'll call you when I'm through," the Shaman said, and turned to go. "Stay away from the house until I've cleaned it, or you'll just be infected again."

Esmeria blew a strand of dark hair out of her eyes and leaned over the tub. Kara remained unconscious. Dammit, she should have woken by now. He could feel the strength leaking out of her at an alarming rate. Goddess help them, she wouldn't last another hour.

"Stay with me, Kara." His grip on her tightened.

Minutes later, Esmeria sat back, swearing. "Now that I'm treating the spell, I'm getting the flow to stop, but it keeps starting up again."

He had to do something. *He would not let her die.* Fear for her pounded through his blood.

"Tighe, I need your assistance."

"Anything, Roar."

Lyon leaned forward, sitting up straight. His heart thudded. "Next time Esmeria stops the bleeding, I'm going to try to heal one of those wounds again. I need you to brace Kara's head while I lift her waist to my mouth."

"All right."

Lyon looked to the healer. "Do it."

Esmeria pulled the blankets away, closed her eyes, and pressed her hands to Kara's wounds as she had before. Seconds later, the bleeding stopped.

"Now," Lyon said, and lifted Kara's too-light body to his mouth, closing his lips around the nearest wound. As he'd done before, deep in the dungeons of Feral House, he stroked the gash with his tongue. Working frantically, he felt the flesh knitting beneath his tongue. He was nearly done with the first of the gashes when the blood-bath resumed.

He pulled back and eyed the wound with knee-weakening relief. "It worked." Only a trickle of blood broke through. He wiped his chin and looked at Esmeria. "Whenever you're ready."

Paenther moved to the side of the tub and took the seat the Shaman had vacated. His hand fell heavily on Lyon's shoulder. Their gazes met for an instant, long enough for Lyon to know that the full force of Paenther's will was behind him.

One after another, Lyon healed the gashes ringing Kara's slender waist. He'd just started licking the last of the eight when he felt Kara stir, felt her fingers slide into the hair at the back of his head.

His body sagged with relief. *Thank the goddess.* "Lyon . . ." she breathed.

With shock, he felt the faint stirring of her passion. Relief flowed through him sharp enough to burn his eyes, tightening his chest until he thought it would crack. If he was able to awaken her passion, she was going to be fine.

"Hold on, Warrior," Esmeria said. "I need to take the stitches out of that last one." Stitches that had been useless.

Once the stitches were removed, Lyon lifted Kara's waist to this mouth once more, his arms shaking from the force of his emotions. He took exquisite pleasure healing this last of her wounds, feeling her own pleasure rise with every stroke of his tongue.

He squeezed his eyes closed against the burn of moisture, reveling in the rising strength of her life's energy, feeling the constriction around his heart ease with every tiny gasp that left her throat.

When her fingers fisted in his hair, and her body arched and trembled gently against his mouth, his beast purred with satisfaction. And a drop of moisture leaked from his eye.

Tighe whistled behind him. "Damn, Roar. I wish you'd teach me that trick."

He wiped his cheek and his chin on his bare shoulder as he lowered Kara onto his lap and cradled her precious body against him.

Kara reached for him, curling her arms around his neck, and melted against him, melting his heart.

"I'll take it from here, Warrior," Esmeria said. "I'll get her cleaned up and into bed."

"No," his beast said, before he could think it through. He wasn't letting Kara out of his arms, let alone his sight, anytime soon. "I'll tend her."

Esmeria nodded. "I'll put clothes on the bed for her, then. And for you."

The healer rose and left, but his men remained. Silence blanketed the room. In his arms, Kara slept.

Tighe sat on the edge of the tub, his gaze on Kara. "Damn."

Jag moved behind Tighe. "Guess it's a good thing we didn't vote to kill her off." But his tone lacked its usual rank attitude. In his voice, Lyon heard the same chill he suspected was going through all of them.

Paenther made a sound of pain deep in his throat. "If it had been up to me, she'd be dead."

"Who could have put it in her?" Tighe asked.

Paenther growled. "Whoever did it *is* dead."

"I'm with you, Geronimo," Jag said.

Tighe reached out and put his hand on her head. "She's been through hell. Great bunch of protectors we turned out to be."

"There was no way we could have known," Lyon said. But Kara had told him almost from the start something was wrong, and he hadn't paid enough attention until nearly too late.

Lyon sighed. "You heard the Shaman. Go find yourselves some sex. As soon as the Shaman's found that dark charm, we'll go home."

"You need help?" Tighe asked him.

"No. I've got her."

Tighe nodded. "Yeah, I hate these tough assignments, but I guess I'd better get at it."

Jag headed for the door. "Dibs on Lily."

Tighe lunged after him. "Only if I can't talk her into taking me instead."

Paenther remained behind after the others left.

"What about you, B.P.?"

But Paenther shook his head, the concern in his dark eyes still running deep. "I'll go later. For now, I'll be right outside the bathroom door, if you need anything." His gaze dipped to Kara. "If she needs anything."

Lyon nodded. If the bleeding spell broke through again, he'd need help. Paenther's guilt was nearly as thick as his own. And Lyon had virtually no ability to sense his emotions as he did Kara's.

"Don't beat yourself up about it, Paenther. You thought she was Mage."

"I'm sworn to protect our Radiant. I would have destroyed her."

"But you didn't."

Paenther nodded once and left.

As Paenther closed the door behind him, Lyon leaned back against the tub, in no hurry to move. He couldn't have let go of Kara in that minute if his life depended on it. And once he let go of her, he might never have her in his arms again. Because it had occurred to him, in that stunned instant when the Shaman pronounced her not Mage, that the Pairing might have been right after all.

Kara, conscious now, if dozing, clung to him sweetly, her body slowly warming. Beneath the blanket, he stroked her back as he marveled at the trust she'd gifted him with. Despite all the ways he'd failed her, he felt her unconditional belief in him like a soft stroke to his heart.

He had been holding her like that for close to an hour when she finally stirred, rubbing her cheek against his collarbone. "Where are we?"

He stroked her silken head and pressed a kiss to her hair. "Safe, Kara. We're safe."

"It looks like a bathtub." She stretched and tried to shift her legs, then melted back against him. He could tell every movement was an effort, requiring more strength than she possessed. "Why do we have blankets in the bath?"

"You bled for hours, little one. This was the only place where it didn't ruin the carpets."

"Sorry."

Her apology, so out of place, made him smile.

"I feel gross," she murmured. "Sticky."

"If you're awake, we should get you cleaned up and into bed."

Her grip on him tightened. "Stay with me. Please."

Always, his beast cried. But the man wasn't at all sure the fates would allow it.

"Of course." He kissed her temple, then called for Paenther's help. As much as he hated to release her, it was time he got her clean and warm.

Paenther took her from him while he climbed out, removed the blood-soaked blankets, and rinsed the tub. Filling it again with warm, clear water, he stripped off the rest of his clothes and took Kara back into his arms.

As Paenther gathered up the soiled linens and left, Lyon sank into the warm water with Kara in his arms and bathed them both, Kara more asleep than awake. He loved touching her, loved the feel of her curled against him, and though his body stirred as it always did whenever she was near, no real need built. Both he and his beast were more than content simply to hold her. To protect her. To cherish her.

When he felt her shiver, he knew he'd squeezed every moment he could out of the bath. He dried them both, then wrapped her in an oversized towel and carried her into the bedroom, where Paenther waited.

"Go, B.P. Get yourself cleared. This battle's won."

Paenther nodded and left.

Lyon dressed Kara in the pajamas Esmeria had left for her, then tucked her into bed already asleep. He pulled on the sweat pants and tee shirt that had been left for him and hesitated, suddenly uncertain where his honor lay. He'd pushed Vhyper aside and claimed Kara for his own when he thought her Mage. Now that he knew better, he should back off. Stay away from her.

Yet he wondered now. Had that cantric, and the dark charm still inside Feral House, fouled the Pairing anyway? That was a question for later. For now, he would watch over Kara and keep her safe as he'd failed to do before. As he slid under the covers and pulled her against him, he told himself he was just taking logical precautions. What if the bleeding broke through again, and he didn't realize it? She could bleed to death without him knowing.

He rubbed his chin against her damp, clean hair and told himself he was just being careful.

But deep inside, his beast shook his maned head, telling him he was a fool if he thought he'd ever allow him to let her go.

Chapter
Nineteen

Kara woke with a jerk, terror lingering in the crevices of her mind.

"Shh, little one. You're safe, now. No one's going to hurt you."

Strong, gentle arms went around her, pressing her against a warm, hard body. Without opening her eyes, she knew she was lying on her side on a bed, Lyon's warm scent surrounding her. She tried to move closer to his warmth, but her strength was gone. The hazy memory of something awful lingered still, but she couldn't remember.

As Lyon's strong hand stroked her hair, she opened her eyes and blinked, but all she could see was the dark tee shirt that covered his chest.

She lifted her head to see him. "What happened?"

Her throat felt dry as sand, the words little more than a rasp. Her head was too heavy, and she let it fall back to his arm.

"I rescued you." A deep shudder went through him as his hold on her tightened. "We locked up Vhyper again and brought you to the healer, at the Georgetown Therian enclave."

His words made no sense. Exhaustion overtook her, and she slept again.

"You going to stay with me, this time?"

Kara blinked and looked up into Lyon's worried face as she woke for the second time. He was still holding her, as before, but she felt different. Stronger, as if that awful weakness had finally left her.

"Did I fall asleep?"

"You did. You lost a lot of blood. Your body needed time to heal."

"What happened, Lyon? I don't remember. All I remember is pain." The memory of it echoed like screams in her head. With a hard shudder, she pressed her face to his chest.

He pulled her tighter and stroked her back, holding her for a long time, until the chill slowly subsided within the warmth of his arms.

Kara finally pulled back. Lyon released her, and she rolled onto her back.

Lyon propped his head on his elbow and looked down at her, hooking his free arm around her waist and pulling her close. She turned toward him, meeting his gaze, his eyes warm and soft.

With a gentle finger, he pushed her hair behind her ear. "How do you feel?"

"Okay. Fine, I think." Her gaze moved outward to take in the simply furnished bedroom. "Where are we?"

"Georgetown. Down in D.C. In one of the Therian enclaves."

"Why?"

His eyes grew more concerned. "What's the last thing you remember?" His thumb brushed her cheek.

"The prison. You took me down to the prison and locked me up. The next thing I remember I was in horrible pain. And you were there. You saved me."

"I did. You don't remember anything in between?"

Did she? There was something teasing her mind, but she couldn't get a grasp on it.

"I feel like there's something I should remember, but it's not coming."

"That's good. It's nothing you want to remember."

"Why?" By the look on his face and the pain in his eyes, she knew it was bad. "I think I need you to tell me."

He brushed her cheek again. "I'd rather not. But if I don't, someone else probably will." He took a deep breath and let it out slowly. "Vhyper escaped from his prison cell and broke you out, too. He took you down to the dungeons deep below the house, tied you up and . . . punished you . . . for being Mage."

She shivered, his words teasing the memory in her head. "How did he punish me?"

"He stabbed you. Multiple times. You bled." His eyes turned bleak and he looked away, his jaw going rigid. "I didn't think you were going to stop bleeding." He turned back to her, his gaze stroking hers softly. "But you're okay, now. It's over. You're safe."

"Why didn't I stop bleeding?"

His brows flicked up. "Interesting story there. Apparently the cantric I took out of your hip wasn't there to increase your magic. It was causing you all kinds of problems. Because you're not Mage."

Kara blinked at him. Then made a sound of disbelief. "You've got to be kidding. After all that, I'm *not* Mage?"

His mouth twisted sheepishly. If a lion could look sheepish. "It *was* a cantric. Even the Shaman's never heard of one being implanted in a Therian before. It shouldn't have done anything to you, and probably didn't until you arrived at Feral House. The Shaman's fairly sure we have a dark charm in the house somewhere that worked with the cantric to make you afraid."

"At least I know it wasn't my imagination."

Lyon's expression turned rueful. "Can you ever forgive me? For doubting you?" His eyes flinched with pain. "For taking the cantric as I did? I don't think I'll ever forgive myself for that."

Kara reached up and ran her fingers through a

thick lock of his golden hair. "You came after me when I ran and saved me from certain death. Then you saved me again when Vhyper hurt me. I'm thinking you're on the right path to forgiveness."

His eyes crinkled at the corners. "But I have a way to go?"

She smiled. "We'll see." His revelations continued to ping-pong through her head, and she dropped her palm onto her own forehead. "First I'm human, then I'm Therian, then I'm Mage. Now I'm Therian again? Are you sure?"

He lifted her palm, kissed her forehead, then resettled her palm over the kiss. "You're Therian. The Radiant. The Shaman's heading out to Feral House this morning to find the dark charm and destroy it."

"And that's it?"

"Hopefully, yes. You should be fine."

"Good. That's good." And it was. But she didn't feel as relieved as maybe she should have. Something was bothering her. Something she couldn't remember. "So, what happens now? Are we back to trying to ascend me?"

Lyon nodded as he looked down at her. "Once the Shaman's through and I'm certain you're okay, we'll go home." His brows drew down in a way that worried her.

"What's the matter?" she asked softly.

"The Pairing. You're the true Therian Radiant, so it may have worked after all. But the magic may still have thrown it off. We can't ascend you unless we're one hundred percent sure we've got the right

Feral as your mate. We're going to have to do another Pairing."

"*Yes*." Kara grinned and sat up, swinging around to face him on her knees. "I know it was off. It's you who's my mate, Lyon. You." But as she caught his grim expression her delight evaporated. "You don't want it to be you."

He sat up until he faced her and slid his palms over her cheeks, cradling her face in his hands. His eyes spoke of fervent need. And sadness.

"I want to be chosen to be your mate more than anything I've ever wanted in my life. *Anything*."

Tears sprang up in her eyes. "Really?"

"Don't, Kara. Don't be happy about that, because it doesn't matter. It's not my choice to make any more than it's yours. The Pairing will decide. Only that. And I fear the results will be no different than they were the first time. Perhaps not Vhyper. But someone. Someone who isn't me."

He leaned in and laid a gentle kiss on her brow. "That may not be a bad thing."

"How can you say that?"

"You deserve someone who can make you happy, sweetheart. Someone like Tighe, who will make you laugh and smile. I'm not that man. I don't have that laughter inside me."

"You're wrong, Lyon. So wrong. You're the only one I need."

His thumbs feathered across her cheekbones. "What happens, happens, Kara. The Pairing will decide, and we'll both live with that decision. The goddess always chooses the best Feral for her Radiant. The one absolute is that once you accept her choice, you'll be happy. And you'll ascend safely. That's all that matters."

"What about you?"

He pulled her onto his lap and tucked her head beneath his chin. "Knowing you're happy will be enough."

Kara pulled away to look at him. "It's not enough for me. Knowing you're unhappy will destroy me." She leaned in and kissed him on the mouth. "But we're getting ahead of ourselves, don't you think? The Pairing may still choose you. And right this minute, I'm free to choose my lovers."

She looped her arms around his neck locking her fingers she looked into his eyes. "I want you. Even if you can't promise me forever, you can give me now. Please, Lyon. Please let me love you as I want to. If only this last time."

Her body tensed, knowing him well enough to know his honor would probably send him stalking from the room. But to her amazement, he kissed her with all the passion of a lover, intending to see the act through to the end.

He pulled back, his mouth damp, his eyes glowing with a fierce, carnal light. "Yes," he growled.

"Really?"

His mouth gave a self-deprecating twist. "I've been ordered to bring you to release to cleanse you of the magic. A full-penetration release."

She shivered at his words. "The Shaman's orders?"

"Yes."

Kara grinned. "I think I love that Shaman."

He glowered at her with mock severity. "I don't know what the future holds, but for this moment, I don't want you thinking of anyone but me. You're mine, Kara MacAllister. *Mine*." His hand slid beneath her shirt to cover her breast, staking his claim.

Lyon covered Kara's sweet mouth in a deep, drugging kiss while his fingers sank into the softness of her breast. She shifted on his lap, swinging her leg around until she straddled him, exploding his senses.

Goddess, he wanted this. Wanted *her*. Today, tomorrow, every day for the rest of his life.

Passion erupted as he shoved his tongue into her warm, welcoming mouth, desperate to get inside her. As their tongues slid against one another, creating a sensuous friction, Kara moaned and ground her hips against his growing erection, her passion rising. With one hand, he cradled her head, with the other he cupped her buttocks, pressing her hard against him. When she shattered on a low cry and clung to him, he held her, keeping her pressed tight as his beast gave a rumble of hot satisfaction.

What would he do if the Pairing gave her to another yet again?

Kara pulled back to look at him with eyes alight with a sexy, slumberous fire. His gaze dropped to her lips, full and damp from his kisses. His chest ached with an overwhelming tenderness.

"You're so beautiful," he murmured. "I need you, Kara." He kissed the corner of her mouth, her jaw, her neck, while his hand cupped and kneaded her breast. "I have to be inside you, sweetheart."

Her eyes melted with heat and tenderness as she laid her palm against his cheek. "I want you inside me. Always."

His conscience rose from the fires of his passion, reminding him what happened last time he'd touched her prior to a Pairing. Did he really want to foul a second one?

His beast growled. The Shaman had ordered Kara penetrated, and he'd kill anyone else who tried to touch her. This was the only way.

Praise the goddess.

Kara kissed his mouth, a gentle peck. "You're waffling. I can see it in your eyes. Tell me you're going to make love to me, Lyon. I want to hear you say it."

Her hand slid down his chest to his abdomen and lower to stroke his growing erection. The need in her eyes shimmered. "Say it, Lyon."

His body shuddered, and he kissed her hard. "I'm going to make love to you, Kara."

"Say it again."

"You doubt my word, woman?" He found himself smiling at her and felt a strange and wonderful lightness he couldn't explain. And had no desire to. All he wanted to do was fulfill the promise he'd just made to the woman in his arms.

She grinned at him. "Just making sure." Her lips

landed at the corner of his mouth, teasing him with infinite gentleness. "I'm going to make love to you, too."

When she would have mirrored the kiss on the other side of his mouth, he flipped her onto her back on the bed, startling a laugh out of her. The sweet sound filled him with such happiness he grinned at her and followed her down. She rewarded him well by flinging her arm around his neck and raining kisses on his cheek and eye and nose. Never had anyone kissed his nose. Or his cheek, for that matter. Not even as a child. Hell, as a child, he hadn't even known what a kiss was.

His grin grew into laughter as the tiny kisses tickled. "What are you doing?"

She stopped kissing him and met his gaze, her eyes glistening with a fine sheen of tears. "I'm loving you," she said softly, the depth of emotion in her eyes almost more than he could bear.

But then she smiled at him, her eyes turning mischievous, easing the sudden aching tension her words had formed deep inside him. "Would you prefer I kiss you somewhere else?" Her grin turned positively wicked. The thought of where he wanted those lips, nearly sent him over the edge.

"Everywhere," he growled. He licked and nibbled his way from the hollow below her ear to the pulse pounding at the base of her throat. "I want your mouth on me, Kara. But first I'm going to lick every single inch of you."

The look she gave him was pure fire. "I dare you."

The lightness inside him erupted like tiny fizzing bubbles, and he laughed. Never had he felt so good. *Goddess, but this must be love.*

He set about proving he was up for her dare, starting with her face, then her neck, until she was moaning and rocking beneath him. But he stopped short of bringing her to release.

When he pulled back, Kara groaned. "No fair."

"Patience, sweet Radiant. You have too many clothes on." But when he pulled up her pajama top, his gut clenched at the fading dashes of scars circling her waist, his body pained by the sight of them. He traced each one with his lips, then his tongue, giving her pleasure where last night she'd only known pain.

But not too much pleasure. At each place his lips touched, he kissed her with tender thoroughness until he felt her passion on the brink, then he moved on without giving her release.

"*Lyon . . .*"

"Patience, little one."

"Payback is going to be hell, I hope you know." Her promise was half laughter, half groan.

He pulled the shirt from her, and laid kisses and small licks on her torso and her arms, then removed her pajama pants and indulged himself on every inch of her slender, shapely legs.

She lay on the bed in nothing but skin damp from his kisses and flushed with heat, her hips rocking with unfulfilled need, her blue eyes flashing with fire and desperation. And promise.

Without a doubt, she was the most glorious creature ever made.

She licked her lips, the movement unstudied and intensely erotic. "I want you, Lyon."

The blood pounded through his veins in answer. He was hot and throbbing and loving every minute of this sweet torment.

"Take off your clothes for me," she said. "I want to see you. All of you."

He complied, stripping off his clothes and tossing them to the floor as her hungry gaze fed on his body, hardening him almost to the point of pain.

Lyon joined her. At the first lick of his tongue on her nipple, she cried out.

"Lyon, I can't take any more. Touch me. *Please.*"

He grinned. As his mouth moved to cover one perfect breast, his hand slid down the plane of her stomach, then farther, dipping between her thighs. His fingers found the drenched center of her need.

At the first stroke of his fingers, she moaned.

He lifted his head and met her heated, frantic gaze. "Come for me."

"*Lyon.*"

Dipping his head again, he slid one finger deep inside her, then a second as he took her breast in his mouth. With his tongue, he stroked her tight, sweet nipple. With his fingers, he pushed in and out of her until he felt her passion rise and finally break as he brought her to a crashing, violent release.

When her shudders subsided, she ran her fingers through his hair. "Oh, that was good. Now it's my turn to have my way with you."

He pulled his fingers out of her and tasted the nectar, far sweeter than any he'd ever known. "Not yet," he told her. He moved down her body until he was kneeling between her legs, then he lifted her hips, opening her to his hungry mouth. The first stroke of his tongue on her most sensitive flesh sent her over the edge, crying out. He kissed her, drank of her, and drove her to orgasm after orgasm, one starting long before the one before had ended, until she was gasping for mercy.

"That was . . ." she struggled as he released her and came to lie beside her, pulling her against him. "That was . . . the most amazing . . . the most . . ."

He kissed her shoulder, smiling. "Want me to do it again?"

"No. Not . . . yet. I'm going to have a heart attack if you start again."

He chuckled. "Therians don't have heart attacks. But I'll give you a short break."

"Not . . . no." She struggled out of his hold to sit up, then looked down at him, meeting his gaze with an expression he couldn't name.

Slowly, her eyes filled with tenderness, her lips lifting in a sweet, sexy smile. "How could you ever think you couldn't make me happy?"

He stared into her eyes. "What I did made you happy?" Her answer suddenly mattered more than he would have thought possible.

She laughed, the sound music to his soul. "Oh, yeah." Her eyes sparkled. "But not just that. Everything you do makes me happy. Every touch, every look, every kiss. Every word. You make me happy, Lyon. *You.*"

He didn't understand how anything she said could be true, and yet he couldn't deny the joy he saw in her face and felt shimmering out of her. Deep inside, he felt the splintering and shattering of a belief he hadn't realized existed inside him until Kara shone the brilliance of her light into the crevices of his heart. The brittle belief that love and smiles were alien to his soul. The belief that love, which he'd never really known, had never been meant for him.

He stared into the glistening gems of her eyes, then pulled her down, kissing her thoroughly, telling her silently how much her words healed the ache of loneliness so long hidden even from himself.

As his hand slid to her breast, she broke off the kiss and rose to her knees, a mischievous smile lurking on her mouth. "It's my turn."

He watched her, smiling, feeling the weight of centuries lifted from his heart even as he banished his doubts that after the next Pairing this woman would be his.

He didn't want to think about that. For once, he wished to live only in this moment. With Kara.

"Your turn for what?" he asked.

"To have my way with you."

Holding his gaze, she bent to kiss his chest, flicking her tongue across his nipple as he had hers. He forced himself to lay unmoving beneath the tender torture of her kisses and her tongue, his chest filling, expanding until he thought maybe Therians could have heart attacks after all.

Kara lifted her head, her blond hair falling in soft waves around her face, her eyes glowing. "You don't respond to me as crazily as I do you."

He lifted a hand to her face. "If I did, it would all be over long before it began."

Her mouth turned up into a wicked smile. "Maybe I'm not kissing you where it counts."

She turned to slide her hand down the plane of his stomach until those warm fingers curled around his erection, and his eyes nearly rolled back in his head. Bending over, she presented him with a first-class view, nearly sending him over the edge when her delicate tongue flicked out and stroked the slit at the tip of him.

"*Kara.*" He slid his hand over the lush, soft flesh of her buttocks, then between her legs, touching her, being drenched by her.

The stroke of her tongue was beyond paradise, beyond erotic, and he knew he wasn't going to last a minute longer.

"Kara, I have to have you. *Now.*"

She was under him in three seconds flat, spreading her thighs, sliding her hands over his shoulders as she welcomed him. He met her gaze, embraced by those blue depths even before he pushed against her slick opening. As he buried himself inside her, her mouth dropped open, her eyes heavy with pleasure, her back arching. But her gaze never left his. Her eyes darkened with desire as she clung to him and softened with an emotion that warmed him, filled him, until he thought his heart couldn't contain it all.

With each thrust, she rose to meet him as he stroked her deeper than the time before, lifted on the rising tide of her passion, riding the storm of his own. Her hands slid up his neck, her fingers digging frantically into his hair as gasps of growing pleasure escaped her throat with each hard meeting of their bodies.

"Lyon," she cried, and he felt the storm breaking over her. "*Lyon.*"

The storm ripped him from his moorings, and he felt himself tumbling in after her—into her eyes, into her body, into her soul—the release like nothing he'd ever experienced. He felt destroyed, demolished, shattered. And utterly and totally reborn.

"Kara." As the last of her contractions milked him, he kissed her, needing to taste her, needing to be joined with her in a thousand ways. When his tongue stroked hers, she turned her head, breaking the kiss on a musical peal of exhausted joy.

"Lyon, I can't," she gasped, her eyes smiling at him. "I can't come again."

"You can." He made a sound of satisfaction deep in his throat, knowing that in this moment, she was his. Completely. Her body the finest of instruments tuned to his touch. He kissed her cheek as she had his. Then her eye. And nose.

Then he drank of the smile he'd put on her lips and slowly ran his tongue across the same, drawing a gasp from her, making the hard knots of her tight breasts press against his chest.

He ran his tongue around the curve of her ear, and that single stroke was all it took to send her back over the edge. Deep inside, her body squeezed him over and over, as her hot gasps bathed his lips, hardening him all over again. He pulled out and shoved himself inside her welcoming body, and she met him thrust for thrust, as ready for him a second time as he was for her.

She stared up into his eyes, her own silently mirroring the longing, the devotion, the beauty of what they'd just shared. And as they crested a second time, she said, "I love you, Lyon."

His beast purred as her words soaked into his heart, but the fear that she wasn't his reached in to pluck away his pleasure. He rolled onto his back, still buried inside her, cradling Kara against his heart.

As her heartbeat raced with his, he stroked the warm, damp silk of her back with one hand while the other buried itself deep in her hair, sliding against her small, precious head. A vicious protectiveness rose inside him as his gut contracted over the thought of losing her.

Mine.

"You're mine, Lyon," she said, as if she'd heard that desperate inner voice of his. "I know you're mine."

"We can't be sure." Despite the certainty of his beast.

She tucked her hand beneath her chin. "How soon do you think we can do another Pairing?"

He stroked her back, wishing he could stay here, like this, for the rest of his life. He sighed, thinking. "As soon as the Shaman clears the house of any dark charms, we'll know if it was those affecting my men or the lack of radiance. If it's the latter, I'm not sure how we're going to do it. I'm not endangering you."

"We may not have a choice, but I guess we can figure that out once the Shaman's done."

"I agree." He kissed her head and held her close.

She might never be his to hold like this again, but that didn't mean he wouldn't watch over her, and protect her, and care for her from a distance. No one would ever hurt her again.

He would die before he let that happen.

Kara's gaze took in the long, narrow interior of a comfortably decorated house as she followed Lyon down the stairs a short while later. As they'd dressed, Lyon had told her this house actually looked like a row of town houses from the outside, while inside it was open, with passages running from one end of the block to the other. The Therians had lived here for well over a century.

Her hand brushed the fashionable pastel floral skirt the Therian, Esmeria, had loaned her along with a long-sleeved coordinated blue sweater. These people might live for centuries, but they kept up with the fashions.

Paenther met them as they reached the bottom step. Lyon extended his arm in greeting and Paenther accepted the greeting with a bow of his head. But when Lyon released him, Paenther's attention went to her.

His usually hard eyes were nothing short of sad. "I'm sorry, Kara. For not protecting you. For believing you were the enemy."

Kara reached for his hand and squeezed it. "It wasn't your fault, Paenther. *I* didn't even know if I was Mage or not."

Paenther lifted their joined hands to his lips and kissed the back of her hand. Not as a chivalrous act, but as an act of deep contrition.

"I'll make it up to you. I'll find a way."

Kara smiled. "Just give me the benefit of the doubt next time, and we'll call it even."

To her amazement, his mouth twisted into what could almost be called a lopsided smile. "You have a deal."

As they started into the main living area, Jag joined them. His eyebrow lifting with surprise as Lyon extended his arm. Jag clasped Lyon's arm in return.

"Chief," Jag said. His gaze slid to her. "You're looking better. Got a little color in those cheeks." He glanced down at the floor, then up at Lyon. "I'd like to speak to our Radiant for a minute."

His jaw clenched, but his eyes remained uncertain. "Alone."

She felt Lyon tense, but he glanced at her with a lift of his eyebrow.

Kara nodded.

"You won't be out of my sight," Lyon promised her.

Jag reached for her, then seemed to think better of it and dropped his hand. "How about we stand by the window over there where the king of beasts can keep my hide in the crosshairs?"

He led her toward the window, then turned and glanced back at Lyon before meeting her gaze.

"Here's the thing, Radiant. Kara. I owe you a humongo apology. I may shift into a jaguar, but I'm a jackass, through and through. Always have been." His mouth twisted. "I'm sure any of the others will agree."

He propped his hip on the back of the sofa behind him and crossed his arms. "We haven't had the best luck with Radiants. I didn't much like either of your last two predecessors, and I didn't expect to like you. I suppose when I first saw you in the media room, I wanted to let you know that in my own charming way."

He smiled at her, but there was no humor in his eyes. There was something about him that made her think he didn't like himself very much.

His smile died, and his eyes turned hard. "I saw what Vhyper did to you. That snake lost it." He looked away, shaking his head with revulsion.

"I'm just saying . . . I'm sorry for being an ass in the way I treated you. You're okay." He said the last as if he were surprised. "Not only have you tamed the beast . . ." His glance flicked to Lyon as if he knew exactly what they'd been doing upstairs.

Kara's cheeks heated.

"But you won Pink over, too, and I'm kind of fond of the bird. She sent me to the grocery yesterday to get a surprise for you for your Ascension celebration."

"Really?" Kara smiled. Pink had forgiven her. "I'm glad to know that, Jag. Thank you." She had an instant's temptation to give him a hug, hesitated, then gave in to it. Stepping forward, she wrapped her arms around his lean, hard waist.

He hugged her back, then tugged on a loose lock of her hair when she pulled away. "See? I can be a good cat."

She laughed. "When you want to be."

He winked at her. "Don't tell anyone." He rose. "Come get some breakfast. Marina's doing waffles. I'm not usually into bread, but her waffles are a treat."

As Kara started back with Jag, Lyon waited for her, his eyes guarded. "Everything okay?"

She smiled. "Perfect."

At Lyon's hooded glare, Jag lifted his hands in surrender as he passed, chuckling.

Lyon shook his head and laid his hand on her shoulder. "Get breakfast. I have some things I need to do."

She nodded and followed Jag, who was entering the kitchen in the middle of the open house. Tighe was already there, seated before a plate piled high with bacon and eggs.

When he saw her, he stood and opened his arms to her, leaving the choice up to her.

With a smile, she accepted his hug. "Hi, Tighe."

"Hi, yourself." When she pulled back, he gripped her shoulders and held her in front of him, his smile dying as he inspected her. "You look a hundred times better than the last time I saw you. I never thought anyone could be that pale." He squeezed her shoulders. "Are you feeling better?" His mouth kicked up, a small gleam entering his eyes. Apparently everyone knew the Shaman had ordered her penetrated.

"I'm feeling much better, thank you," she said primly. But she flashed him a smile that said she knew full well what he'd been asking.

"Roar!"

Tighe was just pulling out a chair for her when Paenther's shout made them all freeze.

The two men beside her started forward, then as one, turned back to her. Jag grabbed her hand and pulled her with them to where Paenther waited in the foyer.

As they rounded the corner, three men she'd never seen before were entering the house, two large men helping a youth with long, dark hair and old-fashioned clothes who looked like he was drunk. Or drugged. Behind them, was Hawke.

"What happened, Shaman?" Lyon demanded.

To her surprise, it was the youth Lyon addressed. A man he'd told her was ancient.

Without looking at her, Lyon reached for her hand, took her from Jag, and pulled her against his side.

The Therians pressed the Shaman into one of two upholstered chairs in the wide foyer, then backed away as the Ferals pushed forward. The Shaman's head tipped against the wall behind him, his body shaking, his flesh white as snow.

"I couldn't get near the house. Halfway up your front walk, I passed out. Hawke drove me back."

"Magic?" Lyon asked. His hand tightened around hers.

"Yes. Stronger than I've felt in millennia. Old magic. And woven throughout that magic . . ." His gaze rose to pin her. "I felt your Radiant."

Chapter
Twenty

Lyon's blood went cold, a warning growl rumbling deep in his throat as he pulled Kara in front of him and wrapped both arms around her, ready to protect her with his life.

"*You said she was innocent.*"

"I did. Innocent, yes. But I felt her in the magic, and I believe the Mage . . . for this is clearly a Mage attack . . . has been using her. The cantric you found in her was doing more than I thought it was. More than it should have been able to."

"There's a Mage in Feral House?" Lyon roared.

"Yes. A strong one. No one else could wield that kind of magic."

Lyon looked at Paenther. "Let's go."

The Shaman held up his hand. "Wait, Warrior.

This attack isn't new. The magic I felt has been there for months. If you haven't found it before now, you're not likely to."

Lyon snarled. "You want me to let the Mage have Feral House?"

"No." His weak gaze went to Kara. "There's another way. She holds the key."

Lyon shook his head, knowing where this was headed. "No mind-skinning. She's been through enough." He looked at his men. "We're going out there. Now."

Jag snorted. "We're going to waltz into a full-scale Mage attack without any clue what's going on? Sounds like a hell of a plan."

Lyon glared at him. "I'm not forsaking my men."

"So said the seventeen," Jag muttered.

A strained silence blanketed the foyer.

"What's the seventeen?" Kara asked, breaking the silence.

Lyon's jaw clenched. "Centuries ago, seventeen Ferals were lost in three days."

Kara turned her head to look up at him. "*Seventeen?* But I thought there were only nine of you."

"There are now," Tighe said. "There were almost thirty at that point. Six warriors walked into a cave they'd never seen before and never came out. Over the course of the next two days, eleven more went into that cave searching for them, every man certain he'd be the one to save the others. The last group included the chief. He gave direct orders to Lyon, his second, that if he failed to return, no more would enter. None did. Fourteen days later the bodies of the seventeen men littered the ground outside the cave. Apparently unharmed, yet quite dead."

"I thought new Ferals were marked when the old ones died, just as new Radiants are."

"They're supposed to be. But none of those animals ever came forth again."

"Jag's right," Paenther said, meeting Lyon's gaze. "We don't know what we're walking into." His gaze went to Kara, regret in his eyes. "We'd be fools not to use the one weapon we have."

"I agree." Kara shoved her way out of Lyon's arms and stood in front of him. "You have to use me."

He gripped her shoulders. "You don't know what you're agreeing to. Trust me on this." He started to turn, but she grabbed his hand, her grip surprisingly strong. Her eyes and voice stronger still.

"Then you're going to do this for me. You owe me this, Lyon. After the hell I went through in that house, I can finally find out why. I want to know. For you, for me, for all the Ferals. We *need* to know."

"She's right, Chief." Paenther's mouth was grim as his gaze met Lyon's. "I swear to you, I searched that place top to bottom when I was looking for the dark charm, and found nothing. Without more to go on, we could be wasting our time."

Lyon's grip tightened on Kara's shoulders as he turned back to her. "It's going to hurt."

She shrugged, her eyes filled with a determination as strong as any warrior's. And he realized it was his own pain he was trying to avoid. The pain of watching her suffer yet again.

But she was right. As was Paenther. He'd be a fool to go into battle blindfolded when sight was but a short, heart-ripping procedure away.

"Let's do it, then." He looked to the Shaman. "Are you up for it?"

"Yes." The man looked at him with weary humor. "I don't suppose you're willing to wait for me to clear this magic?"

"I'm not."

"I didn't think so."

As Tighe helped the Shaman to his feet, Lyon turned to Hawke. "Get yourself laid while we do this. We'll fill you in on the way to Feral House."

Hawke nodded, his eyes grave.

Marina, standing nearby smiled at Hawke and held out her hand. "Come, Warrior."

Lyon gripped Kara's hand as they followed the Shaman to one of the offices off the main living area, lending her strength. And stealing it back again.

The Shaman stood at the door and held up his hand. "The Radiant and one other only. I won't have an audience."

But the Ferals ignored him, brushing past the Shaman's outstretched hand with a rumble of low growls.

"We stay." Lyon spoke for all of them.

The Shaman frowned and looked at Kara. "You may not want them to see this."

But Kara only shrugged. "From what I've pieced together about the scene in the dungeon, they've seen just about all there is to see of me. They stay."

The Shaman shrugged. "All right, then. Sit in the chair." His gaze turned to Lyon. "I have to be standing behind her, but you'll need to keep her in the chair."

Lyon's muscles tensed. He wasn't going to like this. He wasn't going to like it at all.

He led Kara to the chair and knelt in front of her, holding one of her hands as he placed the other on her shoulder.

"I'm here, little one." He looked her in the eye. "Whatever happens, I'm here."

She gave him a small, rueful smile. "If you're trying to reassure me, a nice lie might work better. Something like, it's not going to hurt a bit?"

"I'm not going to lie to you."

Her expression turned serious, her gaze softening. "I'm glad." A soft emotion sifted out of her to wrap around him, dulling the edges of the apprehension they shared.

"I learned this trick from a Mage a long, long time ago and haven't practiced it much. It may not be pretty."

"*Do it.*"

The Shaman began to chant in a language even Lyon couldn't identify. A language probably long gone from the Earth.

Kara's hand clenched his as the first wave of her pain hit him. A moment later, a second, stronger wave hit, making her gasp. As the third ripped through her, she cried out.

He wasn't going to survive this.

"How much more?" he snarled.

"Not much, but the worst is yet to come. Hold her down."

Lyon had barely tightened his grip on her shoulder when the scream rose from her throat, her pain so sharp, so excruciating as it pierced his own flesh, an answering yell escaped his own.

He felt strong hands on his shoulders and knew Paenther was at his back. Through a haze of white-hot pain, he saw Tighe reach for Kara as she fell forward.

"*Kara.*"

Her pain flew at him like daggers, ripping apart his organs, clawing out the chambers of his heart.

He felt a hand go around his wrist.

"Let go of her, Chief," Paenther said.

"No."

"You're not going to do her any good if you pass out, too."

"*No.*" He could take it from her. Take the pain. Or at least help her carry it. He wasn't letting go of her. Ever. *Ever.*

He didn't know how much time had passed when he was finally able to start breathing again.

Kara stirred with a heart-wrenching moan.

His vision cleared enough for him to realize his men were tight around them, having pushed the Shaman out of the way. Tighe was standing beside her and had her head lying on his arm. Jag was kneeling on her other side, her free hand tight in his. Paenther remained at his back.

Lyon struggled to his feet, glaring at the Therian who'd caused such pain. "Can I move her?"

The Shaman lifted his hand, then dropped it again as if he didn't have the strength to hold it up. "Yes. You're not going to cause her any additional pain by moving her."

His men stepped back as Lyon lifted her into his arms, then settled onto the deep leather chair with her on his lap. Kara's pain blanketed him in raw agony, but he wouldn't leave her to fight it alone.

Her head lolled on his shoulder, then jerked, her entire body going tense as a high wire.

And suddenly it wasn't only pain attacking him, but fear. Terror in its purest form.

"Easy, sweetheart. You're safe."

"No. No. Oh, God," she moaned.

"She's remembering," the Shaman said behind him. "Reliving the things she's forgotten. You can talk to her. Ask questions. In fact you need to, before she gets lost in there."

Lyon squeezed her close. "Kara. Kara, I need to know what you see. What's happening?"

"Cut me." She gasped. "*It hurts*. She wants it to hurt. Wants *me* to hurt."

"Who cut you, Kara?"

"*It hurts*."

"Where? Where does it hurt?"

"My hip. So much blood. So much pain."

"Who did this to you, Kara?"

"Can't say. Can't make a sound."

"Try another question," the Shaman suggested.

"Why, Kara? Why do they want you to hurt?"

"To feed her pets."

Paenther stepped into his line of vision. "Did this happen recently, Kara? Or in the past?"

When she didn't respond, Lyon tried the question another way. "Kara, sweetheart, how old are you?"

"Twenty-seven."

"How old were you when they cut you?"

"Twenty-seven."

Lyon met Paenther's gaze. "Kara, where were you when you were cut?"

"My bedroom. The Radiant's bedroom."

"Shit," Jag said behind him.

"Who cut you, Kara? Who did this to you?"

"Vhyper. And Zaphene. She has strange eyes. Copper rings around her eyes."

"Zaphene's Therian," Tighe said. "Kara's not re-membering correctly."

"Maybe she is," the Shaman said. "In the old days, there were Mage who could change small as-pects of their appearance for short periods. Their typical trick was to hide the copper rings of their eyes in order to bewitch a Therian. It takes power-ful magic. But there's no doubt we're dealing with that kind of magic here. The kind I haven't seen in centuries. Tens of centuries."

"Kara, was Vhyper helping Zaphene?"

"Yes."

A muscle leaped in Paenther's jaw. "Vhyper

wouldn't help a Mage. *I know him.* He would never team up with a Mage, not for any reason."

"It's always the ones you don't expect," Jag muttered.

Lyon shook his head. "She's bewitched him."

"Kara, was it Zaphene who freed you and Vhyper from the prison cells?"

"Yes."

"Did she help Vhyper stab you?"

Kara moaned, jerking back as if reliving the pain. "Vhyper didn't stab me. Bleeding spell to bleed me quickly. They knew . . . they knew you'd come for me. Didn't have much time, but the pets needed feeding, and you'd taken the cantric." She began to gasp.

"Easy, Kara. Easy, little one." He pulled the terror and the pain from her as hard and fast as he could. "Who stabbed you?"

"The ones in the robes."

"Did you see their faces? Anything?"

"No. Only their knives."

"How many?" Paenther asked.

"I don't know. More than four."

Lyon stroked her hair. "Where were they? Where was Zaphene? We didn't see anyone but you and Vhyper when we got down there."

"Hiding. Zaphene was hiding with her pets."

"Were her pets the ones that stabbed you?"

"I don't know."

"They have to be somewhere in the dungeons," Paenther said. "I never searched them. I checked that door when I searched the house, Chief, I swear it. I thought it was sealed tight, like it always is. I missed it."

The Shaman lifted his hand and dropped it again. "Warding. Magic to hide the truth from you."

Lyon looked at Paenther. "Call the house. Warn Kougar and Foxx there may be Mage hiding in the dungeon. I want them out of the house until we get there."

"What about Wulfe? We can't just leave him to them."

"Leave him. If it turns to war, he could turn on us as easily as the Mage." Lyon turned back to Kara, his sense of urgency to return to Feral House growing by the second. But there was more he needed to know. "Why, Kara? Why did Vhyper and Zaphene do this to you?"

"She needed my blood."

"Her pets needed your blood?"

"The ritual needed my blood. She didn't have enough, but you were coming. Vhyper told her to hide. He'd get the rest later."

His grip tightened on her. "Like hell. They're never coming near you again." He glanced up as Hawke joined them, then turned his attention back to Kara. "What ritual, sweetheart? Why did they need your blood?"

"To free the Daemons."

Lyon felt his men's shock as clearly as his own.

"They can't free the Daemons." Tighe's voice was hot. Indignant. "No one can do that but us."

"That may be, Stripes, but we've already blooded that blade," Jag drawled. "And if I remember correctly, doesn't the ritual to free the bastards require the blood of an unascended Radiant?"

Silence burst over the room, punctured by Tighe's groan.

"Beatrice. Her death was no accident. She died right after Foxx brought Zaphene home."

Kara's body slowly began to relax against him, the fear and pain draining away.

"Are you still with me?"

"Uh-hmm. I feel like I just went three rounds with a grizzly bear. Or any one of you."

He slid his hand into her hair, pressing her head against his shoulder.

"If the Mage mortgaged their power to imprison the Daemons, too, why would a Mage try to free him?" she murmured.

"I don't know. Evil can take any form. This time it seems to be taking the form of a Mage witch."

"Zaphene probably bewitched Foxx into opening that window," Paenther said. "She's probably had him bewitched all along."

Tighe nodded. "Which is how Foxx wound up bringing that Daemon blade to the goddess stone the night we raised the power of the lion. And why he couldn't remember doing it."

"Dammit to hell." Lyon stood, still holding Kara tight against him. "We've got to get back there and find her. And when we do, she's dead." He looked at the Shaman. "Can you do some research? See if you can figure out what in the hell her pets are and how she means to free the Daemons?"

The Shaman nodded, straightening from the

wall. His color seemed to be coming back. "I'll work on it."

He kissed Kara's head. "Can you stand?"

"Yes. I'm okay."

He let her slide to her feet, but kept her close against him as she rearranged her skirt. "If Kara's memory was right, the witch wants more of her blood. She's still in danger. I need someone to guard her."

"I'll do it," Hawke said.

Lyon nodded. "Jag, get the Hummer. We need to roll." He turned Kara to face him. "Rest while we're gone. I'll come get you as soon as we get this situation straightened out."

"I wish I could come with you." A hot spark of malice lit her eyes. "I'd like to kick Zaphene's butt for what she did to me."

"She won't live another day," he snarled. "I'll take her head myself. I promise you that."

She reached up and touched his face, her soft fingers stroking his heart. "Okay. But you have to make me a second promise as well."

"What's that?"

"Come back to me, Lyon. Whole. I couldn't bear it if anything happened to you. I love you."

And he knew he'd battle a hundred armies if he had to, to keep her by his side.

Kara heard the front door close behind Lyon and the others. She was afraid for them. If what she'd remembered was true, they were in serious danger. The entire world could be in danger.

The Shaman started for the door. "I've got magic sticking to me like glue." He turned to look at her, the eyes in that youthful face as old as the ages. "If you're feeling better, Radiant, I'm going to get myself cleared."

Kara nodded. "I'm fine now. Thank you." She followed the Shaman out of the office and saw Hawke coming toward her from the foyer. She tried to smile at him, despite her worry for Lyon.

"So you're my bodyguard today?"

He nodded. "We need to go."

"Go where?"

"To one of the other enclaves. Lyon doesn't want you to stay here. Too many people know you're here."

"Oh. Okay. Do we have to go right away?"

"Immediately."

The Shaman stripped off his clothes, enjoying, as he always did, the sight of Esmeria removing her own. He felt lousy. Like the magic from that place had seeped into every pore and was eating away at his body like acid. The sooner he got rid of it, the better. He wondered if one release would do it. He might need a second. Or even a third.

He smiled to himself. The life of a Shaman was a trial, to be sure.

Esmeria unhooked her bra, pulled off her panties and lay down on the bed, opening her thighs. She pushed her fingers between her legs, slipping them inside her body until the damp, sucking sound told him she was ready. When she pulled out glistening fingers and motioned for him, opening her arms wide, he joined her, kissed her neck as he positioned his body over hers and pushed himself home.

Oh, yes. This was what he'd needed. Whenever the magic rode him, it took him a while to find his release, as if the magic fought to hold on. But, finally, he felt his body tighten, felt the rush of orgasm and the cleansing of his spirit. As he found completion, and collapsed into Esmeria's warm arms, his mind began to tingle in a way that had him turning to stone.

"What's the matter, Shaman?" Esmeria rubbed her hand along his back.

"Bewitchment." He felt the veil lift from his mind like a fog dissipating in the sun.

And he remembered.

"*Damnation.*"

Esmeria released him as he levered himself out of her. "What's wrong?"

"Get Lyon on the phone and tell him to get back here. *Quickly.*"

"Which enclave are we going to?" Kara asked Hawke as she slid into the front seat of his car.

"You'll see."

Kara flicked the warrior a glance, then turned to look out her own window as he pulled away from the curb. She supposed it didn't matter since she didn't know one from the other. And Lyon would be able to find her no matter where she was, thanks to his finder skills.

"Did you know Zaphene very well?" As soon as

the words were out of her mouth, she wanted to take them back. For all she knew, all the men had slept with her at one point or another.

"No," Hawke replied.

"That must have been a shock. I'm sorry about Beatrice."

"Yes."

Kara quit trying to engage him in conversation. For her, it was an attempt to take her mind off Lyon and the others, but he didn't seem to want the distraction. She knew he had to be immensely worried.

They continued in silence, driving through the busy streets, through traffic unlike anything Kara had ever seen. They didn't have traffic like this in Spearsville.

When Hawke took the on-ramp to I–495, the Washington Beltway, Kara looked at him in surprise. She'd thought the Therian enclaves were all fairly close together.

"Hawke, where are we going?"

He didn't answer.

"*Hawke.*"

He glanced at her, his eyes cold.

"I'm not Hawke."

Chapter Twenty-one

"The witch's pets?" the Shaman said. "They're clones."

"Explain." The phone in Lyon's hand creaked from the white-knuckled pressure of his grip.

"When I got out to Feral House, Hawke and Zaphene met me at the door. Except it wasn't Hawke. The man who drove me back to the enclave is a draden."

"Turn the car around," Lyon barked at Jag. Into the phone he said, "That was no draden."

He held on as Jag made a fast, illegal U-turn across the median. "Back to Georgetown?"

"Yes."

"It started out as a draden," the Shaman said through the phone. "The witch has split your souls, Warrior, and used your souls to animate the draden. She implanted the cantric into Kara to stimulate her fear, then channeled that fear to the draden to feed and grow them into clones of you and your men. It's the clones who will free the Daemons."

Raw fear twisted his guts into knots. "Where's Kara? Get her away from Hawke!"

His heart pounded as he heard the Shaman moving down the stairs. He heard a distant scream.

Kara.

A commotion in the background had his breath catching. He heard shouting.

"Shaman!" he yelled into the phone.

"Marina's dead. Drained as if by draden. She took the clone to bed."

"*Find Kara.*" But she wasn't there. His senses felt her moving. Away from the enclave. Away from Georgetown. "She's gone. He's already got her."

"I'm sorry."

"Jag, get on the Beltway. East." He clutched the phone. "How in the hell did she split our souls?"

"One by one. You trusted her enough to let her touch you, correct? All she had to do was touch you to enthrall you long enough to do what she needed to."

"How can we live with half a soul?"

"You can't indefinitely. In the short term, you probably can't tell the difference, though you may start losing control more quickly than normal. Control of your anger, your actions."

"That's already happening. One of my men has lost control completely."

"He was probably the first to have his soul split."

"How do we get our souls back?"

"Kill the clones."

"Done. The way we kill any draden? By pulling their hearts out?"

"Yes. But be careful, Warrior. They may look identical to you, but they're not. They're energy creatures. They won't bleed. And like any draden, if they get their mouths on you, they'll try to drink your life force. And these draden are as big and strong as you are. They might well kill you."

"Understood."

"Lyon," the Shaman said. "Beware the witch. She's strong. Stronger than any Mage I've run across in more than a thousand years. She's come into possession of old magic. Powerful magic. Be very, very careful."

"I'll do whatever I must to stop her, Shaman. That's the only promise I make."

He snapped his phone closed and reached for his knife.

"Want to explain what's happened to our souls, Chief?" Jag drawled.

"In a minute. Give me your hands."

Without hesitation, the three warriors thrust their palms toward him. Not even Jag complained. Three quick, shallow cuts confirmed that they were flesh and blood. He cut his own and held it up like a badge of honor, but the others only looked at him with confusion.

"What's up, Roar?" Tighe asked.

"Kara's in trouble. Hell, we're all in trouble."

"They've stopped." Lyon kept his eyes closed, his senses firmly on Kara as Jag drove. Fear for her clawed at his insides. He shouldn't have left her. Dammit, when was he going to learn? She belonged with him. By his side.

"Where?" Paenther asked.

"Somewhere between the I–95 and Route 50 exits."

"That doesn't narrow it down much. What exits are around there?"

"I don't think they took an exit. It felt like she stopped. Wait. Now she's moving again. Slowly. Very slowly." His heart lurched on a spark of hope. "I think she's running."

"Good for her," Jag said, his voice little more than a growl.

"The sun sets in less than an hour," Tighe said. Less than an hour before the draden would be on top of her. Then again, with a draden clone chasing her, she might not have even that long.

Ahead, the road curved, revealing a sea of brake lights.

Jag swore and slammed on the breaks.

"Where's that plane of yours when we need it, Tighe?" Paenther growled.

"About two hours west of here this time of night. If only we had Hawke." His words fell into the silence like rocks on glass. "The real Hawke," he amended. "When he could shift."

"He's still not answering his phone?" Jag asked.

"No," Paenther said, his voice grim. "None of them are."

Lyon stared at the stopped cars ahead. No way in hell was he sitting in traffic while Kara fought for her life. As the Hummer came to a complete stop, Lyon reached for the handle.

"I'm running. If you start moving again, pick me up."

He jumped out of the car, slammed the door, and took off along the shoulder. His speed in this form was, unfortunately, no faster than human, but he could keep it up indefinitely. And he was moving a hell of a lot faster than the cars.

His senses stayed on Kara. He couldn't feel her emotions from here and was almost glad for it. He knew she was terrified. If she was running, she'd figured out Hawke wasn't who she'd thought. If that clone caught her, she was going to be in pain.

His own fear was nearly more than he could bear—the fear that his senses would suddenly lose her, and he'd know that the only light that had ever shone in his soul had gone forever dark.

Kara ran for her life, down a steep embankment off the highway, toward a cluster of old buildings. Behind her she heard the blare of horns and looked over her shoulder. The man who was not Hawke had left his car in the middle of the Beltway and was chasing her, a large, lidded bucket swinging from one hand.

She knew what he intended to use the bucket for. To take her blood back to Zaphene. The witch would use it to free the High Daemon and his horde who, in turn, would try to destroy the Ferals. He couldn't get her blood. Never mind that she'd probably die in the process.

Even running as fast as she could, the man was faster, his legs longer. Too late, she realized she'd run into a dead end, a loading dock that was closed and deserted. Her heart stuttered. Sweat rolled between her breasts as she turned around, her skirt flaring around her legs, but the man blocked her escape, his arms spread wide as if daring her to try to get past him.

She wouldn't make it. He was too fast.

Instead, she dashed toward one of three doors lining the loading dock and pulled, praying it was unlocked, but nothing happened. With a groan of frustration, she started for the second, but she never made it. The creature grabbed her from behind and threw her against the wall. Her head collided with concrete.

Dimly, through a haze of pain, she was aware of being dragged to the edge of the raised sidewalk and pinned, facedown, with a knee to her back. She heard the echo of plastic against plastic and the clatter of the bucket being dropped to the ground several feet below. As her head started to clear, the pressure in her back released long enough for her to be pushed forward until her head and shoulders extended over the edge.

She struggled against the impending fall, but the knee slammed into her back, pinning her hard. A hand grabbed a fistful of her hair and yanked her head back.

Her eyes swam with tears at the pulling at her scalp. Her pulse thudded. "Are you going to kill me?"

"My mission is to retrieve your blood. Your body is no longer important to my mistress. I will devour your life force."

"*What are you?*"

"I am what I am."

"Is he . . . is Hawke dead?"

"I cannot live unless he lives."

Thank God for small favors. But the gleam of metal caught her eye and she knew Hawke's survival was the only good news she was going to get.

The searing pain of the knife slicing her tender throat nearly sent her into oblivion. The drip of her blood into the bucket sounded obscenely loud, growing into a steady stream before it slowed again as her body healed. He sliced her throat again.

A second later, he yanked her sweater off her shoulder and sank his teeth into her flesh.

Her scream caught in her throat, finding no way out. Tears ran down her cheeks to mix with her blood as she felt him stealing her energy. Her life. Just like the draden had tried to do.

But the pain of the wounds was nothing compared to the pain in her heart. *Lyon.* He'd find her too late. And he needed her.

She couldn't die.

She wouldn't die, dammit.

In the far reaches of her mind she remembered Lyon's voice telling her draden couldn't feed off her in full radiance.

But radiance had to come through the fire and she needed Earth. No going radiant in the house, Lyon had said. And the concrete would block her just as surely as the house's floor would.

Lyon.

Her love for him turned to desperation. She had to live. For him, she had to live.

The Earth. Connect to the Earth. Struggling to free herself from the fear and the pain, she sent her senses outward. She felt the wind caressing her damp cheeks. Wind. Air. These were of the Earth.

She pulled. Like a vacuum, she pulled and pulled.

Her senses caught on Lyon. Running. Anguish.

She could feel herself growing weaker. *Dammit, she refused to die!*

With a furious effort, Kara called on every scrap of energy left in her body and pulled, envisioning the fire, the radiance.

Envisioning Lyon.

For a moment, she felt him. His determination melding with hers. His power.

The fire erupted inside her, a triumphant rush

of warmth and power racing through her blood, transforming her body into the glowing splendor of full radiance.

The demon released her with a squawk of anger. *Hold it,* she told herself. Now that she had the radiance, she had to hold it. Her life depended on it. But she was so weak.

Sweat broke out on her brow and ran down her temples. Lyon's face swam in her mind's eye. The pain in his eyes when he found her in the dungeon. The heat as he made love to her. And the tenderness when he'd asked her to stay behind. Safe with Hawke.

Finding her dead would destroy him.

She held on to the radiance with everything she had until she was shaking from the effort.

Finally, the creature released her hair. Her chin slammed into the cement, shooting her head full of stars, but she held the radiance, knowing it was her only way back to Lyon.

She heard her assailant jump to the asphalt below, screw the lid on the bucket, and hurry away.

Still, she stayed radiant, feeling the warmth slowly heal her and the glow renew her strength. When she was able, she lifted her head and rolled onto her back, away from the edge. A small, exhausted smile tugged at her mouth.

She'd survived.

Her senses swam outward, seeking Lyon, sharing her triumph. His relief rushed over in a blazing kaleidoscope of emotion she could only believe was love. The gray clouds above turned to silver crystals through her tears. He'd never told her he loved her. He'd never said the words. But the love that flowed out of him, even from this distance, filled her with a warmth that eased all the pain, all the fear, all the loneliness she'd ever known.

She felt him near and managed to push herself up on her elbow as he ran up the ramp. He swept her up and into his arms, burying his face in her hair. For a long time he didn't say a word, just held her, quaking.

Finally, he pulled back, his pained gaze searching her face. "You're okay."

"I'm fine."

His eyes grew tormented. "I felt you slipping away."

"He was feeding off me. Like a draden."

"That's what he was. A draden grown into a clone." His expression shifted, turning amazed. "How did you ever go radiant here?"

Kara lifted her shoulder in a small shrug. "It was either that or die." She looked at him with all the emotion in her heart. "And I couldn't leave you."

The love that shone from his eyes made tears form in her own. He kissed her long and tenderly, then pulled back.

"You'd better put out your light before anybody sees you." He started down the ramp, carrying her as if she weighed nothing.

"He filled a bucket with my blood." Kara let herself release the radiance.

"We believe the witch plans to use the clones to free the Daemons. Probably as soon as this one returns. We're going there now, as soon as Jag gets here with the car."

"Lyon, don't leave me behind again. They've already got what they need from me. I'm not in danger anymore."

"If those Daemons are freed, we're all in danger." His gaze met hers, his amber eyes at once infinitely soft and hard as stone. "But I'm never letting you out of my sight again."

A sense of urgency charged the air in the Hummer as they finally reached Feral House more than an hour later. For the entire drive, Lyon had cradled Kara against him in the backseat, reassuring himself over and over that she was all right. That she was alive. He'd never felt so helpless in his life as when he'd sensed her life draining away and had been too far away to stop it. He'd died a hundred deaths as he'd run, trying to reach her before it was too late.

But his little warrior had saved herself.

"He's already here," Paenther said. The car hadn't come to a full stop when the men flung the doors open and leaped out.

Lyon pulled Kara out behind him. As much as he wanted to keep her away from the witch, he wouldn't leave her behind again. As the breeze rushed over him, something rancid crawled over his skin.

"Ritual magic," Tighe said. "They've already started."

"Let's go!" As Lyon ran for the house, he pointed right. "Paenther and Jag take the rear." All rituals took time to complete, but there was no way to know how long ago they'd started. They might have nearly a half an hour to stop the Daemons from rising. Or mere seconds.

Lyon, Kara, and Tighe ran for the front steps. While Lyon pushed Kara behind him, Tighe opened the door and slipped inside.

"All clear," he called softly. They had no way to know if the real Foxx, Hawke, and Kougar would try to ambush them. No way to know what the witch had done to their minds.

The three raced for the door to the lower chambers, but as Tighe reached for the doorknob, his hand stopped abruptly.

Tighe swore. "A barrier."

Hell. Lyon slammed his fists over every inch of the door and never touched it. The entry was completely sealed off with magic. Tighe slammed his shoulder at the portal and bounced right off.

"It's sealed tight."

Lyon grabbed Kara's hand and nodded. "Back door." But they hadn't even reached the kitchen when Paenther and Jag came bounding into the hallway.

"It's blocked off magically," Jag said. "We can't touch them."

"Are the others here?" Paenther asked.

"Haven't looked. Tighe and Jag, find them." As the two warriors took off, Lyon met Paenther's gaze. "What do you suggest?" he asked his second. "How are we going to break through?"

The black-eyed warrior scowled. "In my animal form, I could breach that kind of magic. We all could."

"How?" Kara asked, the color high in her cheeks, the scars across her throat fading, though paining him still. "Why in your animal forms and not your human?"

Lyon squeezed her hand. "It's through our animal forms that we acquire the mystical power we need to fight this kind of magic."

"So if I were ascended, you could get through?"

"Yes. But you're not."

"How about we try punching a hole in the floor and dropping in on them that way?" Paenther suggested.

"Let's do it."

"I'll grab some tools out of the storeroom."

As Paenther took off, Kara pulled on his hand and stepped in front of him, her blue eyes hard as steel. "Ascend me."

Her words ran through him like a sharp bite of electricity. "No." He refused even to contemplate it.

Tighe and Jag came down the hall. "No sign of them. Not even Pink."

Lyon's fists tightened. At the sound of Kara's wince, he realized he'd about crushed her hand. "Sorry."

"They're not dead," Kara told them. "Hawke's clone said the clones can only live as long as the original lives. She won't kill them until she no longer needs the clones."

"Until she's freed the Daemons," Jag said. "They'll probably be Satanan's first meal."

Frustration and urgency lapped at Lyon's nerves until he thought he'd go mad with it. He had to reach that witch!

"Move the rug," he ordered, pointing to the runner in the hallway. "We're going to try going through the floor."

Paenther returned a minute later with two hatchets, a crowbar, and a pair of heavy mallets. They worked quickly, but it was soon apparent that no matter what they did, they couldn't create a hole.

Jag scowled. "The bitch was thorough."

"You have to ascend me," Kara said loudly enough that every man straightened and stared at her.

"No," Lyon said. "We don't know who your mate is."

She met his gaze, her eyes calm and sure. "It's you. You're going to ascend me." She turned to Tighe. "Can four of you do the ritual?"

Tighe's startled gaze swung to Lyon. "Yes. If necessary." He turned back to Kara. "I think you're right. I think Lyon's your mate. But if he's not, you'll die, Kara. None of us is willing to risk that."

Kara pulled her hand from Lyon's and stepped away from his side, making his beast roar in protest. She faced Tighe. "If the wrong man ascends me, will you still gain the power you need to shift into your animals?"

Tighe looked to Lyon, his eyes pleading for help.

Kara turned impatiently, her gaze flicking between Jag and Paenther. "I need an answer. Will you get what you need to reach the chambers and stop her from freeing the Daemons?"

"Yes," Jag said, the word low and pained.

Paenther nodded. "But if the Feral who ascends you isn't your mate, the power that renews us will kill you, Kara."

She turned back to Lyon. He felt the strength in those eyes, strength that outweighed his by two metric tons. "If you don't stop that ritual, the Daemons will kill your friends. And then you. And then me. They'll go on a rampage that will destroy everything and everyone we know and love." She shook her head slowly. "There's no choice, Lyon. And there's no time. You need to ascend me, and you need to do it now."

She was right. Dammit to hell, she was right. And it was killing him.

He couldn't lose her. None of them could afford to lose her. She'd demanded they use her once and would do it again even knowing she might die. He marveled at her courage and knew she was the finest Radiant they'd ever had. Would probably ever have. The Ferals needed her in their midst. At their heart.

She *was* their heart.

She was his life.

Lyon shook his head. "I can't lose you."

Kara's eyes softened and she stepped in front of him and took his hands in hers. "I'm not going to die, Lyon. You're my mate. I'm sure of it." She squeezed his hands with strength like steel. "You can't let those Daemons be freed, Lyon. And right this minute, the witch is down there freeing them."

Though his beast roared its denial, Lyon knew she was right. Nothing mattered but stopping the Daemons. No single life weighed in that balance.

He closed his eyes against the pain of what he must do, then opened them and met her certain gaze, and he nodded. "Paenther, prepare the circle out back. We'll meet you there in a minute. She needs to be prepared."

"Roar . . ." Tighe's voice held a pain they all shared.

But Lyon didn't relent. He couldn't. "We're shifting, but for Kara's sake, keep your clothes on. You can buy new ones later."

His blood was like ice at the thought of what he must do.

But it was the only way to save his world and the people he cared about. The people he loved.

The only way.

"Get undressed," Lyon said, stepping over the wreckage to reach the largest of the three closets in the Radiant's bedchambers.

Kara stripped out of her clothes as she watched him, her love for him stronger than anything she'd ever felt. She was sure of what she was doing. They had to be able to reach their animals.

But she wasn't positive she was going to live through it. Deep in her soul, she knew Lyon was the love of her life, but whether the Earth knew that was another matter. And if the Earth disagreed, she was dead. But this death would be different than the one she'd faced before. This time it was on her terms. For the right reason. In the arms of the man she loved.

Lyon came to her with a blue gown, its sleeves long and full. She lifted her arms for him to put it over her head.

"Not yet," he said. He tossed the gown on the bed, yanked off his shirt, and pulled the armband with the lion's head off his arm.

"What are you doing?" she asked, as he hooked it around her upper arm, squeezing it tight. "I thought you needed that."

"This is the way it's done." He picked up her gown and she lifted her arms for him to slide it over her. The dress fell to her ankles in a soft, silken cloud, the wide sleeves brushing the backs of her hands.

Lyon pulled his shirt back on, then gripped her shoulders, his hands steady and firm, his eyes dark, deep, and pained. "You are the most amazing woman I've ever known." His hands slid to frame her face. "I love you, Kara. If there was any way but this, I would choose it. But this is the way it has to be."

She covered his hands with her own. "I'm not going to die, Lyon. You're my mate. I know it's you."

He kissed her softly, then pulled away, closing his eyes as if he couldn't bear for her to see the pain in them. "Let's go."

As they went out the back door, she looked at the dark sky with trepidation. "What about the draden?"

"We have a sacred circle in the backyard. The men have already raised the Feral Circle. We'll be as well protected here as on the goddess stone."

The sacred fires were already lit and the flames cast shadows over the faces of the three men waiting for them. Tighe, Paenther, and Jag stood barefoot, divested of jackets and belts, but otherwise fully clothed. She suspected they usually shifted in the nude and was glad for Lyon's intervention. It was hard enough to accept what she was going to have to do in front of them, but to watch their bodies reacting to it would have been too much.

No, she amended. It would have been uncomfortable, but that was all. She was more than prepared to do whatever she must to give these men the power they needed to defeat Zaphene and save the world.

Lyon squeezed her hand. "Don't call the fire until I say." He pulled her into the center of the circle and into his arms. His mouth covered hers in a fierce kiss of love and possession and aching loss.

He thought he was going to lose her. She could feel it in the way he held her, could sense his sorrow in every touch. He thought she was going to die.

But when she tried to pull away to reassure him, he held her fast. His tongue slid against hers with frantic strokes, sending fire pouring through her body until she was clinging to him, moaning with need, a second away from release.

He pulled back, leaving her wanting, and gripped her head, his gaze boring into hers. "I love you. I've lived more these past days with you than I have in seven hundred years. Live for me, Kara. You have to live."

She smiled, tears gathering in her eyes. He loved her. What's more he knew it. "I'm not going to die," she whispered, despite the fear beginning to lap at her courage.

"No. You're not."

He shoved his tongue into her mouth once more, nearly sending her over the edge, then pulled back and turned her around to face the three men.

To her surprise, Jag leaned forward to kiss her cheek.

Paenther did the same on the other side. "Stay with us, Kara." He pulled out his knife. "I'll make the cuts shallow. Give me your hand."

He made a tiny cut in her palm, then a mirroring cut in Tighe's. Tighe held out his hands to her. "I'll hold you steady." When she placed her hands in his, he kissed her forehead. "This is going to work, Kara. We're not going to lose you."

Jag and Paenther knelt on one knee on either side of her. Paenther sliced each of their palms, made small cuts in each of her ankles, then tossed the knife into the grass.

Kara looked over her shoulder, needing to see the man she loved more than life, meeting Lyon's gaze for perhaps the last time. His eyes caressed her and loved her as hers did him.

"Turn around, sweetheart," he said softly. "Tighe."

While Lyon gripped her hips, Tighe stepped back, forcing her to bend over.

Paenther murmured odd words, intoning the ritual chant.

Her pulse began to race with an odd mixture of embarrassment, excitement, and fear. Lyon's hands squeezed her hips gently, reassuring her, sending a cascade of warm, damp need to her throbbing center.

"Call the fire, Kara," Lyon said softly. "But don't go radiant. Not until I say."

Tighe squeezed her hands, telegraphing his tension, a tension she suspected they all shared. She didn't want to die. Not now. Not when she'd found her place. Her heart.

She took a deep breath, finding her courage, then concentrated on pulling the fire.

"Done," Tighe said. Tendrils of blue flame leaked out between their clasped hands.

The sound of Lyon's zipper sliding and the faint rustle of clothing behind her sent her pulse into orbit. She felt him lift her dress, felt the cool breeze waft over her bare flesh. Lyon's fingers curled around her hips.

"Spread your legs, Kara."

She did as he asked, the men's hands retaining their grip on her ankles. She felt the damp tip of Lyon's erection slide against the hot center of her need. Then he slid inside her with a single perfect thrust. Kara gasped and arched at the rush of pleasure.

Lyon pulled out, then pushed himself into her again, filling her, his entry slow and careful, as if he wanted to savor every moment, every touch. He pulled out, then pushed into her again and again until her body quickened and she was on the verge of shattering.

"Now, Kara," Lyon said, his voice strained. "Call the radiance. *Now.*"

She could barely think. Struggling against the thick swirl of pleasure, she drew the fire in one hard pull at the very instant Lyon thrust hard into her, sending her over the edge. Her body tightened and burst on an incredible release, the radiance rushing through her in a torrent of heat, licking at her skin, filling her with a powerful blend of pleasure and strength, life and rightness.

A scream tore from her throat, pure triumph.

A scream mirrored in the triumphant yells of the men. As Lyon pulled out of her, the hands holding her fell away and she opened her eyes to find three huge, feral cats shimmering to life before her. Chills raced over her skin.

It worked! *She was alive.* She grinned and whirled to Lyon.

And watched in horror as he collapsed to the ground. Not a lion. A man. A man who appeared to all the world to be dead.

"No!" She fell to her knees beside him as her fingers flew to his neck, searching for a pulse that wasn't there.

"*Lyon.*"

"*Roar.*" Tighe dropped on the other side of him, a man once more. "What happened?"

"I don't know," she cried. "It worked. I thought it worked."

"Look." Paenther grabbed her wrist and yanked up the sleeve of her gown, exposing the armband Lyon had given her, the lion's eyes glowing bright amber.

"*Shit,*" Jag said.

Kara looked at Tighe, her blood turning to ice. "He told me this is the way it's done, but it's not, is it?"

Tighe shook his head. "Dammit, Roar."

Her gaze flew from one man to the next. "How do we help him?"

Jag just shook his head.

"We don't," Paenther said, releasing her arm. "Not even a Feral can survive a blast like that without the means to channel it. He sacrificed himself rather than risk your life, Kara."

"He loved you," Tighe said, simply, his voice hollow.

Kara couldn't believe it. They were giving up. "There's got to be a way!"

Tighe's eyes burned with pain. "If only there were."

Kara's mind went white with shock as if all the color had drained from the world.

"We've got to stop those Daemons," Jag said.

"Go." She flung her arm out. "Don't let him have made this sacrifice in vain."

Around her, the three men shifted back into a life-sized tiger, panther, and jaguar, and leaped away. As she watched, through a haze of pain, they crashed through the doors into the underground chambers and disappeared.

Chapter
Twenty-two

Kara turned on Lyon, her anguish turning to fury. "I hate you for this! It would have worked, Lyon. I know it. And if it didn't, *I'd* have been the one to die. It should have been me. *Me*."

Tears blurred her vision and ran down her cheeks. "Oh, God, Lyon, how am I supposed to live without you? I love you, dammit. I love you."

She was buzzing like a power station with enough energy running through her to light up half the state of Virginia, yet she couldn't save the man she loved.

Lyon needed her power. He needed . . .

Her mind started to spin. *He needed his heart jump-started.*

She ripped the gold band off her arm and curled it around his far larger one. Her pulse began to thrum. Humans came back from stopped hearts all the time, didn't they? There had to be a way to use this power to help him. Dammit, she wasn't going to let him go without a fight.

She sniffled, wiping her eyes on her sleeve, then ripped his shirt open.

Blood. She needed blood to blood, a conduit for the power. A knife. She leaped up and retrieved the one Paenther had tossed in the grass. Sparing no time, she sliced two deep cuts in Lyon's chest and matching cuts in her palms, then dropped the blade and straddled Lyon, pressing her palms to his chest, mingling their blood.

She was running on instinct now. With her shins and bare feet on the ground, she called to the Earth and was amazed at how easily she went to radiance now that she was ascended. Power burst through her, nearly more than she could contain. She struggled to control it, then focused it through her hands and into Lyon.

"Please, Mother," she prayed to the Earth. "Please give this warrior life again. Help me save him. I need him. *I love him.*"

Tears streamed down her cheeks. "Lyon, come back to me," she choked, and on a wave of fury and desperation, pulled more power and more and more until her skin glowed so brightly she had to close her eyes against the near-painful brilliance. She grabbed the knife and reopened the healing cuts on her hands, then slid her palms into the seeping blood on Lyon's chest, cuts that weren't healing. With a scream of fury, she poured everything she had into him, over and over until she was drenched with sweat.

"You're not going to die!" she screamed. "You're not!"

"Kara." The sound of her name from Lyon's lips was the sweetest she'd ever heard.

"You're alive," Kara gasped. She was glowing too brightly to be able to see him.

She felt his hands sliding up her hips, their grip weak. "Passion and pain," he whispered. "Blood and sex."

"Sex." My God, how was she to do it with him when he was barely alive? But as she tried to scoot past his loins, she came upon a massive, hard erection. "Gotcha."

She rose onto her knees, pulled the dress to her waist, and took him deep inside her again. As she rode him, she grabbed the knife, cut her palms and reached for his chest, clasping her hands to his own still-open cuts.

Mind spinning, she remembered how he'd had her pull the radiance as she came. With an effort, she released the glow and let her skin go dark as she pressed down on him, released him, then pressed down again. Lyon's hands fell from her hips.

Her heart clutched. She shouldn't have released the radiance. He needed the power and now he was too weak.

"Lyon, kiss me. *Make me come.*" She leaned low and covered his mouth with hers, sliding her tongue between his lips.

She felt him stir, felt the gentle slide of his tongue and the almost instantaneous race of fire to her core. She kissed him, rode him, pressed her bloody hands to his open chest and rose, gasping with the growing pressure between her legs. Cresting.

As the orgasm exploded, she reared up, pulling the power harder than she ever had before. Light flared, lighting the entire backyard, turning night to day.

Strong hands gripped her hips. "Kara," Lyon groaned, taking over, pushing hard inside her. "Goddess, but I love you." He thrust into her until she came again, screaming. And suddenly the man beneath her began to change.

With a gasp, Kara dove sideways into the grass and watched as the man she loved turned into the king of beasts, an exquisite, full-maned lion. He rolled onto his feet and shook, then looked at her, joy and love shining in the amber eyes she'd come to know so well. She scrambled to her feet and ran her hands through his mane.

"We're going in together."

He shook his massive head, but she ignored him and climbed onto his back. "You told me you were never leaving me behind again. I'm taking you at your word. Besides, I'm not helpless, in case you hadn't noticed. This is my fight, too. And your men may need my help."

The lion beneath her lifted his head and gave a roar that shook the ground and could have crumbled less sturdy buildings, but when his emotions washed over her, she felt the strength and warmth of his pride in her. And his love.

Kara patted his lion's shoulder. "Let's kill us a witch, my heart." Grabbing tight hold of his mane, she held on as he bounded forward and leaped through the mangled remains of the doors, to the deep bowels of Feral House. And into the heart of the battle.

Kara took in the scene of devastation in the dim, smoky dungeon. Horror ripped along her spine at the sight of three strong Feral bodies littering the floor, headless.

Bloodless.

Not Ferals. *Clones. Thank God.*

Zaphene stood back from the action, dressed much as she'd been the first time Kara saw her, in a slinky dress and high, strappy heels, her red hair loose and stylish, her gaze locked on Kara with malice and dismay. A chill rippled over Kara's flesh, the icy shadow of remembered terror as she met the witch's copper-ringed eyes.

Her pulse skittered, her body flushed cold, then hot as fury slowly overtook the fear. This woman, this . . . *thing* . . . threatened everything she'd come to hold dear. Lyon. The other Ferals. The *world.*

And Kara wasn't helpless anymore.

"Get them!" Zaphene shrieked at the clones. "I want them alive."

Kara's quick gaze scanned the room, looking for Vhyper, remembering now, all too well, how he'd strung her up and stripped her down, then directed the clones to shove the blades deep inside her. Her courage steadied as she saw no sign of him.

Jag and Paenther were engaged in battle with two clones each. Tighe was nowhere to be seen. But at the sight of their leader returned, the two great cats let out long, feral cries.

Kara could almost feel their gladness and the leaping of their spirits.

As she watched, Paenther flew at one of the clones, taking a blade deep in his gut as the second clone rushed him.

Beneath her, Lyon's muscles bunched. *Get down, little one.* Lyon's voice sounded in her head. *Be safe.*

She slid quickly off his back and watched him join Paenther. With a single, massive paw, he knocked Kougar back, then leaped on him, grabbing the Feral's head with his massive jaws and ripped it clean off his body.

The violence of the act sent shock jangling along her nerve endings until the startling absence of blood jerked her back to her senses. Not Kougar. Draden clone.

As the Wulfe clone beat off Lyon with a sword, Kara saw a flash of blue and turned to see Zaphene hurrying toward the door.

"The witch! She's escaping."

Paenther lunged after her, leaving Lyon to battle the Wulfe clone.

Kara turned to find Jag battling valiantly, but the two clones were getting the better of him. Jag's fur was matted with blood, one hip partly cleaved from his body. He needed help.

While one clone, a draden who looked exactly like Lyon, hacked at the sleek animal, the other attempted to avoid Jag's raking claws and tie him with a thick rope. Her heart fought with her mind as she watched the twin of the man she loved attacking this animal she knew to be a friend. When a vicious swipe of the sword nearly took off Jag's other hind leg, she moved, fury sweeping caution to the winds. That cat was *hers*. They weren't going to harm him.

She remembered something Lyon had said about a Radiant who'd thrown fire. Focusing inward, she pulled the power into her palm and threw it, hard, watching it land well short of its target, disappearing in a puff of smoke as it hit the floor. But she wasn't deterred.

Magic, she reminded herself, worked . . . well . . . like magic.

Jag attacked Lyon's clone, biting the hand that held the sword. But the other clone leaped in to attack him.

The great cat went down.

Moving closer, Kara pulled more fire, this time visualizing the flame hitting the second clone and spreading, consuming him. With a heave, she threw the fire and watched her visualization turn to reality, the flame spreading over his body like an oil slick. The clone yelled with pain, falling backward as fire engulfed him.

Before she could call the fire again, let alone find the steel to destroy the man who looked so much like the one she loved, Lyon's clone leaped at her, tackling her to the ground. Her breath rushed out of her body, her head cracking against the floor, the radiance evaporating as it if had never been.

In her head she heard Lyon's voice. *Kara!*

Lyon's face swam before her dazed vision, then disappeared as sharp teeth dug into the side of her neck and began to suck the life's energy from her battered body.

The weight left her in a flash of spotted fur.

Kara gasped for breath, feeling the blood trickle down her neck from where the clone had fed from her. Her ribs cried with pain, but she struggled to sit up, then stumbled to her feet as Jag ripped out the heart of Lyon's clone and tore its head from its body. The last of the clones had gone down.

Her gaze searched frantically for the real Lyon, needing reassurance, and found the cat with Paenther, surrounding the witch.

Are you all right? His voice rang through her head as the cat's head swung toward her. Not certain how to answer a voice in her head she just nodded.

She's trying to shield herself from us, magically, but she's weakening. Can you help Jag?

Her mind slowly clearing, she realized the spotted fur that had saved her was lying at her feet, his blood spreading in a pool around them both. She gripped her aching ribs and reached for the downed cat.

"It's me, Jag. I'm going to try to heal us both." Forcing her hands away from their protective cage around her middle, she pressed her palms to Jag's blood-soaked fur and pulled.

The fire came slowly, but it came, filling her with warmth, then heat, then light as she went fully radiant. Little by little, she felt the pain ease from her body, and sensed the strength flowing into Jag, mending his torn flesh. When his jaguar's head gently butted her arm, she knew she'd succeeded. He leaped to his feet, then startled her with a quick lick of his tongue on her cheek.

A soft burst of laughter eased from her throat, and she stroked the spotted cat as he passed her to join the others.

Kara bent down to pick up one of the blood-soaked swords lying on the ground and slowly went to face the woman who'd caused her so much pain.

The three cats snapped and clawed at the witch, wearing down the unnatural barrier she hid behind.

Zaphene laughed. "You can't touch me!" But her voice rang with false bravado. In her eyes, Kara saw the hard shine of fear.

Kara went to stand beside Lyon, seeing bloody streaks across his back. She laid her hand lightly

on one of the cuts and poured healing energy into
him.

I love you, he said in her mind.

She stroked his muscled back. "And I you." She
met the witch's copper-ringed gaze. "You're not
going anywhere, Zaphene."

"Vhyper will be back."

"Vhyper will be free of you once you're dead."

Something in the witch's eyes made Kara shiver.

Zaphene shook her head, her smile certain.
"Vhyper is not under my control. He's no longer
one of you."

"What is he, then?" Kara repeated the question
Lyon put in her head.

"The Daemon blade, when it drank of the Ferals'
blood, stole Vhyper's soul. Vhyper does Satanan's
work, now."

She dies, Lyon said.

Kara patted Lyon's back. "I want the killing
blow."

She sensed his approval.

Agreed, my little warrior.

"If I add my power to yours, can we break
through her barrier sooner?"

Yes. Do it.

Kara laid the sword at her feet, then pressed her
palms to the backs of the cats on either side of her,
Lyon's, and Paenther's. "Jag, come lean against my
leg, please."

The cat trotted obediently to her side and slid
his head against her. With her gaze locked on Zaphene's, Kara pulled a great fist of power from the

Earth and directly into the cats until their very fur began to glow.

Then, as one, the three huge cats flew at the witch, tackling her to the ground in a tumble of fur, high heels, and Mage blood.

Zaphene screamed as the cats' strong jaws ripped at her limbs. Lyon's paw covered her face, holding her down as he lifted his maned head to Kara, pride shining in his eyes.

Your turn, little warrior.

Kara picked up the sword. Never in her wildest dreams could she have imagined intentionally taking a life. But this *thing* needed to die.

"Let her see me," she told Lyon.

Lyon lifted his massive paw. Copper-ringed eyes stared up at her with terror.

"You'll never mess with me or mine again," Kara vowed. She lifted the blade high over her head, and plunged it down in a shower of fire and blood.

Lyon lifted his head on a powerful, satisfied roar. As one, the three cats shimmered in a rainbow of light, changing to bloody, naked warriors. So like their clones until she looked into their eyes and saw raw admiration.

And in Lyon's, love.

His arm curled around her shoulders and he pulled her into his arms. "You were magnificent."

"Where's Tighe?" Jag asked. "And Vhyper?"

Kara's smile died before it was fully born.

"Vhyper fled, and Tighe followed." Paenther grabbed one of the torches off the wall and took off at a run, deeper into the dungeons.

Lyon grabbed her hand, and together they and Jag followed close behind. As they rounded the corner, they found the great orange-and-black-striped cat lying unmoving in a damp, empty chamber.

The men knelt at the cat's side, Paenther digging his fingers into the tiger's neck fur.

"He's alive, but barely. His pulse is slow, Roar." Disbelief shimmered in his eyes. "Vhyper poisoned him. I smell it."

Lyon shook his head. "How could Vhyper have shifted? He wasn't with us during the Ascension."

Jag snorted. "There's been some heavy shit magic going on down here. The witch must be right about the blade stealing Vhype's soul. That snake knows his venom can be deadly, even to us."

"Find him," Lyon ordered. "And find the rest of my men."

As Paenther and Jag ran from the room, Kara fell to her knees beside Tighe, her heart clenched in fear, her stomach tight with misery. She stroked her hand into his fur, settling it on his chest as she searched for sign of life.

"Can a Feral survive Vhyper's poison?"

"For a short time, though we've never had to test it. He's used it against the Mage before. That poison attacks even immortal bodies and will eventually destroy them."

Kara felt movement, the slight rise and fall of Tighe's breast. "He's still alive."

She pressed both palms to his fur and poured her radiance into him. Lyon squatted on the other side of the tiger and slid his hand into his friend's fur, his expression grim as he watched her.

"Do you feel anything?" he asked.

"No. Nothing's happening." She pressed power into Tighe until sweat rolled down her temples, but still he didn't respond.

"Look what I found," Jag said and she looked up to see Wulfe, Kougar, Foxx, and the real Hawke standing behind him, fully clothed. Wulfe was blinking as if he'd just woken from a long sleep. Behind them, Pink entered in her birdlike gait.

Hawke frowned at Tighe. "What happened?"

"Long story," Jag countered. To Lyon he said, "Wulfe seems to be back to normal now that he's got the other half of his soul back. I found Kougar, Hawke, Foxx, and Pink in the prison cells, too. The witch wasn't taking any chances."

"Where's Zaphene?" Foxx demanded.

Kara grimaced, feeling sorry for the young warrior and hoping his emotions had only been manipulated by the witch and not truly engaged. Or he was going to be hurting.

Jag put his hand on Foxx's shoulder and led him away from the others to talk to him.

Beneath Kara's hands, Tighe wasn't responding. She turned off the radiance, letting herself go dark as she held up her hand. "I need a knife."

"No," Lyon said. "His blood's been poisoned. You're not going to mix it with yours."

Love for him overflowed even as she met his gaze with calm certainty. "This is my purpose. To heal and empower the Ferals. He's mine. You're all mine. I love you, Lyon, but don't stand in my way of what I have to do."

He stared at her for one long moment before scowling. "Damn, you're bossy."

She grinned at him. "That's why I'm so sure we belong together."

A smile twitched at his mouth, but never quite erased the worry in his eyes. "Don't make the cuts any deeper than you have to."

"I won't."

Lyon's mouth compressed, but he pulled out one of his switchblades and made small cuts in the centers of her upturned palms. He turned to Tighe and dug the blade into the fur at the animal's shoulder.

Silence blanketed the room as Kara pressed her bloody hands to the tiger's fresh wound. "Come back to us, Tighe." She paused before pulling the fire, visualizing what she wanted. A blast of energy so strong it charged into Tighe and shot him to his feet, whole and alive. Kara took a deep breath and pulled hard.

Power leaped into her in a blinding rush and poured into the animal beneath her hands. More. *More.*

"Damn," someone muttered behind her.

Tighe stirred, filling with the power as Lyon and Jag had before him. Strong arms gripped her and pulled her back as Tighe shook like a great cat coming awake, then shifted into human form, immediately covering his eyes. Unlike the other three cats, Tighe retained his clothes when he shifted and looked strangely and completely normal.

"Someone turn off the lights or get me my shades," he growled.

Kara laughed, relief and joy bubbling through her as she let go of the radiance and went to slide into Lyon's arms.

Tighe's face took on a sudden fury. "Kara get away from him! He's a clone."

Lyon held up his free arm, crisscrossed with barely healed cuts. "The clones are dead, Tighe."

Kara nodded. "You missed a lot."

Paenther moved into the circle, pants now covering his lower half, two extra pairs in his hands. He tossed one each to Jag and Lyon, then pressed his fist to Tighe's shoulder.

"Welcome back."

"Did you find Vhyper?" Lyon asked.

"He's gone, along with his car."

"Hell."

Tighe shook his head, still staring at Lyon. "I saw you die."

Lyon released her as Tighe closed the distance between the two men and flung his arms around Lyon in a hard, warrior's embrace. He pulled back, thrust his hand out, and when Lyon grasped his arm, gripped Lyon's shoulder with his free hand. A grin slowly swallowed his face.

"Damn I'm glad to see you. How . . . ?"

Lyon looked down at Kara with a suspicious sheen of moisture in his eyes. "Our Radiant might just be the most stubborn woman who ever lived."

"You should have seen her, Stripes," Jag drawled, pulling on his pants. "Kara demanded the witch's head. And took it."

Paenther turned to her, the hard intensity of his eyes softened by gratitude. And maybe respect. To her surprise, he dropped to one knee in front of her and slammed his fist to his heart.

"I pledge my life to the defense of you and yours, Radiant. Not out of duty, though I would have for that alone, but because you've proven yourself worthy in every way. Courageous, devoted, selfless. May we be as worthy of you."

Jag dropped to one knee beside Paenther without hesitation. Tighe released Lyon and joined them. The other Ferals stared at the three, then dropped more slowly.

Lyon knelt with his men. "For those who weren't in on the battle, our Radiant has proven herself a true warrior today, risking her safety and her life over and over to advance our purpose and to fight beside us. It was thanks to her courage and sacrifice that we're all still here. And that we prevailed."

The four new arrivals stared at her with curiosity and confusion, then one by one, bowed their heads to her. Behind the men, Pink stood watching her and, like the men, dropped her head in acknowledgment and gratitude.

"I'm honored," Kara said softly, her cheeks growing warm. "And completely overwhelmed."

"We've still got the Daemon blade, right?" Tighe asked.

Paenther and Jag exchanged looks. As one, they leaped to their feet and ran from the room.

"The Daemon blade's gone," Jag said grimly, joining the group in the hallway outside the ritual room a short time later.

Paenther followed close behind him. "Vhyper's car isn't the only one missing. Tighe's Land Rover's gone, and there's no sign of his clone."

"Hell," Lyon said, his men gathered around him after the unfruitful search. Kara stood beside him, her hand tight in his. And damned if his muscles weren't shaking.

They had serious trouble, still. But he could handle it. He could handle the whole world as long as Kara remained by his side.

He didn't want to do another Pairing. He'd already decided it didn't matter who the goddess chose for her. She was his.

But he needed to know. If for no other reason than to know the face of the son of a bitch who would try to steal her away.

If it wasn't him.

Please, Goddess, let it be me.

"We're doing a Pairing," Lyon announced. "Now."

Paenther nodded. "I'll start getting things ready."

"I thought we already did the Pairing," Wulfe said. He looked at Hawke, shaking his head. "I feel like I stumbled into the Twilight Zone."

"Join the club," Hawke muttered.

Ten minutes later, the men stood once more in a circle around the Radiant's pedestal, the ritual fires lit, the blood drawn. Kara was still locked against his side.

Mine, his beast roared.

"It's time," Kougar said.

Kara slipped out of his hold, meeting his gaze with eyes alight with love and promise. A promise he could read clear as day, for it echoed that in his own. No ritual was keeping them apart.

She stepped onto the pedestal without help, proud and confident, so different from the scared, confused woman he'd lifted onto that platform just two days ago. Her gaze met his, held his as Kougar intoned the incantation.

All eyes turned to him.

Kara held out her hand, and he went to her and took her hands, linking her fingers with his.

"You're mine," he said, staking his claim for all to hear.

Tears shimmered in her eyes. "As you're mine. No matter what happens, Lyon. You're my heart and my breath. My soul. And I will love you until the day I die."

Her words echoed the declaration in his heart. "Why are we doing this?" he growled. She was already ascended.

For a terrifying moment, he wondered what he'd do if he wasn't the one chosen to be her mate. Because despite her words, he'd lose her. Sooner or later she'd fall in love with the man who was meant for her. *The Pairing never failed.*

She lifted their joint hands and pressed them against her lips one after the other. "We're doing this because you need to know. Because if we don't, you'll always doubt that my love for you is for always." She released his hands and slid her palm against his cheek. "Kiss me, my warrior."

With shaking hands, Lyon slid his fingers into her hair and prayed, *prayed*, she was right because he would never love another.

Slowly, so slowly, he leaned toward her, praying to the heavens and the Earth. *Let her be mine.*

The moment their lips touched, he knew. Even before the cheers nearly brought the walls down around them, he knew. Power, energy, fire, and love rushed through him into her and back again, filling him with a gladness, a completeness, he'd never known a man could feel.

Kara pulled back from the kiss first, tears streaming down her cheeks, her smile brilliant.

"Let me see your hands."

Letting go of her in that moment was the hardest thing he'd ever done, but he did what she asked and pulled his hands between them so they could both admire the blue fire burning from his fingertips.

"It was always you," she said, choking on her happiness.

"It was always *us*," he countered. Then he hauled her into his arms and kissed her. His mate. His love.

His heart.

The celebration feast was, necessarily, makeshift given that Pink had spent the day locked up with the Ferals, but two hours after the happiest moment of her life, Kara found herself with tears in her eyes again as Pink took her hand in her feathered one and led her to the dining table. In the middle of the buckets of fried chicken and barbecued ribs, sat a perfect, round chocolate cake. In pink frosting on the top were the words, "Welcome, Kara."

Kara wrapped her arms gently around the bird-woman. "Thank you. Chocolate is my absolute favorite."

She couldn't be certain, but she thought she saw tears in the flamingo's eyes.

As the men ate, the discussion returned to Vhyper.

"If that blade stole his soul, he may be lost to us," Hawke said dismally.

Paenther growled. "If magic took him, magic can bring him back. I'm going after him."

"And it looks like we're going to have to track down my evil twin," Tighe muttered.

Kara walked to the end of the table, behind Lyon, and slid her arms around his neck from behind.

"Have a seat," he murmured.

"In a minute." She liked touching him too much.

Lyon reached up, clasping her hands in his.

"What about the Daemon blade?" Tighe asked. "The witch didn't complete her ritual, but it doesn't mean someone else won't find another way to free those bastards. That blade holds all our blood. No one's safe until we get that thing back in our hands."

"We've got our work cut out for us. But we're strong again. Stronger than we've ever been, thanks to Kara." Lyon raised one of their joined hands to his mouth and kissed her knuckles, then lifted their hands in the air like a fist.

"Victory to the Feral Warriors!" Lyon yelled, like some kind of Marine sergeant.

"Victory to the Feral Warriors!" the other men responded, fists thrust into the air in unison, and Kara realized this was for real. A true Feral war cry.

Behind them, Pink thrust her fists into the air, one after the other, like a pink-feathered cheerleader, grinning as she winked at Kara. If Kara had ever wondered if the flamingo could smile, she did no longer.

Kara burst into laughter, drawing the attention of all the males.

Tighe, having seen the whole thing, wadded up two napkins and lobbed one at each of the women, dimples flashing. "Show some respect, you two."

Kara only laughed harder, drawing chuckles and grins from every one of the men.

"We're not going to solve anything tonight." Lyon rose and with a single fluid move, scooped her into his arms, like a bridegroom about to carry his bride over the threshold. He proceeded to kiss her thoroughly.

"Oh, hell, here they go again," Jag drawled. "Someone get the fire extinguisher."

Lyon pulled back, gazing down at her with such love, such need, her vision blurred all over again. "How hungry are you?" he asked.

"Ravenous," she replied softly. "For you."

A growl rumbled low in his throat. "Right answer."

As he carried her from the room, Kara yelled, "Pink, save me some cake!"

Ribald laughter followed them down the hall, melding with Lyon's own.

"What's so funny?" she teased him, then dissolved into a fit of giggles, too giddy with happiness to do anything else.

Lyon laughed with her, then turned almost serious as he stopped at the foot of the stairs and looked into her eyes.

"You're mine," he said simply, his own eyes overflowing with rivers of love. His gaze deepened until she felt as if she were tumbling all the way to the center of his soul. "Seven hundred years I've waited for this moment. You in my arms. *Mine.*"

Kara pressed her hand to his warm, beloved cheek, the love inside her too much for her heart to hold, love that had to be shared. "Yours, Lyon. I'm yours. For always."

She and her heart had found their home, at last.

Turn the page for an exciting sneak peek from

OBSESSION UNTAMED,

the second book in the Feral Warriors series
available now from Avon Books

The Feral Warriors were in a world of hurt.

Tighe lifted his face to the night wind, trying to cool the frustration lodged beneath the surface of his skin as he traversed the rugged, rocky woods high above the Potomac River.

The Mage had lost their freaking minds and were apparently *trying* to free the Daemons. After sacrificing so much five millennia ago to imprison them, Tighe couldn't fathom why, but there was no denying at least one Mage, the witch Zaphene, had been determined to free Satanan. Zaphene was dead, but she'd left a hell of a legacy.

One of the Ferals, Vhyper, was missing. The Daemon blade itself was gone. And one of Zaphene's creations had run off with half Tighe's soul. Literally.

Where the Mage witch had come by the magic to split souls, no one knew, but she'd done so to make clones of the Ferals. Clones who would raise the Daemons from the blade in the real Ferals' stead, since the real Ferals weren't *stupid* enough to want that plague freed again. *What were the Mage thinking?*

A growl rumbled deep in his throat as he climbed the last of the stone outcroppings onto the cliffs above the river. The night was clear, the brightest stars little more than a dull glow, thanks to the damned humans and their incessant need to battle back the dark.

His clone was, by all indications, currently wreaking havoc on the human population. Tighe and two other Ferals had been tracking him for three days as he'd left a path of dead between Great Falls, Virginia, and nearby Washington, D.C.

And while, yes, the clone's deadly rampage needed to be stopped, Tighe's stake in his capture was a lot more personal. He needed his damned soul back. No one knew for sure how long he could survive with it split like this, but the consensus was, *not long*. At least not with his sanity intact.

Dammit.

Which was why he returned to Great Falls and Feral House each night instead of remaining on the trail of his clone. He'd seen what could happen to a Feral with a split soul and it wasn't pretty. Hell, it gave him nightmares.

He was determined to hold onto his sanity, even if every Feral watched him as if they expected to have to lock him up in the prison deep below Feral House at any moment.

Wulfe stepped onto the rock beside him. "Any sign of draden?" Wulfe was the biggest of the Ferals, a monster of man close to seven feet tall with a face that looked like it had once been used as a cat's scratching post.

Tighe released his frustration on a huff. "Not yet. They'll come." Then he'd rip their hearts out, as he did every night, and release some of this gut-eating frustration. Enough to feel relatively safe returning to the hunt for his clone in human-infested D.C.

"I'm surprised Lyon let us take you out without a leash," Jag drawled behind him.

A growl rumbled in Tighe's chest. The idiot wasn't satisfied until he had every Feral ready to rip his throat out. And Tighe was in a foul enough mood to accommodate him.

"Shut up, Jag," Wulfe snarled. "The last thing he needs right now is your needling."

The last thing he *needed* was everyone treating him like he was filled with gunpowder, a lit fuse dangling from the corner of his mouth. He was *fine*.

But the burn in his fingertips gave lie to that little assertion. He struggled for control, struggled to pull back from the feral rage engulfing him. Under normal circumstances the feral state was merely a place of lost tempers and healthy fighting. The place halfway between man and beast where human teeth elongated into fangs, claws erupted from fingertips, and human eyes no longer looked human. A place where a hawk and a tiger could access their wilder natures, yet fight on equal footing.

But these were not normal circumstances. Thanks to the rending of his soul, he didn't know how much longer he'd have the strength or control to pull himself back out of that state again.

He fought against the fury engulfing his body, clenching his teeth even as he willed himself calm, but it was too late. Claws unsheathed from the tips of his fingers. Fangs dropped from the top of his jaw. Daggerlike incisors rose from below as a backload of damned-up rage ripped free of his control. In a rush of feral anger, he lunged, tackling Jag to the rocky ground.

In a haze of bloodlust, he felt the slash of claws and the ripping of flesh as Jag went feral, too. Blood spilled into his mouth, both his own and Jag's, tasting warm and fine. His vision hazed in a wild bloodlust that had him suddenly longing to sink his teeth into Jag's neck and rip out the bastard's throat for real.

His logical mind recoiled. He was losing it. He could almost see the dark, swirling waters of chaos lapping at his sanity. As his sane mind clawed its way back from the precipice, Wulfe wedged himself between the two warriors, jerking Jag out of his grasp.

Tighe slowly struggled back to his controlled, human, form. As his claws and fangs retracted, Wulfe balled up his fist and hit Jag in the jaw with a hard right hook.

Jag went sprawling. "What'd you do that for?"

"You can be such an ass," Wulfe snarled. "Do you *want* to see him locked up? *Now?* Would it be too much to ask you to *not* hasten the destruction of one of our strongest warriors?"

Jag scowled and pushed to his feet. "Fuck you."

"I'm not heading for destruction," Tighe growled, standing and adjusting his ripped shirt so that it continued to hang, *barely,* from his body. He wouldn't let it happen. He *refused* to let it happen.

But he couldn't deny he was shaken.

"Let's kill some draden, then," Wulfe said.

Tighe compressed his mouth and nodded. They hunted draden by waiting for the little fiends to smell their Therian energy, energy the Ferals emitted in their human forms. It wasn't much longer before a faint dark cloud appeared over the cliffs across the river.

"Incoming," Wulfe said quietly. The draden had found them.

Wulfe yanked off his tee shirt and unzipped his jeans, tossing his clothes onto the rocks. Jag stripped out of his camouflage pants and army-green tee. Tighe did nothing. He was one of the Ferals who possessed the strain of Mage blood that allowed him to retain his clothes when he shifted. A damn handy trick, especially when he hunted among humans.

The dark cloud of draden moved quickly toward them over the gleaming river, a smudge against the stars and the shadowy distant cliffs. A *huge* smudge.

"Holy *shit*." Jag whistled low. "Is it just me, or is that five times the usual number?"

There had to be hundreds coming at them. Maybe more than a thousand. Holy shit, was right. They'd known the draden were multiplying faster than usual, but the evidence was alarming. If they didn't get them under control, there wouldn't be enough Therian energy for them to feed on. They'd turn to humans.

And if that happened, they'd decimate the population in no time, without the humans ever knowing what hit them.

"Then let's get 'em, boys," Jag said.

"I'll take first bait." Tighe pulled his knives. One of them had to remain in his human, or Therian form, or the draden would fly off. But as *first bait*, he would absolutely be fighting for his life.

In a sudden, heart-jarring instant, a veil of darkness dropped over his eyes, swallowing everything. Tighe's blood went cold.

He couldn't see. "What the hell?"

"What's the matter?" Wulfe asked beside him, as if nothing were wrong.

Shit. His pulse began to pound in his ears. This must only be happening to him. His vision was gone. Totally. Was this the first step to losing his sanity?

As quickly as his sight vanished, it reappeared, but his relief lifted and plummeted in the same instant. He wasn't actually seeing. Like a movie lighting a dark screen, a scene appeared before his sightless eyes.

A harsh, bright light lit a rough room, nothing but half a dozen washers and dryers on a cement floor. A public laundry room. Two heavy-set women worked, one shoving wet laundry from the washer into the dryer, the other standing before a nearby table, folding clothes. The standing one glanced toward him, her expression at once appreciative and wary.

"Hi," she said cautiously.

Suddenly, her face grew in his vision as if a camera lens were pulling in close. Her eyes widened with terror as the room lurched dizzily. As if he'd attacked her and taken her to the ground.

Was this a premonition? *Heaven help him.* Of what he was to become?

Behind him, the other woman screamed, piercing his eardrums.

"No!" His victim threw up her hands, the terror in her eyes churning up rancid memories buried deep in his mind.

Memories of another time, another place.

His gut knotted until he thought he'd be sick. But he couldn't deny the evidence. It seemed he was finally doomed to become the very thing he'd been accused of being all those long, miserable years ago.

A monster.

Visit

AvonRomance.com

to discover our

complete digital

book library

More Romance
More Dish
More Fun

AVON